Cahill Cowboys

Texas's Finest

In the heart of America's Wild West,
only one family matters—the legendary Cahills.

Once a dynasty to be reckoned with,
their name has been dragged through the cattle-worn mud,
and their family torn apart.

Now the three Cahill cowboys
and their scandalous sister reunite.

With a past as dark as the Texas night sky, it's
time for the family to heal their hearts and seek justice....

Author Note

Are you as excited about this release as I am?

This is my first continuity. The collaboration between Carol Finch, Debra Cowan and Carol Arens has been the most rewarding part of constructing this story. Together we created a town full of people who felt real to me—streets, businesses, life. What fun!

I've been waiting for Chance to ride back into Cahill Crossing and now he has finally returned. You know he's going to shake things up and cause trouble, because that is what he does best. Quin would like him to be more responsible, Bowie would settle for just having him stay out of jail and Leanna wishes he'd settle down, but Chance has his own ideas. Get ready for a rough ride!

I have more about Ellie and Chance and the writing of this story on my website, www.jennakernan.com, and readers who want more insight into my day-to-day writing life can follow me on Twitter at http://twitter.com/jennakernan.

Finally, I'd like to thank my editor Ann Leslie Tuttle and the UK editorial team for all their hard work on this series.

Enjoy the adventure and giddy-up!

Jenna Kernan

JENNA KERNAN

THE LAST
CAHILL COWBOY

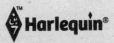

TORONTO NEW YORK LONDON
AMSTERDAM PARIS SYDNEY HAMBURG
STOCKHOLM ATHENS TOKYO MILAN MADRID
PRAGUE WARSAW BUDAPEST AUCKLAND

Recycling programs
for this product may
not exist in your area.

ISBN-13: 978-0-373-29675-0

THE LAST CAHILL COWBOY

www.Harlequin.com

Printed in U.S.A.

JENNA KERNAN

is every bit as adventurous as her heroines. Her hobbies include recreational gold prospecting, scuba diving and rock climbing. Indoor pursuits encompass jewelry-making, writing, photography and quilting. Jenna lives in New York State with her husband and two gregarious little parrots. Visit Jenna at www.jennakernan.com for excerpts from her latest release, giveaways and monthly contests.

Prologue

Texas, 1880

Chance Cahill checked the soles of his boots before entering Ma's parlor and then felt the gut punch as he remembered where he'd just been. Ruby Cahill would never again care if he tracked mud into her house. His sister, Leanna, squeezed his elbow and he glanced down at her pretty face, marred with dark smudges beneath her red-rimmed eyes. The black silk dress did not suit her normally cheerful personality and seeing her in her mourning garb only served to make Chance feel worse.

His two older brothers were already going at it. Quin, the eldest, had been ordering them around for as long as he could remember and it looked as though today would be no different.

He ushered Leanna in and then they separated as she took the center spot on the sofa and he moved to the fireplace, to watch and wait—wait for orders, wait to be noticed, wait for an opportunity that would never come. He'd given up on hoping he'd earn an equal place with his brothers. They couldn't see he'd grown up. Twenty-five now with a man's wants and desires for independence. Foremost, he wanted out of here. He'd known it before the wagon accident that had ripped their parents from them forever. He just hadn't gotten up the nerve to tell his pa. Now he'd never have to.

He glanced out the window. They were both out there now, buried on the land they'd ranched. He clenched his fists in rage and guilt. He couldn't stay here; he didn't belong, not anymore. He'd made a terrible mistake, one that could never be put right. Now all he wanted to do was run.

He scanned the room, seeing his mother everywhere except in his father's big leather chair, which Quin now used as a coat hanger. Chance wanted to knock his brother's black jacket to the floor. Instead, he closed his eyes, shutting out the sight, but not the voices.

"Pa talked about expansion and that's what I'm aiming for. We'll pour the profits of the ranch and the town rents back into the 4C."

One hour before, they had been standing by two open graves. Quin did not even have the decency to allow them to grieve. One glance at Leanna's tightly pressed lips told him she felt the same. She cast him a look of frustration, but neither Quin nor Bowie noticed, because Quin was all over Bowie like grease on an axle. The two had butted heads about everything and only Pa could ever make them stop. But Pa was gone and Chance felt his stomach cramp as he watched Bowie's jaw tick.

"I'm assigning you to raising, breeding, training and sale of the horses," said Quin.

Neither cared that Chance's only joy, besides shooting, was working with horses.

"I have a job, in case you've forgotten, brother," snapped Bowie. "I can hardly oversee the horse operation, the livestock and hired hands if I'm already working as the sheriff in Deer County."

Quin didn't seem to hear a word, just ignored him as usual, so he missed the murderous look Bowie shot him when he turned to face their sister.

"Annie, you're in charge of the household, meals, staff and supplies…everything Ma did."

Leanna's eyes rounded at the mention of Ma, then narrowed on Quin. Her anger did not stem the tears that had been streaming down her cheeks all day.

Quin turned next to him, ticking down the list and the pecking order all at once.

"You're working under me."

The hell he was. Chance stood in silence.

"Helping with the breeding and cattle and you'll give the orders to the cowboys while I'm gone on roundup come spring and fall."

Quin had been gone when the accident had occurred, although he'd promised to be back. It was that promise that had made Chance decide it was safe to skip out and go shooting instead of driving the wagon as Pa had requested. Quin was always where he was supposed to be—just not this time.

"So, I'm your hired hand?" Chance ground out.

Bowie cut in. "Now just hold on. We should all have a say in what we do."

Chance nearly laughed. *A say,* that was rich. Like they'd listen. Leanna was trying to get Quin to lay off, taking exception to his timing, which was lousy as usual. The neighbors would be arriving any minute with their pies and casseroles. Chance glanced out the window again, looking for escape from the lecture Quin had started on family responsibility. Bowie butted in again, arguing about his job.

Chance was jealous that Bowie had escaped and understood it perfectly. Pa had been a tough taskmaster and Quin was unbearable. Bowie had had the guts to leave and Chance admired him for it. Plus Bowie had found something to do that he loved and was good at. But Chance had also seen how his leaving had disappointed Pa and that stopped Chance from doing the same. But it hadn't stopped him wanting to.

Quin didn't miss the opportunity to jab Bowie by repeating Pa's harsh words about walking away to defend strangers instead of doing his duty at the ranch. Chance watched the barbed tip of the arrow hit home.

"And who do you think got stuck with the extra work? It sure wasn't Annie or Chance."

No matter how quiet he was he still got dragged into their fight every time. The raised voices and heated words made Chance's head pound. He just wanted quiet.

Bowie and Quin always clashed as Bowie tried to get the upper hand, while Quin was determined not to lose his place on top. They made it easy for Chance to just disappear. The two of them together filled the room without any help from him.

Bowie countered by reminding Quin that it was a whore in Dodge that had kept him from being here to drive Pa. Quin winced as Bowie's words tore flesh and he doubled down, leaning in and lifting his finger like a cocked pistol.

"You knew I was gone." He jabbed a finger at Bowie. "You should have been here, taking up the slack. Especially when you learned about Pa's broken wrist. You knew he couldn't drive that wagon."

"I was working that day," Bowie gritted out. "I had a dangerous prisoner in my jail."

Any minute now they'd recall that he was the one Pa had asked to drive him, not Quin, not Bowie—*him*. But he hadn't wanted to go to Wolf Grove. Hadn't wanted the new suit that Ma had insisted he have for the family photo commemorating the founding of the new town, Cahill Crossing. So he had snuck off before they left to practice target shooting with his new repeater. Chance fingered the crisp trouser seam of the stiff black pants that Ma had picked out for him, realizing she'd managed to get him into this damned suit, anyway. Chance steeled himself against the burning in his throat, fearing he might cry.

It was his fault they were gone and he had to get out of here before Bowie or Quin said aloud the words that were already tearing at his heart.

He stepped between them. "I'm not staying to take orders from either of you anymore. If I do, I'll never be anything but y'all's kid brother. Pa's gone and I'm through being a ranch hand."

Quin rounded on him. "You're part owner of this ranch! As such, you have to work just like the rest of us." He glared at them all, his quicksilver eyes flashing. "We are doing what is best for the 4C."

Chance had expected that, but he'd steered the conversation away from the accident, away from his shame.

"Ranching isn't in my blood. I only stayed this long for Pa," he said.

Quin exploded. "Ma and Pa are barely in the ground and y'all are jumping ship. I'm trying to hold everything together so we can become the family and the ranch Pa worked so hard to build. We're the most influential ranching family in Texas. Pa wanted it to stay that way."

"That's what *you* want, Quin," Bowie snapped.

Chance nodded. "I'm going."

"Me, too," Leanna said.

Quin stared at the three of them. "You aren't going anywhere."

"Watch me," said Bowie.

Leanna tried to get between them, but they brushed her aside.

Quin leaned in, his jaw locking like a wolf trap as he fixed his cold silver eyes on Bowie for a long moment before he threw down his challenge. "Be a man and do your part."

Bowie shoved Quin against the wall. Quin fell into Ma's treasured porcelain bowl. Chance took a step in that direction, but too late, as the bowl exploded on the hardwood planking. Leanna gave a cry and fell to her knees before the scattered pieces, the silk of her skirts billowing out around her like a black ocean. Quin lowered his shoulder and shoved Bowie back, sending him sprawling over Pa's big leather chair.

Bowie scrambled to his feet, his face flushed a deep red. "Go to hell and take your orders with you!"

Leanna let the single shard of blue and white porcelain fall from her fingers as she stood and stepped between her brothers again. Their fighting always upset her and she'd tried to stop them more times than Chance could count.

"Stop it." She latched on to Bowie's arm, clasping his clenched fist with both her hands. "What do you suppose Mama and Papa would think of us? Can't this wait…?"

"Stay out of this, Annie," Quin ordered.

But she didn't. She never could disappear like Chance because she felt everyone's pain as if it were her own. He'd told her that her big heart would get her into trouble and she had countered by telling him that someday he'd find a problem that was too important for him to walk away from.

Maybe they were both right. But why did she have to bait Quin to protect Bowie? He knew that look and saw it all coming before she let the words fly.

She rose on her tiptoes and still didn't reach Quin's shoulder. "No one made you ruler of us all, Quin!"

She'd done it. Chance could tell by the look on Quin's face that he'd forgotten all about Bowie. She had succeeded in stopping the fight by getting Quin to turn on her instead.

Chance had never before seen Quin so mad that the blood vessels at his throat pulsed. Chance stepped closer, ready to do whatever he had to in order to protect Leanna. But Quin never lifted his hand. Instead, he opened his mouth.

"Grow up," Quin growled. "You're not fit for anything other than looking pretty and playing games."

Bowie stepped up beside Chance. One of the few things they'd ever agreed on was protecting Leanna, even from herself.

Leanna glanced at them and Chance silently begged her to back down. But there was fire in her blue eyes and a familiar set of her jaw that Chance knew spelled trouble. She turned back to Quin.

"I say we sell the ranch and each take our share."

Chance froze. Bowie's head jerked toward her. It was as if she had thrown a live mortar into their midst. The silence in the room was so loud Chance could hear the ticking of the clock in the hall.

Quin recovered from the bomb Leanna had hurled first.

"Have you lost your damned mind?"

Leanna flushed as if only just realizing what she had said. But Chance knew she'd never take it back. She was too damned stubborn for that, and anyway, it was what they all were thinking—all, that is, except Quin.

"Ma and Pa are buried on this land, you spoiled little brat." Quin no longer raised his voice, but there was a cold inflexibility there that was more brutal than his shouting.

"You can't run it alone. It belongs to all of us. Bowie has his own life. Chance doesn't want yours and neither do I."

"And just what are you fit for, Miss China Doll? We sell over my dead body. Ranching is who we are. That's our destiny."

"Yours, maybe. Not mine," said Chance to Quin. Then to Leanna. "You coming?"

She nodded and he took her elbow, heading out of the room.

Quin bellowed from behind them. "You're not worthy to be called Cahills."

They reached the front door.

"This ranch stays intact, as Pa stated in his will," he shouted.

Chance held the door and waited for Leanna. To her credit, she hesitated only an instant before leaving the only home she had ever known. A moment later, Bowie joined them. Chance lifted his twin holsters from the peg beside the entrance and strapped the gun belt beneath his new black jacket.

Quin stilled, realizing perhaps that Chance was really going, for he knew his little brother well enough to understand how much those pistols meant to him.

Chance followed Leanna and Bowie out.

"Don't come back!" yelled Quin. "You hear me? If you walk away now, don't you ever come back."

The three crossed the porch with Quin dogging them as far as the steps.

"Fine. You go and see how you do without your family to back you! But I'll be here where I belong, keeping the 4C Ranch alive like Pa wanted. And if you're going, you go with a horse and the clothes on your back."

"More than I expected," muttered Chance, and then cursed.

"You think leaving here will help you find out who you are?" Quin stood on the porch waving his fists. "I can save you the trip. You're *quitters* and I'm ashamed to call you family. None of you are worthy to bear the Cahill name."

Chance kept walking. He'd gotten his wish. He'd severed the ties between himself and this ranch. But the price was high. He'd earned his freedom at the cost of his family.

At the middle of the yard, he took a last look at his home.

"Don't think I'll beg you to come back, because I won't!" hollered Quin.

That would be a cold day in hell, thought Chance as he saddled up and rode out.

Chapter One

Two years later

Chance Cahill returned to Deadwood, South Dakota, with another body tied to the dead man's horse. The jail had been among the first structures rebuilt after the May floods, brick and mortar this time, but much of the rest of the town was in shambles. Still, rebuilding was underway.

Chance glanced toward the saloon where his sister, Leanna, dealt cards, half expecting her to come out to greet him as she often did. She didn't like the sight of blood and disapproved of Chance's current profession, although why she thought killing murderers was beneath him, he had no idea. The pay was good, real good, and shooting was the one thing that Chance did well.

The new Deadwood Dick, Richard Bullock, stepped into the street to meet him. The man had the kind of toughness necessary for a lawman out here and did not hesitate to flip back the stained oiled canvas.

"Another head shot?"

The hole where Chance's bullet had exited the back of Meyler's head seemed to speak to that question.

"Find they spend less time escaping that way."

Bullock gave a snort that might have been a laugh.

"Looks like he saw you coming. You do know that you don't have to give outlaws a chance to draw, don't you?"

He knew. But he always gave a man a chance, not out of some sense of fair play but with the hope that one day he'd meet someone faster. He was dead inside already, but somehow he remained aboveground. Meyler had been too damn slow and so Chance was here collecting another bounty.

"Come in and I'll fill out the paperwork. What's the pay on this one?"

"Only five hundred dollars. Give it to Annie. I'll bring him over to Hannon." The undertaker paid Chance twenty-five dollars for the body and then charged folks a dime to see the outlaws Chance brought in.

"Yeah, about that."

Chance's gaze flicked to Bullock and read his expression. Something had happened to Leanna. Cold terror washed over him. He knew it, knew that working in a bar was no place for her, but damned if he could talk her out of it.

"What happened to her?"

"Nothing. Well, something, I imagine, but I'm not privy to it. She left a letter for you with Mrs. Jameston, her landlady."

Chance glanced back at the saloon and then narrowed his eyes on Bullock. "What's going on?"

"All I know is that she pulled out, lock, stock and barrel. Took the girls with her and that baby, too."

Chance pushed back his gray Stetson, trying to sort out what was happening. Leanna wouldn't just go without telling him. Something had happened. Something bad.

"Where to?"

"Home, she said. Texas. That where you're from?"

Chance's stomach flipped. Leanna had said she'd never go back there and he'd sworn the same. Nothing on this earth could compel him. If she expected him to trail after her again, she was dead wrong. He had followed her to Deadwood, but that was where it ended. Chance stared bleakly across the street knowing that he'd lost the last thing on earth he cared about. Leanna had left him.

Why would she ever go back there? And then it hit him like hot lead in his guts. Something had happened to his brothers. Bowie came to mind first. Had his position as the new town marshal of Cahill Crossing placed him in harm's way? Chance's knees buckled and he sat hard on the stoop. But Quin worked with stock and all beeves were stupid and unpredictable. Were they dead, too?

"Cahill?" said Bullock. "You okay?"

"My brothers? Are they alive?"

Bullock peered down at him. "Didn't know you had brothers. Damn, man, you look white as a bedsheet. Come out of the sun."

Bullock swung into the office and Chance followed, spotting Mrs. Jameston, Leanna's landlady, clutching a pristine white envelope before her in gloved hands.

Chance glanced to Bullock.

"Called her when we saw you coming."

She scowled up at him, or rather at his battered

gray Stetson. He dragged it off belatedly, holding it before him.

"Welcome back, Mr. Cahill. I trust you are well?"

"Yes'm."

"Your sister left me with this letter for you. I promised that I would put it in your hands personally upon your return." She did just that.

"Thank you, ma'am."

"Least I can do. You're still cleaning up the territory single-handedly, I see." She waved a hand at the pig-eyed appaloosa holding the remains of Meyler before shifting her gaze to him again. "Did that young man find your sister?"

"Ma'am?"

"Well dressed, extremely handsome and charming, oh, my. Cleve Holden was his name. Said he was a friend of your sister. I told him she headed home to Cahill Crossing in Texas and he lit out after her."

Chance scowled. He didn't know the man and thought it likely that Leanna didn't, either. Who was he and what did he want? Chance had that bad feeling. The one he got before gunplay.

"Why, what is it, Mr. Cahill?"

"Did it occur to you, Mrs. Jameston, that he might not be a friend and that telling him exactly where to find Annie might have put her in danger?"

"Well, he seemed such a gentleman."

"Not everyone in this world is what they seem, ma'am."

"My gracious. I would be positively beside myself if difficulty befell her on my account. Mercy, I shall write her this very day. Please do come by for supper, Mr. Cahill. You need filling up." With that Mrs. Jameston scurried off, looking like a fast-moving lumpy sofa.

He replaced his hat and accepted the chair Bullock offered. Seated, he spun the envelope in a circle, knowing he didn't want to see what was in there. Leanna had written his name on the front with a blue fountain pen, her looping handwriting as familiar to him as his own.

Chance tapped the envelope to send the letter in the other direction and then tore the side seam, reached into the gap and pulled out a page and a telegram, both neatly folded in two. He knew that Annie and Bowie were in touch, that she had let him know where they had landed after the fight that had broken the family apart.

So Bowie was alive. Chance found he could breathe again. But what about Quin? His oldest brother, the boy he'd wanted to become, the man who he'd grown to hate.

Chance flipped open the telegram and read the words carefully printed on the form.

WESTERN UNION TELEGRAM COMPANY
Sent by: JM
Rec'd by: NH
Check: paid
Dated: August 3, 1882
Received at: 1:08 p.m.
To: Leanna Cahill, Deadwood, SD
Parents' death no accident.
Come home.
Quin

Chance rose like a phoenix. For two years he'd blamed himself for the deaths of his parents. Two years of hell on earth, trying to find his way in the dark, blaming himself for a mistake he could never set right, knowing that if he'd driven that wagon to Wolf Grove he never would have lost control of that team. But if it hadn't been an accident... A tiny pinprick of light appeared, a reason to go on.

He scanned the words again. Parents' death not accident. *Murder,* that was what Quin meant. His parents had been murdered.

By whom?

Chance dearly hoped they hadn't caught him yet, because he needed to be there to put a bullet in the man who had taken his parents from them.

Chance read the next line again—an order, how typical of Quin to issue an edict. The remarkable thing was that Annie had done as he had demanded.

He wondered if Quin would be surprised to see him. One thing was sure. Chance wouldn't be welcomed back with open arms, not after leaving the family ranch, not after turning his back on them all.

Chance flicked open Annie's letter.

August 4, 1882
Dear Chance,
I hope that when you read this you will forgive my haste. I am leaving for Cahill Crossing to help our brothers discover who is responsible and see they are brought to justice.
Your loving sister,
Annie

He checked the dates. Leanna had written this the day after she'd received the telegram. What day was it now, September 26 or the 27? She had nearly two months' head start. Bullock said she'd taken the girls along with that baby she'd decided to raise. She'd gone by rail, would have had to, of course.

Chance slipped the letter into the breast pocket of his black oiled duster and turned to Bullock.

"You leaving?" asked Bullock.

Chance nodded.

"Money will be here in a day or two," said the sheriff.

"Can't wait." He turned to Bullock. "Will you wire it to Cahill Crossing, Texas, care of Leanna Cahill?"

His gaze turned icy. "I'm not your errand boy."

"Keep it, then."

Bullock's scowl deepened, dragging down the corners of his bushy mustache. "I'll send it."

"I'm obliged." Chance left the office, untied the appaloosa holding his bounty, leaving the body on Bullock's doorstep. Then he swung up into his saddle, lifted his reins and pointed Rip south, back to the land of his birth. Back to a town named after his folks, a town he had never expected to see again.

Chance arrived in Cahill Crossing by rail on the second Friday of October, dirty and sorer than he'd ever been from riding. He wondered if his horse had fared better as he stared out the passenger car window at the familiar landscape, not realizing until now how much he'd missed the green rolling hills of his boyhood home. It was strange to ride through the 4C in a passenger car.

The engine slowed and Chance peered at the town that had arisen where once there had been only ropes and stakes.

The very first building he spotted was three stories tall with a sign above the porch roof reading Leanna's Place, all capital letters.

Chance smiled. He'd found his sister without even getting off the train. The locomotive rolled slowly past a string of impressive new businesses lining the tracks, blasting steam across the platform. Beyond the gaming hall stood Stokes's general store, then a boutique, a bakery, Steven's Restaurant and then the biggest damned hotel he'd seen since Dodge City. Château Royale said the sign in flowing gilded script. He gave a low whistle. Things sure had changed.

He disembarked, checked on Rip, paying the porter to take his horse to the livery. Then he stepped along the new planks that still smelled of sawdust and into the hotel, pausing to stare at the glittering interior, taking in the huge crystal chandelier, sweeping staircase and opulent furnishings set before a fireplace upon a large oriental rug. Generally you had to be in a high-class whorehouse to see this much flash.

But why was it so empty?

The answer came an instant later when a gunshot cracked somewhere beyond the grand staircase.

Chance drew both pistols and stepped into the lobby. A thin man in a black suit and dark hair slicked to his head cowered behind one of the red velvet sofas. To the left was a reception desk behind which crouched another man with a brown goatee, raised pistol and a nervous expression. He glanced toward Chance, revealing the silver star pinned on the front of his hatband. It made a fine target.

He turned to the man behind the sofa.

"What's going on?"

"A gambler's trying to kill his wife."

"Where's Bowie?"

"He's not back yet. But Glen Whitaker's pinned by the stairs."

"That his deputy?"

The man nodded. "The gambler is shooting at anything that moves."

Chance made it to the deputy without another shot fired, but he heard someone pounding on a door.

"Whitaker! His wife still alive?"

"Don't know. Ellie Jenkins locked herself in a room with her and he can't get at them."

Ellie Jenkins was Leanna's best friend.

Chance recalled a girl in pigtails tied with yellow ribbons. She'd lived in Wolf Grove with her folks in the hotel they owned, but had spent a lot of time at the 4C with Leanna over the years. Chance didn't mind Leanna's company, but he cleared out when there were other females about. Except for Ellie. That girl interested him. When Ellie was around, she and Leanna could disappear in broad daylight and he never could find them unless they wanted to be found. She didn't seem a stupid girl but locking oneself in a room with a woman whose husband is bent on murder didn't seem wise.

Chance made it to the stairs, peering through the gaps in the balusters, seeing nothing.

"Don't go up there," whispered Whitaker as he flopped his empty hand at Chance.

Chance ignored him and headed around the newel post and up the stairs two at a time, guns out, chin down. Someone fired a shot from the dark hallway above. Chance started shooting, aiming for the barrel flash. Someone yelped and then ran. Chance pursued, running now.

The gunman must have knocked out every lamp on the floor and drawn the heavy curtains over the window at the end of the hall. A beam of light knifed between the two drapes, sending a ray across one wall. Chance searched for the shooter as his eyes tried to adjust to the gloom.

Next came the sound of splintering wood as a door crashed open and light spilled into the hall.

Two women screamed.

The gambler had reached his target. Chance ran down the hall and into the room.

He took in the scene at a glance. There stood a beefy man holding a Colt repeater aimed at Chance and a derringer aimed at the two women huddled in the corner of the room. If he shot the gambler, the man might still pull the trigger as he fell.

His gaze flicked to the women. The braver of the two was small but slim as a willow branch, wearing an ordinary navy blue skirt with a small fitted jacket. Her white starched blouse had an unfortunate cascade of ruffles that tumbled like a waterfall down the front of her bodice, completely obscuring her shape. Her dark brown hair was gathered in a functional little bun that made her neck look long and slim. Chance stared into big hazel eyes. Ellie? The other woman cowered behind her, clinging and shivering in a fitted pink jacket, skirt of the same garish color and a hat rimmed with ostrich feathers dyed to match. She looked like an entertainer. His gaze flicked back to the husband.

Chance stepped forward.

"She cheated on me," he said.

Chance looked past the barrel of the raised pistol leveled at his guts to the man who stood no more than eighteen inches away. "Don't care."

"Another step and I'll shoot."

Would he? He was sweating like a long-distance runner.

"You gonna shoot me? Then aim here." Chance tapped his chest with one of his pistols. "Not my guts. I can still kill you with a belly wound."

Ellie gasped. He didn't look at her.

The man's hands shook like an old drunk on Sunday morning. "I got no quarrel with you, mister. Clear out, now."

Chance shook his head, waiting for the bullet. Waiting for the peace that would come afterward. But the shooter swung both weapons toward the women.

Chance fired. The bullet passed through the man's forehead and out the back, leaving a hell of a mess on the bed coverlet and rug. He crumpled to the ground as the wife started screaming.

"Bobby!" She fell across his chest, then glared at Chance. "You killed him!"

"You're welcome," said Chance. He turned toward the hall. "Deputy! Come up."

Ellie stepped forward as Chance holstered his gun. Her brow descended over her hazel eyes. She looked different from how he recalled. Taller certainly, and the sunlight pouring in the open window gave her brown hair a reddish cast. Her upper lip was full and the corners of her mouth tipped down in disapproval. Likely he'd catch hell over the blood and such.

"Chance?" she whispered.

He nodded, holstering his repeaters, surprised she could recognize him under the dust and stubble.

"Oh, Chance!" She threw herself into his arms.

Now this was more like it. He tucked Ellie close, feeling her curves pressed to him as he held her tight. She clutched the lapel of his rumpled duster and made a choking sound. His hand swept down the velvet of her nape and down her narrow back, feeling a wellspring of unexpected tenderness for the woman who was his sister's best friend. What was happening here?

Ellie straightened and her hazel eyes narrowed as she stepped back. Chance didn't want to let her go but he did.

"That was a crazy thing to do."

Why had he expected thanks?

"No crazier than locking yourself in here. Why didn't you head the other way?"

She raised her chin. "Why didn't you?"

The corner of his mouth twitched. He still liked her. She had more spunk than he remembered and was a damn sight prettier. Her pale skin positively glowed in the sunlight, revealing the lovely pink color dusting her cheekbones.

"Sorry about the carpet."

Footsteps sounded in the hall. A moment later Bowie cleared the doorway, pistol drawn, looking mean and deadly as hell.

Chance raised his hands. Bowie holstered his weapon.

"Hells bells, Chance."

"Nice to see you, too, big brother."

Bowie's clear blue eyes flicked about the room and settled on Ellie. "You two all right?"

The woman on the floor wailed. "He killed my Bobby."

"What took you so long?" asked Chance.

"Drowning upriver. The tanner's little girl. They're bringing her into town now."

Ellie gave a startled cry at this.

"Martinez?"

Bowie's nod confirmed it. Chance knew the family. They'd lived on the river as long as he could recall.

"That's a pity," he said.

"Get Ellie out of here. But don't go far. I got to talk to you," ordered Bowie.

Chance frowned. Mostly his older brothers talked at him, not to him. Seemed nothing had changed in that regard.

Chance motioned to Ellie. She preceded him out of the room, turning toward the windows and drawing back the thick velvet draperies. He waited; they walked side by side down the empty hallway.

"Welcome home, Chance," Ellie murmured.

He nodded, thinking about hugging her again.

"I've heard you're a bounty hunter and that you've killed over a dozen outlaws."

Chance said nothing to this. Did the number impress her or sicken her?

"But not one person mentioned you had a death wish."

Chance drew up short. Ellie halted beside him, regarding him with a disconcerting fixed stare. It took him a moment to mask his surprise.

"I don't know what you're talking about."

"I saw you back there, Chance Cahill. Are you trying to kill yourself?"

He gave her a look that usually made grown men run, but she continued to stare, her thin brows now descending low over her eyes. This was Ellie, and she knew him or had known him back when he was another person. The little spitfire didn't retreat. Instead, she stood toe to toe and lifted her chin in a defiant attitude. If a man looked at him like that, he'd knock him down. As it was he'd a good mind to kiss her, just to teach her a lesson.

"Why do you care?"

"Your mother would roll right over in her grave if

she saw what you pulled in there. You were going to let that man shoot you."

He folded his arms across his chest. "What do you want me to say, that sometimes I think about it? Well, I do. Now get out of my way, Ellen Louise, or I swear you'll be sorry."

Her jaw dropped open, though whether from the threat or what he had said before that, he wasn't certain. He left her there, wondering what had possessed him to tell her the truth. And why was it that Ellen Jenkins was the only one who had noticed that he no longer cared if he lived or died?

Her voice followed him. "What's happened to you?"

He kept on walking.

Ellie descended the stairs on legs that suddenly felt wobbly and found Chance Cahill already gone and her father speaking to the deputy. He left Glen Whitaker to meet her as she reached the bottom step. Oscar Jenkins had once been the best of the Confederacy's blockade runners, and was thin and tough, with deep brown eyes now filled with concern for his daughter. Ellie threw herself into his strong arms.

She had expected her father to rescue her, and had been holding out until he could return from his morning business at the bank. But Chance had gotten there first.

"Y'all right, Buttercup?" He gathered her in.

"Yes, sir."

"Chance all right?"

"He killed Mr. Rogers."

Her father tucked her under his arm and headed toward his office. "I hear Mr. Rogers killed himself when he decided to draw a gun at the Royale. I owe that boy my thanks."

"Mr. Rogers thought Mrs. Rogers was cheating on him," said Ellie.

"Was she?"

Ellie nodded.

"You always know what's going on here, don't you? I've said before that you would have made a fine spy for the Confederacy." Did that mean her father also thought her plain enough to blend into the background?

"You could have slipped through enemy lines with a thousand vials of morphine sewn into your petticoats and not a one of those Yankee boys would have lifted an eyebrow."

"Or a skirt?"

Oscar chuckled. Ellie liked the sound of his laugh; it was as comforting as rain against her windowpane.

"Papa, is that just a nice way of saying I'm invisible, like mother always says?"

Oscar stopped abruptly. "No, Ellie, that's not so. Being quiet and observant, that's not the same as disappearing. I figure you just haven't met anyone yet who makes you want to step into center stage."

Her mother, Minnie, emerged like a prairie dog from her burrow.

"Is it safe?" she whispered.

Oscar nodded. "Chance Cahill disarmed him, Minnie."

It did not escape Ellie that her father had omitted telling his wife that Chance had shot a man in her establishment. He often told this kind of half-truth, but Ellie was sure that her mother would get to the bottom of the matter right down to the last bullet hole in her new wallpaper.

Oscar left Ellie to comfort his wife.

"A shooting at our hotel. I just can't believe it." Her mother's eyes welled up.

"Minnie, darling, he just rescued a woman right here in our place. Don't you think that will be good for business?"

Ellie stepped back, silent as the furniture. Just two more steps and she'd be out of sight and mind. She had a feeling that when word got out about the shooting, they'd have many more patrons in her restaurant and she needed to rally the kitchen staff and escape her parents.

"Shooting, good for business?" cried her mother. "Honestly, Oscar, you have absolutely…" Minnie stared at Ellie.

Ellie stilled.

"What's that on your face?"

Ellie lifted a hand and rubbed it over her cheek. When she pulled it back she found a tiny smear of crimson on her index finger. Her stomach gave a lurch. Her father took hold of her elbow and steered her toward the kitchens.

"Is that blood?" cried Minnie.

She followed them into the kitchen where Oscar offered Ellie a wet towel and the following words in a hushed voice, "Don't you faint, now. It will frighten your mother."

Ellie's mouth suddenly began to fill with saliva and she knew she would not faint because she was going to be ill.

She dashed outside and made it only as far as the back porch before losing what remained of her breakfast. Her mother's raised voice followed her. Ellie used the wet cloth to bathe her hot face and lifted her chin to the cool breeze.

"Feeling better?"

Ellie stilled. *No. No. Please don't let that be Chance Cahill out there in the yard, by the woodpile.* But it was and he'd clearly witnessed her humiliation. He stepped into view and she descended the stairs to meet him, still holding the cloth to her burning cheeks.

He looked dangerous, dark and forbidding. She had to remind herself that this was Chance, a man she'd known her whole life.

"Seeing a man killed does that to a lot of folks. Surprised you lasted this long."

"I'll have you know I have had a stomach ailment since yesterday."

A grin teased at the corner of his sensual mouth and his blue eyes sparkled like sunlight on a lake. "You're a pretty fair liar, Ellie Jenkins."

She stood gawking like the schoolgirl she no longer was. Something about Chance always made her pulse jump and the inside of her belly quiver like minnows in a bucket. Was it his clear blue eyes or that bad-boy smile? She dropped her gaze and discovered her mistake. The man wore no kerchief, perhaps because he no longer drove cattle, and so she stared at the healthy bronze skin at his throat and the crisp black hairs at the V of his shirt.

She had known Chance Cahill for many years, yet just now they felt like strangers. His name wasn't really Chance. It was Earl, but no one called him that. He'd been named after his father. Chance was a nickname given to him by his ma after the doctor told her that this little baby boy didn't have much of a chance of living. He'd proved that doc all wrong, growing tall and straight as a cornstalk. Too strong to die, but now he didn't seem to want to live. It troubled her greatly. She cared about him, even if she scarcely crossed his mind.

When she'd visited the ranch, he'd paid her as much attention as Quin and Bowie, which is to say, none at all.

But she had noticed him. It was hard to ignore eyes that blue, or a mouth that sensual. His beard now covered the cleft in his chin, but it was there; she recalled it. He moved closer and then placed a dusty boot on the woodpile, looking down at her with those crystal-clear eyes. Her stomach gave a jump and quiver that she hadn't felt since the last time he'd stared at her years ago. Then as now, she'd fought to keep from making an utter fool of herself before him. And now he'd seen her throw up. Her cheeks burned clear up to her tingling ears. Ellie twisted the damn cloth in her hands in frustration.

"Your face is flushed," he said.

She decided her best course was to run him off and the easiest way to do that was to pepper him with questions. That strategy had generally worked in the past on more than one occasion.

"Why are you out here?"

"Hiding from Bowie."

"You're not afraid of him. Are you?"

"I'm not afraid of radishes, either. Just know they give me hives every time I get near them."

She laughed at that. He could usually make her laugh if he tried. "Might be different after all this time."

Chance grinned. "I just killed a man. Bowie is town marshal, so I guess he feels like shooting folks is his job. Expect he'd take offense."

"You saved our lives, back there."

He leaned his mouth a few inches from hers. "You want to show me your gratitude?"

Chapter Two

Ellie moved closer and rested her hands on the great expanse of Chance's broad chest. His mouth twitched in what might have been an unpracticed smile that shot straight through her like a ray of sunlight. She gave him the tight smile she saved for difficult guests, then whispered to him.

"Not if you were the last man in Texas."

Ellie shoved him with all her might. But her act of extreme violence only served to cause her to ricochet backward. She lost her balance and would have tumbled head over heels if Chance hadn't captured her wrist and dragged her back against him. She had, on some occasions, imagined being in Chance's arms, but never in her fantasy had he held her merely to keep her from breaking her neck.

"Now you owe me twice." He gave her a quick kiss on the cheek and then stepped back. "I'll collect the other one later."

She didn't like being teased and that was what his kiss had been, a prank, like a schoolboy pulling her braid. Nothing like the enveloping embrace he'd shared with her after rescuing them from the woman's crazed husband. Ellie closed her eyes, pushing back the memories of the tenderness of his touch and the aching need to experience again the welcome of his arms. Steeling herself, she met his devilish eyes and playful grin.

She gave him a look she hoped embodied her complete disinterest, for it would not be wise to let Chance know that his proximity played havoc with her emotions.

"I don't think so," she said coolly.

"Ellie?"

It was her mother's voice.

Chance disappeared behind the stacks of cordwood so fast he was as much a blur as a fast-moving train. Yes, her mother had that effect on people.

Ellie's mother and father stepped out onto the wide back porch. Chance continued his retreat until he was certain neither of Ellie's parents could see him. But then he stopped. Why, he was not sure, nor was he sure why he enjoyed teasing Ellie so much.

He looked back at the porch, seeing her parents. They were an odd pair. Minnie was short and curvy, but she had not grown fat as she had aged. Mrs. Jenkins had too much vanity for that. Her elaborate hairstyle was no longer in fashion and included ringlets all about the back of her head. Despite being in her forties, her hair remained a bright reddish brown that was not exactly a color found in nature. Oscar, on the other hand, was exceedingly thin, with an angular face, receding hairline, wide forehead and heavy lines that creased his brow and flanked his mouth. His hair had been the same dark brown as Ellie's but now gray had overrun his sideburns and mustache. Chance had heard stories about Oscar being a privateer and knew his outward gentility was but a thin veneer. Jenkins was as tough and leathery as rawhide.

Chance knew he should go but he just couldn't make himself leave Ellie. If she was going to catch hell, he'd step up to take the heat and not just because Ellie was Leanna's best friend. Truth be told, he liked her better now than before he had left. She had sand and a new glint in her eye that made her more interesting. Lately, women were less and less of a challenge and none of them had ever tried to shove him. He chuckled at the memory. Had Ellie actually tried to knock him down?

Where was she? He craned his neck. Suddenly, something moved beside him. Ellie crouched just behind him.

"You're a little old for this game," he whispered.

"Hush up, they'll hear you."

"You just faced down a gunman, but you're afraid of your parents?"

"I'm not," she said with a little too much force. Chance lifted an eyebrow and motioned to the hotel, challenging her to put up or shut up.

From the porch, Minnie called her daughter again. Ellie's chin sunk to her chest. Then she stood and walked with a slow, steady step back to the hotel, looking as reluctant as a man heading for a tooth-pulling.

"There you are. What happened up there?"

Ellie relayed a version of events in which Chance stopped the crazed husband, but she omitted that she had been standing between the shooter and his intended target. In her version, she had crouched behind the armoire, safely out of harm's way. And Chance suspected that Mrs. Rogers had not just happened into the room Ellie occupied, either. Ellie, it seemed, was quite a competent embellisher, which surprised him greatly. What other secrets had his little brown mouse been keeping?

"That Cahill boy," said Minnie, her voice dripping with distain.

Chance bristled, then reminded himself that he was eavesdropping. People who did that never heard good things about themselves.

He hoped Ellie would stick up for him, but it was Oscar who came to his defense.

"He's hardly a boy, dear. Remember that Chance Cahill saved our daughter's life. We owe him for that."

Minnie gave a little humphing sound to this. "He also turned the Royale into a shooting gallery. This is a quality establishment, not Dodge City. Our clientele expects safe, clean and opulent surroundings. It will hurt our business. You mark me."

"You know you'll be able to charge double for that room starting tomorrow."

Minnie paused to consider and then dismissed the idea. "Nonsense." She turned to her daughter. "And what were you thinking, locking yourself in with that woman?"

"I saw him coming down the hall with the gun, so I just…" Her voice trailed off.

"When you see a man draw a gun, you go the other way. I'd think a daughter of mine would have more sense."

"Brave thing to do," said Oscar, resting a hand on Ellie's shoulder.

"Foolish! We only have one daughter and I still have hopes for her, despite past failures. Quin and Bowie may be off the menu but there are the Fitzgerald boys, both single and well-to-do."

"And running wild as young colts in a spring pasture," added Oscar.

Chance set his jaw, galled at the realization that even Ira and Johny were placed ahead of him on Minnie's eligibility list.

"Ellen Louise could be the settling influence they need."

"There's one Cahill left," said Oscar.

Chance stilled, craning his neck so far that he almost fell clean over the woodpile. Did Oscar favor him?

Hold on a second! How has it suddenly come to this? One minute I'm riding into town after Leanna, and the next we're talking about...marriage...to Ellie?

But for all that, Ellie had thrown down a challenge refusing to kiss him and he did love a challenge....

But his thoughts were scattered when Ellie and Minnie spoke in unison.

"No," said Ellie.

"Absolutely not!"

It seemed the two women had finally found something they agreed on.

"Bowie is waiting in the office to speak to you, Ellen." Minnie dismissed Ellie as if she were a servant instead of a young woman who stood to inherit the largest hotel in town.

She went without a word, but Chance noted she paused just inside the door, looking back at him. Neither parent noticed her.

Chance would have left if he could have made it around the woodpile without notice, but he couldn't risk being caught overhearing such a conversation. With luck he'd get clear of the hotel before Bowie tracked him down. The longer he put off that conversation, the better.

"What are we going to do with the girl?" asked Minnie, her voice laced with despair.

"Let her be. Someone will come along when the time is right."

"Oh, Oscar!" she huffed. "The right man doesn't just come along. You have to lure him and bewitch him. Our daughter does not understand what it takes to make a good match. Lord knows I've tried to get her to see it."

"Now, Minnie."

"And she won't wear any of the lovely things I bought for her. She dresses like a shopkeeper, instead of one of the most eligible ladies in Cahill Crossing. She has a lovely figure, if she'd just show it off."

"Not everyone favors pink."

"Doesn't have the coloring for it, you mean. I swear she's as plain as brown paper wrapping. No wonder the shooter didn't see her. I can't see her even when I'm looking right at her."

Chance watched this thoughtless comment tear into Ellie. Her head dropped so he could no longer read her face. A flare of skirts made him think she had fled at this final humiliation.

What was wrong with the woman? Ellie wasn't flashy, like her mother, but neither was she brass and cloying. She had class—certainly more than her mother, who seemed more interested in clawing her way up the social ladder than in looking for a man who would treat Ellie with the dignity she deserved. If there was one thing Chance hated, it was a bully, and Minnie was just a tyrant in petticoats.

The Fitzgerald boys? From what he recalled those two were the terrors of the county. Not exactly husband material. And, in any case, not for Ellie.

Oscar hugged his wife and she melted against him.

Chance stood transfixed at the sight. Then Oscar kissed his wife. Not like a married man, but like a young buck with his girl on a Saturday night.

Minnie kissed him back and Chance had to look away.

"You go on in, dear. I'm going to smoke a cigar."

"Filthy habit." Minnie withdrew to the hotel, but her cheeks now held a healthy flush that made Chance squirm. He glanced to the kitchen, but Ellie seemed to have disappeared.

Mr. Jenkins retrieved a cigar and lit it. Then he lit another. He held out the second cigar.

"Do you smoke, Chance?"

Chance froze as his heart sprang into his throat. Suddenly he was a boy again, caught spying.

He stepped out from the woodpile and crossed the dusty backyard between the railroad tracks and the wide expanse of balconies flanking the hotel. Seemed every room had either a view of the town or the tracks.

"How'd you know I was here, sir?"

"Because if you weren't out here with my Ellie, you're not the man I think you are."

Knowing the former blockade runner thought him of such low character as to be outside trying to seduce his daughter did nothing to improve Chance's spirits. "I'm sorry. It's not what you—"

"You misunderstand me, son. I mean to say I'd be disappointed."

He offered the lit cigar and Chance accepted it.

Oscar clamped his teeth around the end and puffed a moment. "My wife cannot stand the smoke." He grinned as he removed the cigar. "And so I find myself smoking more and more."

Chance remembered the kiss and thought Oscar

enjoyed his wife more than he let on. He glanced at the glowing tip of the thick cigar, before placing the other end in his mouth. He gave it no encouragement to continue to burn as he clamped down on the rolled tobacco leaves.

"I do not share my wife's opinions where you are concerned. I'm sorry you had to hear my wife's harangue. She only wants what's best for her daughter. Unfortunately, she simply does not understand our girl well enough to know what that is. Ellie's more like me, you see, and she just baffles Minnie. She isn't plain."

"No, sir, she isn't."

"I want to thank you for getting Ellie out unharmed. And if you need a place to stay, I'd be happy to have you here in this hotel."

"I don't think your wife would approve."

Oscar laughed and rested a hand on Chance's shoulder, giving his muscle a quick knead. It was a gesture that his father would have used and it made Chance achingly aware of what he had lost. Oscar's hand slid away.

"Nonsense. You think an old rum runner like me can't get around a blockade? You just leave Minnie to me."

"Thanks for the offer, but I plan on staying with Leanna. She has a gaming hall. I saw it from the train. Seemed like it had rooms upstairs."

"Don't the girls stay there?"

Chance smiled. "Why, I guess they do."

"Well, if that doesn't work out as you expect, the offer stands." Oscar puffed on his cigar. "Your father was a friend of mine. Funny things have been happening since his passing."

What kind of things? "Sir?"

"You seen Leanna yet?"

Chance shook his head.

"Well, she'll fill you in. Expect you haven't met her husband then."

Chance cocked his head. "Come again?"

"Caused quite a stir. She married a gambler name of Holden, Cleve Holden. They're newly wed."

Chance's muscles tensed. That was the man Leanna's landlady had mentioned. The man who had followed Leanna from Deadwood. What on earth was going on?

Chapter Three

Oscar Jenkins did not seem to note Chance clenching his teeth, for he continued on.

"Not everyone is pleased that Leanna placed her business this side of the tracks, Chance," said Ellie's father. "I'm not one of them, but she's had a fight on her hands. Just wanted you to know."

"Obliged," said Chance, and replaced his gray Stetson. He headed out of the Royale, coming to the street and heading west. This row of businesses had two fronts, he realized, one for those arriving by rail and one for those arriving from the street.

Seemed the town was not all that had changed. Leanna was married! Chance wondered if she'd lost her damned mind. First the whores and then adopting that baby, and now she'd wed a gambler. It seemed his little sister was determined to live a life of ruination.

Well, good for her. He was certain her decisions chaffed both Quin and Bowie and that pleased him even more. However, he had to admit he didn't like what he had heard about her husband.

Chance reached the gaming hall with its wide welcoming porch set with a row of chairs occupied by men drinking in the shade of the roof. A sign above them read Leanna's Place. Below that the sign advertised Gaming and Spirits for Gentlemen of Refined Taste.

He stepped from the sunny, dusty street to the cool lively interior. Inside, Cassie Magill, the piano player, plunked out a tune from her seat beside several dining tables, all occupied by male customers enjoying a meal. The floors were polished to a shine and the long bar held padded stools that were also occupied. He'd never seen a saloon with couches and armchairs before, but there were several lining the walls, allowing guests to have conversation and enjoy their tobacco. Chance made a full circle to take it all in, impressed as hell. This place was a palace. He felt proud and amazed all at once.

He stopped when he faced the large stained-glass window. The outside sunlight made the image instantly recognizable. Leanna had chosen to have her artist recreate the 4C, with the ranch house in the center top and the horses grazing peacefully at the bottom. There was Night, Bowie's black gelding, and Quin's big bay, Cactus. Chance stared at Rip, his grulla Morgan, wondering how they found blue-gray glass. There they were, the horses of her three brothers, frozen in time and glass. Chance felt a hitch in his throat. He turned his back on the window and scanned the room, recognizing several of the female dealers as the former whores that Leanna had rescued from a life of shame. But he didn't see his sister. He headed for the closest table and the tall raven-haired woman dealing cards.

"Lucinda, where's Annie?"

The woman stood in surprise, then recalled the half-dealt hands and finished distributing the cards with haste. As the men looked at their cards, Lucinda looked at him.

"Why, Chance, didn't you make time? Miss Leanna is in the back at the high-stakes tables." She pointed. "Just through there."

Chance headed toward the back of the hall.

"Sure is good to see you, Chance, honey."

Several of Leanna's girls had decided that he'd be a fine catch, so he steered clear of them when possible. He wasn't the marrying sort. Why any woman would want to tie herself to him was beyond Chance. He sure had proved himself to be as irresponsible as they came. And bounty hunters didn't exactly make good husbands.

The piano music stopped so abruptly Chance wondered if someone had kicked the stool out from under Cassie.

"Chance, sweetie, that you?" The piano player now had custody of his arm. Cassie clung to him like a tick on a dog, batting her lashes over green eyes. "My, aren't you a sight?" She scratched his thick whiskers and then pushed playfully at his chest. "You need a bath, Chance. We got a tub upstairs."

His sister would break his legs if he let Cassie give him a bath.

"Annie?"

"Oh, I'll take you to her. She sure will be happy to see you. Lots happened since we seen you last, sweetie. Though you ain't changed any, still handsome as the devil hisself." She led him along, her arm looped in his, as if she belonged there. Chance didn't have the energy to shake her off.

Cassie drew back a velvet curtain and there sat

Leanna, looking pretty as ever in a shiny blue gown with a modest, tight-fitting bodice. Beside her lounged a tall, dark-headed stranger with deep brown eyes and a set of duds that were clean and pressed. Chance scowled, not liking his fancy, satiny, bone-colored waistcoat or anything else about the man.

"Table's full, sir," he said, his accent telling Chance he hailed from the south. So this was the gambler who had married his sister.

Chance curled his lip and threw back his duster to show his guns. The man did not cower or rise, simply retrieved a small pistol from one of the four waistcoat pockets, placing it before him on the table and then laying his hand across the grip as he looked to Chance to make his move.

"Chance!"

His sister, Leanna, sprang to her feet and bounded toward him as if she were still ten instead of nearly twenty-eight.

The gambler returned his weapon to his vest.

Chance released his gun grips and hugged her and then drew back to look at her. She was as pretty as a blooming rose, her cheeks flushed pink and her blue eyes sparkling. Her black hair was swept up in an elaborate, elegant coiffure that made him realize with a jolt that she was no longer a girl, but a woman full-grown.

"You got my letter?"

Chance nodded, taking hold of Annie's elbow to lead her…where?

"Cassie, my blossom, could you take over the table?" said the stranger who had been seated beside Leanna.

Cassie seemed grieved to leave Chance, but she did as the man bid her. Chance stared at the gambler as he unfolded from his seat. He was big, lean and his charming half grin peeved Chance to extremes.

"Chance, this is my husband, Cleve Holden. We were married very recently."

Cleve extended his hand. "A pleasure, Mr. Cahill. I've heard so much about you, I feel as though we're old friends."

Chance narrowed his eyes on the man and did not take his hand. "That right?"

Leanna looked anxious now. "Aren't you going to congratulate us?"

He looked at his sister. She seemed hale and happy, but this whole thing had sprung on him like a wildcat.

"I don't know yet. Give me a minute, Annie."

Cleve dropped his hand, sliding both into his satiny waistcoat pockets. He reminded Chance of every gambler he'd ever met, amiable and untrustworthy. He didn't like him, not one little bit.

"We need to talk," he said to Leanna, then glanced back at Holden as he spoke again. "Privately."

His welcoming smile never faltered and he took no visible insult. "I've got to get back to the table. A pleasure to meet you, Mr. Cahill. Welcome home, sir."

Chance lifted his brow. This town was no more his home than this man was family.

"Come on," said Leanna, gripping him about the arm. "Let's go find a table."

His sister fed him a fine lunch of strong black coffee, sour pickles, slabs of white bread and a stew so thick you could stand a spoon in it and so good that he ate two full bowls. When he looked up it was to find Leanna looking both shocked and amused at the speed with which he had downed her fine meal.

"You still eat like a wolf," she mused. "Come on. Let's go to my office."

He followed her to a room dominated by a large cluttered desk and a tall safe painted with an elaborate gilding. Chance leaned against the windowsill while Leanna sat behind the desk.

Chance folded his arms, not realizing until that instant how bone-weary his body was. Days and days with little rest had made him as surly as a wet badger.

"Tell me," he said.

"Quin and Bowie found out that Tobias Hobbs had hired some men to murder our folks."

"Names?"

"Huck Allen, Vernon Pettit and Saul Bream. But they're all dead."

Chance didn't hide his disappointment.

"Hobbs murdered two of his own men, but the third, Bream, agreed to testify against Hobbs, but he killed him, too."

"You mean *Marshal* Hobbs, the lawman?"

Leanna nodded. "Before Bowie could catch him, a sharpshooter killed Hobbs. Quin said all along that Hobbs was working for someone. Seems he was right."

"Any idea who that might be?"

She shook her head. "Bowie is working on that."

Chance didn't know where to begin. His head was spinning so fast he felt like he was breaking horses.

"I've been helping with Bowie. Before Hobbs died he made mention of Van Slyck. Bowie asked me to find out what I could about them. Of course we didn't know which one he meant, Preston or Willem." She must have seen his confusion for she elaborated. "You know him. He was Pa's banker. We think he's embezzling money from the 4C."

"That make him the killer?"

Leanna gave him a look of impatience. "We don't know yet. He has the money to hire help. And if he's not our man it seems likely that he'll know who is. When Quin gets back from Dodge, he's demanding an audit. He's bringing a bank examiner from Austin to look at the books. You know, someone from the outside."

"So we still don't know who did kill Ma and Pa?"

Annie sighed. "There's no wanted poster, if that's what you mean. Did you expect to just ride in here and shoot someone?"

Pretty much.

"If it were that simple, Bowie would have arrested someone. We just don't know if Van Slyck is working alone. Someone has been cutting fences and rebranding cattle. Might be a partner or more hired help. And then there's the sharpshooter who killed Hobbs. We just don't know."

"So what am I suppose to do?"

"Help us, of course."

"I don't work for outfits anymore."

"Fiddlesticks. This is Mama and Papa we're talking about."

"And you're married?"

"Don't you take that tone with me. He's a good man and you'd like him if you weren't dead set against it."

"You know he followed you from Deadwood?"

"I know it." Her eyes flashed defiance. It was a look he had enjoyed watching her cast out on more than one occasion but was not in the habit of receiving it himself.

"I don't trust a man who spends more on his suit than his horse."

Leanna lifted her chin in an arrogant pose that used to drive Quin crazy. "You haven't seen his horse yet."

The door creaked open. If it was her husband, he vowed to poke him in the nose. Instead, a little boy peeked in. His face was covered with freckles and his two front teeth were growing in, making him look like a speckled rabbit. This was another of the strays that Leanna had taken under her wide wings, a Deadwood orphan.

"What is it, Melvin?" Leanna's voice had gone all soft and she suddenly reminded Chance of their mother.

"I heard Bowie was here." He looked at Chance and his face lit up.

"Melvin, you remember Chance?"

He bounded in, stopping just before Chance to bounce as if he were on springs.

"Hi, Chance. You remember me? I've been practicing my draw and shoot." Melvin did an imitation of a fast draw from an imaginary holster using his finger as a gun. "You staying? You can sleep in my room. I got my own bed!"

Leanna laughed and pulled him beside her with an easy hug. Melvin scrambled up into her lap and kicked his legs back and forth.

Chance wondered how he'd gotten a scab on the bridge of his nose.

Melvin stared at the twin pistols that crisscrossed Chance's hips.

"You catch any more outlaws?"

Chance glanced at Leanna and she smiled encouragingly. He didn't often speak to children and always felt awkward. The boy's stare was too direct and his expression completely unguarded.

"A few."

"Boy, I sure would like to be a bounty hunter and ride a fast horse." He slipped from Leanna's embrace and inched forward in a slow, steady advance, firing questions like bullets. "What kind of guns you got? Can I hold one? Will you teach me to shoot?"

Chance found himself backing away until he hit the safe. Leanna giggled. "The mighty Chance Cahill run to ground by a boy."

"He asks a lot of questions."

"That's sure."

The door creaked open to reveal the massive head of a large animal. Chance drew his gun as a huge dabble-gray hound stepped in.

"Stretch!" Leanna's sharp tone caused the enormous dog to halt on the spot. She turned to the boy. "He's not allowed in my office. Please, take him out."

"Aww!"

"Go on."

That was a tone he recalled from their mother, as well. When had Leanna become so maternal? Chance thought it suited her somehow.

She had a hand on the boy's bony back between his shoulder blades.

"Is he staying with us? He could share my room. I wouldn't mind." Melvin turned to Chance. "Will you tell me a story before bed?"

"No."

Leanna scowled at Chance, then spoke to the boy. "Scoot now."

She stood in the door watching the boy and dog retreat.

"I almost shot that dog," said Chance.

"He'd never forgive you. He loves that dog and so do I."

"Whose is he?" asked Chance, coming up to stand in the doorway beside her.

"Well, he's ours, of course."

"Like that baby?"

Leanna spun on him so quick he had time only to fall back against the door frame before she had her finger pressed deep into the muscle of his chest. Chance retreated a step.

"Cabe is *mine*. You understand? Mine and Cleve's. You tell anyone otherwise and I'll never speak to you again."

Clearly, his sister had lost her damned mind. "All right. Understood. He's yours." Even though he knew different.

Leanna continued to glare for another long moment.

He dropped his scowl and lifted his hands in surrender. Leanna accepted her victory with good grace.

"Where are you staying?" she asked.

"Thinking of bunking here."

"In my office?"

Chance pointed toward the ceiling. "You got two more floors."

"Chance, the girls stay upstairs." Leanna spoke to him with the tone one uses on someone who is addled.

Chance glanced out at the gaming hall, expecting Bowie to track him down any minute. Being town marshal, he'd need to speak to the man who'd killed a gambler at the Château Royale.

His older brother was always good at finding the strays and cutting them back to the herd. Well, Chance wasn't interested in rejoining the Cahill herd. He was in town for a reason. When he'd killed the man who did this to his family, he'd blow out of here as fast as the north wind.

"Chance, you can't stay here without ruining their reputations."

"They're whores."

Leanna fisted her hips and Chance knew he'd stepped too far, again. Used to be he and Leanna got on without words.

"Not anymore they're not. Now they are respectable, working women and they deserve to be treated as such. They work the tables, play the piano, and that's *all* they play. And, I'll have you know, I'm in the process of turning this place over to them. Soon they'll be business owners."

Leanna cared for her strays like family. Chance stilled with the recognition that she'd built herself a new family from the ashes of the old. She had sisters, true sisters, among these women, and now she had a husband and children, too. Where did he fit in?

Like a lost calf in a blizzard, Chance saw himself drifting farther and farther afield.

Leanna had built something to be proud of here. What had he to show for two years of work as a bounty hunter? He looked at the worn grip of his pistols.

He only took the worst of the bounties, feeling certain that the world was a better place because of the removal of those outlaws. But the experience had changed him. Shooting a man will do that. It's not the same as picking off tin cans from the tops of fence posts.

"Chance? Are you listening?"

He roused himself.

Leanna was now leaning back on her desk. She pushed off, coming to stand before him. "I was inviting you to supper. Meet my Cleve properly. You sure are welcome to stay at our place for as long as you like. We're renting a darling little house with plenty of room, until we get the ranch house built."

Oscar Jenkins's words spun in his head. Leanna and Cleve were newly wed. The very last thing a new husband wants in his upstairs bedroom is his wife's brother.

"I'll pass."

"Well, where will you stay?"

"With Bowie?"

"He's sleeping at the jail until the wedding. Wouldn't be proper for him to stay at the Morning Glory any longer."

Chance stared blankly.

"What with them being engaged. You see?"

He continued to stare, trying to understand her. "With who being engaged?"

"Bowie, silly. He's engaged to Merritt Dixon?"

"Who's Merritt Dixon?"

Leanna flounced back in her chair. "Why, Chance, I told you he had a girl the last time we talked."

"Yeah, but you didn't say he was marrying her."

"He hadn't asked her then. But now he has. She's pretty and smart and just the best thing ever to happen to Bowie. Chance, soon you'll be the only one of us not married."

Chance didn't want a wife, but somehow Leanna pointing out that he was alone didn't cheer him. In fact, it soured his mood still further.

"Now that he and Merritt are engaged, he can't very well stay in her boardinghouse, can he? I imagine it's hard for him after keeping company with her. He's been grumpy as an old bear since he moved out. Wedding can't come quick enough for him, I think. It's her second, and her first was a Texas Ranger. So she had some doubts about Bowie, him being a lawman, as well, you see."

Chance was still trying to get his mind around the

idea of Bowie being someone's husband. He sure was serious enough. He hoped the gal had some fun in her because his brother was as grim as death most days.

"He still takes his supper there. But now that I think of it, his room is unoccupied. And Merritt would be happy to have you. I mean, you'll be family soon."

Chance gave her a look.

"Well, Chance, you'd have to give her time to get used to the idea. Bowie could take it up for you."

"I'm not taking up residence under his woman's roof. I swear, Annie, you are just plain crazy sometimes."

"I hadn't thought of it that way."

Plus he had only eight dollars and sixty cents to his name until Bullock wired him the money. "Oscar Jenkins said I can stay at the Royale." Though Chance couldn't pay for it until he got his bounty.

He had given Leanna every bounty he'd earned for two years. He hadn't had much need for money, bedding out wherever he found himself. Now he found himself in the unenviable position of needing to ask for some of it back. He glanced at her but pride kept his jaw locked shut.

Her dark eyebrows lifted. "Oh, well, if you prefer. You understand why you can't stay above this place, don't you? My goodness, the way Callie looks at you, I just don't know. She's young and impressionable."

"She's no younger than you, I expect."

"But she seems younger. Doesn't she?" Leanna reached out to him and clasped one of his hands with both of hers. "I'm so glad to have you back, Chance. I love Quin and Bowie, but they just don't understand me like you do."

"You mean you can't lead them around by the nose."

She giggled and released his hand with a soft little

pat. "That's true. Are you sure you don't want to stay with us? We certainly have the room."

"I'll stay at the Royale, for now." Chance ambled toward the door and Leanna followed, walking at his side.

"Well, I won't stop you, though I don't know what you can do in a hotel that you can't do right under my roof."

He gave her the look.

She straightened and flushed. "Oh, well. I see. But the Royale won't abide drunkenness or loose women and you need a bath before you go over there again."

Chance brushed his hand over his forehead. He hadn't had a headache in years, but Leanna seemed bound and determined to give him one.

"Annie, I don't want to stay with my baby sister and her new husband. It's not right."

"That's silly. We're family."

"Is it? Then why didn't you go and stay with Quin when you came back?"

The color in her cheeks now spread down her neck. "That's not the same. Quin and I have differences. And he did not approve of my status as an unwed mother."

"Your…"

Leanna raised a finger to chasten him and Chance fell silent, reminding him of their earlier discussion about the child she called her own.

"You're going to have to explain this to me sometime."

She looked so sad that he was sorry he'd brought it up. "Sometime, maybe." She patted his cheek. "I'm glad you're finally here. We'll figure this out now. I'm certain of it."

"We'd better, because I can't stand to stay anywhere for long."

Leanna gasped. "But this is your home."

Chance snorted. "No, Annie. My home is long ago. It doesn't even exist anymore."

"That ranch belongs to all of us."

"He can keep my share so long as I don't have to see him to do it."

"But we have to work together on this."

He rose. "No, Annie, we don't. I work alone. You know that."

He put his hat on his head, adjusting it low over his eyes. "Got to go find Bowie before he sends a search party after me."

"A search party? Why?" She must have read his look because her eyes widened. "Chance? What happened?"

He told her about the gambler and Ellie. Leanna wobbled and Chance clasped her elbow to steady her a moment.

She gripped his forearm tight. "Are y'all right?"

He gave her a grin and a wink. "You know how fast I am."

Too damn fast, he thought. His words only served to earn him a lecture about being more careful and how much he worried her. She even gave him a little hell afterward. When she ran out of steam, he stepped through her door and she walked him out, her expression still troubled.

"Dinner?"

"Not tonight."

"You are not going to avoid me for long, Chance Cahill. I want you to meet Cleve properly."

He kissed her cheek and then headed out to find his brother. With any luck Bowie would arrest him and he'd have a place to sleep for the night.

Chapter Four

Chance found only Bowie's deputy, Glen Whitaker, at the jail. Whitaker somewhat resembled an image Chance had once seen of General Custer because of his wide forehead and bushy mustache, which was fixed above a neatly trimmed narrow brown beard that covered only his chin. Unlike Custer, Whitaker had vacant blue eyes that did not indicate a deep thinker. He directed Chance to the undertakers, which was conveniently right next door.

Once there, Chance was greeted by Wallace Druckman, the undertaker, a short barrel of a man in a clean white shirt, paper collar and a resplendent peacock-green waistcoat complete with gold watch chain and a fob. At first glance it looked like a gold nugget, but on closer inspection, Chance decided it was a human skull. Druckman's trousers also looked new and sported a narrow gray-and-black striped pattern. Business, it seemed, was good.

"Mr. Cahill. A pleasure to meet you at last." He took up Chance's hand in two of his before Chance offered it. Then he shook it in a deferential, disingenuous way that Chance despised. Chance came away smelling of chemicals. "I have just been admiring your work. A clean shot, sir, very clean, indeed. I see you are not undeserving of your reputation and tales of your deadly accuracy are surprisingly, well, accurate, if you don't mind the pun."

He didn't mind a pun when he heard one, which he still hadn't.

"Bowie?" he said.

"Yes, sir. Right this way." He motioned to a curtain, still grinning. "He's in the back. We've just received another delivery. A child. Very sad for all concerned." His face went from jubilant to regretful in an eye blink. "Even someone as hardened by death as I am is still touched when I see one so young taken from this world by…"

Chance stepped past him, leaving him to finish his speech without the benefit of an audience. Druckman's words trailed off and he hustled to follow.

"Yes. Right this way," he said from behind him. "I wondered, Mr. Cahill, if you would object to my public display of the gambler's remains."

"Do as you like."

Chance ducked past the red velvet curtain and into the storage room, surprised to find the back wall completely missing so the space more resembled a barn than mortuary. The man he'd shot was already laid out on a board, balanced between two sawhorses, his fancy coat and clothing in perfect order, but his mouth was open and his eyes seemed to stare fixedly at the bullet hole that marred his otherwise unblemished complexion.

"Shouldn't aim your pistols at women," he muttered

as he continued on to Bowie, who stood beside a man he didn't recognize.

As he drew near he saw the body of a young Mexican girl of perhaps seven, her long black hair wrapped about her like ropes and her pretty green dress now sodden and clinging. Unlike the other corpse, this girl's eyes were closed and her mouth tipped in a smile. If not for her pallor and the blue tinge to her lips, she might have been asleep. Chance wondered if her death had been hard. Drowning seemed to him a bad end, as you had time to see it coming, time to fight and then realize you were not going to win. Still, she was at peace now and Chance felt a familiar but still unsettling twinge of jealousy.

He flanked the table and Bowie glanced up at him. "Chance, meet Doc Lewis."

He offered his hand over the body to a man with kindly brown eyes and a welcoming smile. The doctor's handshake was firm, but he did not try to impress Chance with either his grip strength or his demeanor. Chance liked him.

"Also the town coroner," said Bowie as the men dropped hands as if both had just realized they were clasped over the remains of a child.

"I've examined Mr. Rogers over there." He indicated the other corpse. "Told the marshal that you shot from close range, that the man was facing you at the time and that the bullet was the cause of death."

Chance nodded and then caught Bowie glaring at him. His brother was just dying to lay into him, but the doctor's presence checked him. Chance considered following the doctor home.

Lewis drew a long intake of breath and then lowered

his gaze to the girl. He placed a hand on the child's stomach and pushed. Water gurgled from her mouth.

"Looks like a drowning to me," he said to Bowie.

"Fell in the river according to her father," said Bowie, his expression as grim as Chance had ever seen it.

Chance had seen more dead men than most, but he felt queasy now. He'd never looked at a death like this.

"She didn't fall."

Chance looked up to see a dark-skinned man in jeans, a checked work shirt, yellow kerchief and a sombrero who was standing at the wide opening in the back of the building. He lifted his head to reveal skin browned by the sun, dark brown eyes and a thick black mustache that did not completely hide his frown.

"Miguel," said Bowie, acknowledging the man.

Chance recognized him now as Miguel Martinez stepped from the harsh sunlight and into the shade of the morgue. This was the tanner's son. His father, Jose, had been tanning hides from all the area ranches for years, just for local use. Miguel brought them downriver to town or sold them elsewhere. That meant this child was one of his sisters.

Chance looked again, recalling a younger version of this girl playing with her siblings outside their adobe house up on the South Kiowa across the river from the border between the 4C and Fitzgerald spread.

"You see something?" asked Bowie.

Jose arrived, trotting into the room, his shirt stained with sweat as if he'd run all the way from the river. He was a shorter, darker version of his son with muscular arms and thick calloused hands. Jose grabbed his son in a bear hug as he shouted in Spanish. Miguel wrestled with his father as the smaller man pulled him out into the sun.

"You check her body, Doc," shouted Miguel. "You'll see."

Father and son faced off. Bowie followed them out into the yard trailed by the undertaker. The shouting grew louder. Chance was about to follow when the doctor pulled the girl's dress up over her head. Chance stilled. There across the child's torso were the clear marks left by a rope. The men exchanged looks.

"Someone lassoed this girl," said Lewis.

Chance scratched his whiskered cheek. "Maybe to haul her out?"

"Or drag her in."

Bowie had sent his deputy out to the Martinez place to talk to the family and find out what had happened. Chance thought it a fool's errand, since Jose wasn't talking and Miguel had gone dumb after his father had gotten hold of him.

Now Bowie sat tilted back in his office chair with one boot resting on his scarred wooden desk, eyeing Chance, who leaned against a window frame, arms folded tight across his chest.

"I haven't had a single unnatural death since Saul Bream and now you show up and I got two bodies in one day," said Bowie. Thanks to Leanna, Chance knew that Bream was the last of the three hired murderers to die.

"You telling me you would have done different?"

Bowie dragged his foot off the desk and his boot heel struck the floor hard. He looked tired. "Just an observation."

"Annie left me the telegram Quin sent. She said Ma's and Pa's deaths were no accident."

Bowie pressed his lips together and his blue eyes

turned cold. All three of them had inherited various shades of their mother's blue eyes, except Quin, who had their father's gray eyes.

"We looking at a murder here?"

"Appears so. Made to look like a robbery gone bad, but it's much more than that. Three men, hired by Marshal Hobbs to make their deaths look like an accident."

"Vernon Pettit, Huck Allen and Saul Bream."

"All dead. The first one tried extortion on Quin."

Chance raised his eyebrows and Bowie nodded as if to confirm someone would really be that stupid.

"Quin shot him. That was Allen." Bowie paused.

Chance shook his head. "Don't know him. Never seen a dodger on him, either." A dodger was a wanted poster, most of which Bowie would also have seen.

"Addie K. stabbed his accomplice, but he got away with two thousand dollars."

"Who's Addie?"

"Quin's wife. Adrianna McKnight Cahill."

"See, I wouldn't think a bleeding man with that kind of money would be hard to find."

"Quin was also shot in the exchange."

Chance pushed off the wall. Surely Leanna would have mentioned if Quin was...

Bowie lifted a hand. "He's all right. Mostly healed up and gone to Dodge with the fall cattle drive at present. Should be back anytime. I know you two can't wait to catch up."

"I can wait."

The two exchanged a smile.

"He got married?"

"She owns the ranch adjoining the 4C just north of Fitzgerald's spread. She's from Boston."

Chance scowled at this piece of information.

"When she moved in, cattle went missing, fences got cut. They each thought the other one was behind it."

"Who was?"

"Not sure. But the trouble seems to have stopped for now."

"He still as bossy as God Almighty?"

Bowie didn't ask who he meant. "His wife has settled him some."

"Like to see that."

"You will, I guess. You stay around long enough."

"Only staying to see this through."

Bowie nodded.

"What about the other two? How'd they die?"

"Marshal Hobbs killed Vernon Pettit. The third man was a childhood friend of Merritt's."

Another detail Leanna had omitted. Chance narrowed his eyes and Bowie pressed his hands flat to his desk, his eyes daring Chance to say just one word. He'd fought Bowie before and knew his older brother was the stronger man. He kept quiet, letting the accusation burn inside.

Bowie sat back. "I know. I felt the same way at first. Man alive, I was steamed. But if it wasn't for him, we'd never have known that Hobbs hired them. Bream told us that Hobbs hired Pettit specifically to kill our parents, Chance. Then Pettit rounded up a couple of his buddies to help him."

"That doesn't make any sense. Hobbs had no bone to pick with our folks."

"I know. So we need to find out who hired Hobbs."

"Van Slyck? Annie mentioned him." Chance toyed with one of the bullets on his gun belt, lifting it half out of the leather sheath and absently pressing it back down as he did when restless.

"Merritt's friend exposed him before he died. Said he heard Hobbs mention Van Slyck."

Chance rested a hand upon his favorite gun. "Which one?"

"That's the trouble, isn't it? We didn't know, but Quin and I think he meant Willem, the banker."

Chance pushed off the ledge. Bowie followed him to his feet. "Chance, you can't just walk over there and stick a gun in his face."

"Why not?"

"Because I'll have to arrest you, for one thing."

"Bowie, you may have to work inside the law, but I sure as hell don't."

"You break the law and I'll lock you up."

"Fine. What did Hobbs say?"

"Nothing. I tracked him down but a sniper got him before he said a word."

"You catch the sniper?"

Bowie looked at his desk blotter.

"Hell, Bowie, you let him get away?"

Bowie slapped both hands down on the blotter, making the ink bottle and pen rest jump.

Chance kicked at nothing in particular.

"Ah, hell." Chance dragged a chair before Bowie's desk and turned it backward, straddling the seat. "So some murderer tries to sell information to Quin. Quin gets shot, kills two men and the other guy gets away. Hobbs kills that one and Merritt's friend." He looked at Bowie. "This sure got complicated real fast."

"But Quin only killed one. Hobbs got the others. Bream is the one who mentioned Van Slyck."

Chance cradled his head. "Then someone else killed Hobbs?"

"From a good distance. I found the shell casing. Hell

of an aim, that. He made that shot from seven hundred and fifty yards."

That got Chance's attention. A shot from such a distance demanded a rare combination of skill and precision. "That doesn't sound like the kind of shot a banker can generally make."

Bowie lifted his brow and Chance knew he'd already thought of that.

"Was Quin with you?"

"Recuperating from the gunshot."

The men exchanged a long look. Chance knew Bowie could use the help and that he wouldn't approve of his methods. Question was, did he tell Bowie what he planned to do or just go do it?

Most of his life Chance had done as he pleased and then dealt with the consequences afterward. He figured this was little different.

Bowie cleared his throat. "If you're going to do anything illegal, I can't be a part of it."

Seemed his big brother had become a mind reader.

"I know it."

"But if you need me, I'll back you up with everything I got."

Chance blinked at him. Bowie had just offered him an olive branch.

Chance nodded. "You know I'll do the same. Don't shut me out, Bowie. I'm not a kid anymore. I can help you."

"I know it."

Bowie stood and collected his hat from the peg by the door. "Time to head over to the Morning Glory for supper. Come along. You can meet Merritt."

Chance shook his head.

"I'm gonna marry her, Chance. You'll have to meet her sometime."

"Not stinking from the trail and covered with dust."

Bowie nodded. "That's probably best. Where you headed now?"

"The Royale. I fancy trying one of their steaks." What he really fancied was seeing Ellen Louise Jenkins and trying to collect that second kiss. Something about that girl just made him want to aggravate her. My, she was a sight when she was riled.

"Fine choice. You know I got an extra cot in the back. I can drag it out for you."

"Naw."

"Bunkhouse at the 4C?"

Chance glared.

Bowie laughed and slapped him on the back as they headed out the door. "Didn't think so. But I've been back out there. It's changed a bit."

"I don't give a damn about it. I just want to find who killed our folks, then put this town behind me."

"I see." Bowie paused outside the door under the wide porch. "I hope you'll stay for the wedding."

Chance felt regret bubbling up like groundwater. "No promises."

"All right. Don't know what Merritt will say. She's got place cards for everyone who's attending."

"Place cards. What the hell?"

Bowie grinned. "You have no idea."

They walked past the new opera house. Chance paused to look at it.

Bowie pointed toward the sign. "Ma would have liked that. A real opera house."

Chance ground his teeth as he always did when he

thought of their mother and then kept walking. The boardinghouse was right next door.

"Good location," said Bowie. "Right at the end of the street. You can see it from Steven's Restaurant and it's close to the depot."

Chance rubbed his neck, anxious to be gone. "Yeah. I'll see you tomorrow in case you want to arrest me."

Bowie clamped him on the shoulder. Chance realized that he was the same height as Bowie now, though still slightly leaner.

"Don't shoot anyone."

"You know where Van Slyck spends his evenings?"

Bowie's smile faded. "The gentlemen's room at the Château Royale or at Leanna's Place. Why?"

"Thought I might have a talk with him."

"Chance, I don't want him tipped off that Quin is getting a bank examiner. He can't know ahead of time. You steer clear of him or you'll ruin my investigation."

"Well, good thing I'm not one of your deputies or I'd have to listen to you. 'Night, brother." He tipped his hat.

Chance turned up the street toward the railroad feeling Bowie's eyes boring into his back like hot coals.

Chance spent half his remaining resources at the bathhouse. Once shaved and shorn, he slipped into a clean white shirt from his saddlebags. The bathhouse had done a fine job brushing his trousers and oiling up his leather vest and boots, so you could hardly see the scars and scuffs. They'd also brushed the grime and mud off his black duster, which he returned to his bags. He would have liked to put on a jacket, but he had none, preferring waistcoats, which allowed his arms to move more freely. Thus appointed and smelling of musk and bay rum, Chance ventured toward the Royale, certain that his reception would be no more than lukewarm.

He wondered if Ellie would even recognize him without two weeks' growth of whiskers on his face. He thought of her standing with that cowering woman in her arms, just daring that bastard to shoot at them. Brave and foolish thing to do. Oscar Jenkins was right about one thing—his daughter definitely took after him. Question was, why had she stayed in that hotel so long?

He'd heard what her mother had had to say and it burned him like staring up at the summer sun. Most girls would have lit out with the first likely man they came across. Why hadn't she?

He wondered if she was like Quin, determined to stick, no matter what. Was she waiting to inherit that hotel? He hoped not, because she was paying for it every day she let her mother talk her down.

Chance passed Leanna's Place and the string of other businesses that must be paying through the nose to have their establishments sit between the tracks and the depot.

He stepped across the wide porch that skirted the street side of the Château Royale and marched back into the fancy lobby, noting how the little crystals in the chandelier caught the afternoon light and sent rainbows skittering across the ceiling.

The next thing he noticed was Ellie.

Chapter Five

The Château Royale was where one came to see and be seen, but to Ellie it was just a pretty cage. She stood beside the open frosted-glass door that led to the dining room, her gaze sweeping the lobby. The hardwood floors gleamed, the fireplace and clusters of opulently upholstered sofas beckoned guests to linger and the ornate tin ceiling and elaborate fixtures added touches of sophistication.

They even had a gentlemen's room, though Ellie was not allowed to enter it. Her mother said it was less busy than usual and blamed Leanna for drawing away some of the most influential men in town. Ellie was happy for her friend's success, envious of her freedom and horrified over how the town had treated her because of it. Heaven knew, Leanna had been through the mill and she could think of no one more deserving of happiness.

Ellie glanced at the open doors leading to the street, likening herself to a bird perched in a cage with the door left wide-open and still she did not fly away. Where would she go?

Guests passed from the stairs and through the lobby. Ellie watched from her place in the elaborate archway that marked the dining area, greeting guests by name and seeing them to their tables before turning them over to the waitstaff with introductions.

She had run the waiters and the chambermaids since she was fifteen years old, back at the old hotel in Wolf Grove, and turnover was rare, unless Ellie's mother decided to "help." Then people tended to quit without notice.

When her mom moved to the hotel reception, and left the running of the place to Ellie and her father, things went back to normal. Her mother did prefer conversation and shopping to the daily running of the hotel, and Ellie had to admit, the Château Royale was a glittering bastion of refinement that leaned just shy of ostentation. Flamboyant would be an adequate description.

Ellie greeted Dr. Lewis as he paused before her. The doctor was only slightly older than she and had recently spent more than the necessary time with her before taking his usual seat for dinner. His long looks made her uncomfortable, but she held her smile.

"I hear you had a very trying day," said Lewis. "You'd never suspect it to look at you. Most women I know would require smelling salts. But you're not one for smelling salts or headaches or dizzy spells, are you, Miss Jenkins? In fact, I only recall treating you that one time."

Ellie rubbed her thumb over her index finger absently as she recalled slicing herself with a knife and Dr. Lewis, then newly arrived in town, stitching her up.

"Clumsy of me."

The good doctor continued to stare, holding his brown derby before him with both hands.

Ellie cleared her throat and tried to think. Her mother was so much more natural at making small talk. He'd mentioned the shooting.

"It was a pity that Mr. Rogers could not hear reason," she said at last. Should she not have mentioned that? Ladies didn't speak of killings to gentlemen. She glanced toward her mother to find her watching like a cat from her place behind the ornately carved reception desk.

"Men can be jealous creatures," said Lewis. "They don't always see straight where beautiful women are concerned." He smiled at that and Ellie shifted restlessly.

"I have your table ready." She swept her arm toward the dining area and then led the way, leaving him to follow. She left him at his usual place, just beyond her post, and he chose to sit facing her as usual.

When she returned to her station, it was to find her mother regarding her with lifted brows, speculatively, as if Ellie had done something surprising.

The sour taste returned to her mouth. She did not share her mother's lust for her to wed a wealthy man.

She did not need wealth to be happy, which was a mercy, since neither Quin nor Bowie had shown interest in her whatsoever. She recalled the soup incident and drew a heavy sigh. Her mother's disappointment in her daughter's failure was matched by Ellie's relief.

Minnie sidled over, her heavy taffeta skirts rustling with each sinuous step. Ellie wished she could walk like that.

"The good doctor seems to be taking an interest in you."

"I don't think so."

Minnie rolled her eyes. "Honestly, Ellen, if you do

not seize such opportunities, they will pass you by. Admittedly, I had hoped you could do better. But marriage to a physician would be acceptable. He's a professional man, after all."

"He's never even spoken to me outside of this dining room."

"He's shy. You have to make excuses to see him. Feign a headache and make a call."

"And he smells of iodine."

"Oh, for heaven's sake."

Ellie looked at the young couple just entering the hotel lobby, pausing, as newcomers were wont to do, to sweep the room with their gazes. They must have come by ferry or stage, because the guests on the noon train had unfortunately arrived just as Mr. Rogers had gone on his rampage.

"Customers," said Ellie.

Her mother fixed a perfect smile on her face and left Ellie.

"Welcome to the Château Royale. I'm Mrs. Jenkins, the owner."

Ellie suddenly could breathe again. There had to be more to life than her mother's constant badgering and her father's sad looks. She glanced again toward the open door.

Ellie was not simple. She knew what her mother wanted. She also knew what *she* wanted, a good man who owned a bit of land. Ellie had spent all her life confined in this hotel or the last one. While her mother thrived on the constant noise and bustle, all the people coming and going, Ellie longed for a view of open sky and a horse of her own. It seemed the ultimate freedom to be able to just throw a saddle on a willing mount and off you go. She and her husband would build a ranch house and fill it with children who were all as plain as brown paper wrapping. She just needed to find a man who would put down roots and love her like crazy. She would find him or remain unwed, for she would not settle for less.

It was a small dream, but it was hers. So she would not be taking buggy rides with the doctor, living in the rooms above his practice and spending her days and nights tending the sick and wounded here in Cahill Crossing.

"Just because I don't faint at the sight of blood doesn't mean I want to see it," she whispered.

Her mother was greeting a powerfully built young man who wore a familiar gray hat.

"Dining room is just that way," she said, her drawl more evident whenever she spoke to men.

He tipped his hat.

"Would you like me to hold your saddlebags? We have a room that is secure."

Just then Maria Martinez strode though the dining room carrying a tray of tea for an upstairs guest. At the sight of Maria, Ellie's spirits fell. Her friend was married to the tanner's son, Miguel, who had just lost one of his sisters in the river to drowning. Ellie had told Maria to go home, but she insisted that she would finish her shift. If Ellie didn't know better she'd think Maria didn't want to go home.

Ellie's attention flicked back to the man who told her mother that he'd hold on to the scuffed twin pouches now resting on his wide shoulders. For an instant Ellie thought the man was Quin, back from the drive, but as he lifted his chin, she saw it was Chance, transformed by hot water and a sharp razor.

At the moment of recognition she startled, as if

waking from one of those dreams when you think you are falling. He looked so different. Clean shirt, dress trousers, gleaming vest and boots. He had been handsome before, but now he positively stopped her heart.

Her mother had not recognized him yet and when she did... What? Ellie wasn't sure, but she had a rising sense of foreboding.

Ellie hurried to her father's office.

"Daddy! Chance Cahill just walked in."

He did not look up, but quickly laid the pen back on the rest and blotted the ledger, then closed the book. He lifted his gaze and gave a reassuring smile.

"Right behind you, Button."

Ellie stepped back out in time to hear her mother.

"If I could just have your name?"

Chance glanced at Ellie as if he'd known where she was all along and winked. She was so startled she did a double take and then was not certain she had seen correctly. No one winked at her, ever.

Then Chance gave her mother his name.

The smile fell from her mother's face like bricks falling from scaffolding. Minnie Jenkins stiffened, looking as if Chance had slapped her.

"Do you have any idea of the damage you did to that room?"

Her father swept past her.

"Chance, my boy. Welcome back."

Minnie had her hands folded tightly upon the guest registry as her glare shifted from Chance to her husband.

"I was just about to tell Mr. Cahill here that he shot a hole through my new wallpaper, completely ruined the carpet and the duvet, in addition to shattering an oak door and frame."

"Rogers splintered the door, ma'am, but I'd be glad to pay for all the damages."

Chance glanced Ellie's way again. His smile sent a jolt right through her.

"If you'd be willing to run me a tab. I'm expecting a bounty from Deadwood any day."

"Under no circumstances," said Minnie.

"Why, of course," said Oscar. "That includes the dining room and gentlemen's room, as well. We have a fine assortment of drink."

"I don't drink. Well, beer, on occasion."

Her father looked surprised, which astonished Ellie as nothing seemed to shock her father.

"We have beer, of course."

Minnie huffed and then faced her husband, lowering her voice to an angry whisper. "I will not have him here."

Oscar stared his wife down. On most occasions he tried charm or flattery and to good result. But this was different. Ellie could feel it. She took a step closer, drawn by the invisible force that keeps one from looking away before an accident.

"Minnie, this boy saved a woman's life. He saved our daughter's life and he is welcome in my hotel for as long as he likes."

"Your hotel? I like that," she huffed, turning so she looked at her husband over her shoulder. "Unfortunately, I don't have any rooms at present."

"You have the one Rogers occupied."

Minnie glowered. "It isn't ready for guests."

Oscar took hold of his wife's arm and steered her into his office. Chance lifted his brows and stared at Ellie in question. She shook her head, not sure what would happen next.

"Y'all right?" he asked.

"Yes. Are you?"

Chance removed his hat. Ellie couldn't keep herself from a sharp intake of breath. All the dark growth of beard had been scraped from his cheeks revealing a face that was familiar and yet not. He seemed leaner than she recalled and his features more striking. His dark hair was now slicked neatly back so she could see his stunning pale blue eyes. They reminded her of blue topaz, clear and bright.

"What's the matter? I got mud on my nose?" asked Chance.

Ellie blinked, suddenly mortified to have been caught gawking.

"You look different."

"Yup, no trail dust." He ran a hand nervously through his hair. It was the very first gesture that did not radiate supreme confidence.

That gave Ellie hope. Perhaps Chance was not the man she supposed. Was it possible that he, too, was not always as self-assured as he seemed? She mentally compared the man who had come barreling through the door with the one that now stood before her and smiled.

"You look very nice."

He nodded and the devilish grin returned.

"Don't worry about them," she said by way of reassurance, motioning toward the office.

"I'm not."

"Oh," she said, off balance again. If he wasn't concerned about the disagreement her parents were having, what could have unsettled him? Perhaps she'd misread him.

Ellie rested a hand flat on the big solid reassurance of the long reception desk, specially made for this very spot. The smooth grain of the waxed wood grounded her and she lifted her chin a notch, meeting his sky-blue eyes.

He stepped closer and she smelled the bay rum splash the barber had used. She could now see the gray flecks about his black pupils and the dark lashes that framed his unsettling eyes.

"Why do you stay here?"

The question caught her off guard. Immediately, she retreated behind her defenses. What right did he have to come in here and ask her such personal questions?

"This is my home."

He held her gaze a long moment.

"When it makes you unhappy, it's time to go."

That comment, so close to her own musings, starched her spine. "Not everyone solves their problems by running away when things do not turn out precisely as they would like."

The corners of his mouth dropped and his eyes went cold as stone. She knew then what those men he chased saw in their final moments and it was more frightening than a bullet.

He placed his palm down and her hand completely disappeared beneath it. A shiver of excitement began at the point of contact and tingled straight up her arm. His hand was warm but his eyes were cold.

Ellie braced herself for a fight. He'd forgotten that she'd known him since he was a boy in short trousers.

"You trying to run me off?"

"You don't need me for that. I recall that you're a mighty good runner."

"And you. Seems your specialty is running men off."

"I don't know what you mean."

His smile said he wasn't buying.

"You can do as you like. You always have." She pulled her hand free of his. "I'm sure it's nothing to me."

Did her voice sound strange to him, as well? She swallowed and tried to compose herself, folding her hands before her.

"Nothing to you? Sounds like a challenge."

She stammered now, fearing she had unwittingly kicked a hornet's nest. This was not the fun-loving, irresponsible boy she remembered. She did not know this man, did not know if she *wanted* to know him.

"It most certainly is not. Nothing of the kind."

Chance smiled, but his eyes remained fixed on her like a hawk sighting a rabbit.

"Your father invited me to stay."

"But my mother is against it."

"She always win?"

Ellie nodded as Oscar and Minnie Jenkins reappeared from the office. Her mother's face was flushed and Oscar's lips were tight. He carried Chance's saddlebags in his right hand.

Ellie glanced at Chance, giving him a look of victory.

Minnie spoke first. "Mr. Cahill, we are in debt to you for protecting Ellen Louise and if you are not disinclined to staying in a room without a lock, we would be most happy to accommodate you."

Ellie's jaw dropped as she stared first at her mother and then her father. Her mother had given way. What in the world had gone on in there?

"We'll have that door fixed in the morning, son," said Oscar. Then he turned to Ellie. "You show Chance up to his room. I'll see to things down here until you get him situated."

Ellie was about to refuse. She was not a porter and

she had duties at the restaurant. But something about the look in her father's eyes made her back down, as she always did. Most of her defiance happened only in her head, as she never did get around to speaking her mind.

"Yes, Papa." She reached for the bag, but Chance beat her to it and their hands brushed again.

Ellie clenched her fingers against the same quivering awareness that rippled through her the first time he touched her and pulled back.

"This way, Chance."

They both knew the way. So why had her father sent her above stairs alone with a man who was said to be more dangerous than a war party of Comanche?

Chapter Six

Ellie mounted the stairs. Behind her, Chance's slow, steady tread told her that he matched her pace step for step. She regretted her comment about him running and felt ashamed of herself. She meant to tell him so when they reached his room.

She knew how unbearable Earl's and Ruby's deaths had been for all the family. She had been with Leanna at the 4C when they'd received the news and her friend had wept as if her heart had broken. Chance, on the other hand, had vanished as he often did until Bowie had tracked him down. After the funeral, Ellie had watched helplessly as the family broke apart. All she knew was that there had been words and that Bowie, Leanna and Chance had left Quin to handle the ranch alone. She'd seen Quin struggle under the burden of that responsibility and was glad he had his new wife to help him.

Then Bowie had come home and the next thing she knew the former marshal had murdered two men and tried to kill Bowie. She could scarcely believe that

Tobias Hobbs had headed the rustling ring and had died in the shootout. Leanna had returned only two months back and caused the first real scandal in the new town. Ellie had found a way to see her friend despite her mother forbidding it. Leanna was no more a fallen woman than Ellie was and she was proud of the work Leanna was doing with women in need. Leanna was willing to help those that everyone else disdained. It showed the kind of guts that all the Cahills shared.

Ellie mulled over all that had been happening. Trouble with rustlers at all the ranches in the spring, Bowie's return and his exposure of Tobias Hobbs in the summer and Leanna's deadly confrontation with the banker's son, Presley Van Slyck. Now Chance had returned.

What did it mean?

Chance drew up beside her. He appeared bigger here in this confined space of the corridor and as out of place as a tumbleweed in a parlor. Even without the dust and growth of beard, Chance didn't belong here. Not that his mother hadn't taught him proper manners. No, Ruby had done her duty with all her children. She'd be proud of them, but saddened, as well, to see the rift between her boys. Leanna had mended fences with Bowie, but Ellie wasn't sure about Quin. He'd objected to Leanna arriving in town with a baby and no husband, as if the child was at fault for Leanna's troubles.

Ellie didn't know who the father was, but neither did she need to. He was Leanna's and that was good enough. She couldn't think of another woman alive who would have endured what Leanna had to protect that child.

Chance gently clasped Ellie's elbow.

"This one. Isn't it?"

Had she really been about to walk right by?

"Woolgathering?" asked Chance.

Ellie made a noise that was neither yes nor no, but more like the sound a dog makes when it's dreaming.

She held out the key like a miniature sword and bent slightly, realizing too late that the key was rendered superfluous by the door being cracked off its hinges and the lock having been torn from its housing. Chance placed his fingers on the solid oak and pushed. The strike plate and lock moved together with the wood earlier splintered from the frame. Had that really only been a few hours ago?

Ellie had not been back in this room since she'd pulled Mrs. Rogers from her husband's remains. She glanced within. The maids had removed the carpet and replaced the bedding.

Chance took in his surroundings and then returned to her, as if checking for her reaction. Without taking his eyes from her, he tossed his saddlebags, succeeding in hitting the bed rail. He retained possession of his hat, holding it in his left hand, down at his side below his holster.

"What are you thinking, Ellie-Lou?"

"No one calls me that anymore."

"How about Squirt?"

She shook her head and laughed. "No, never."

"Well, you aren't a squirt anymore, I guess." His gentle smile was back and with it that trembling in her belly and dryness in her mouth.

She took a step closer, drawn by the warmth of his smile, the cleft in his chin and the glint in his eyes. From this vantage point she could see where the body had lain. Her eyes tracked across the room to the bullet hole just this side of the window and the place where she had been standing.

Chance followed her line of sight.

"Ellie, sometimes, when a person sees a thing like this, well, sometimes the mind dwells on it, like at night when you're trying to sleep. Or it might spring up at you unexpectedly during the day, like a rattlesnake."

Did that happen to him? Was he haunted by the men he had killed? Ellie felt a pang of empathy for the man who slayed dangerous outlaws and then had to live with the consequences.

"If your mind is uneasy, you can talk to me about it," he said.

"I appreciate that, Chance. And I'm sorry for what I said before."

His eyes were tender once more. She thought of the gentle embrace. She wanted that connection again. Ellie held her breath. She wanted to kiss him. Not that silly, childish peck he'd given her on the cheek, but a real kiss. It wasn't wise.

But he would do it if their roles were reversed.

Chance didn't ask permission. He didn't have to placate or try to disappear. He needed no one's approval. No one told him what to do, while it seemed people had been ordering her around her entire life.

She stepped closer, her heart already hammering at what she meant to do.

For some reason it was important for him to see her, not as some little mouse, but as a woman with courage—or if not courage, exactly, at least daring.

Chance remained still as glass as she took another step forward and rested her hands upon the lapels of his newly oiled vest.

The top of her head didn't even reach his chin. When had he gotten so tall, and how would she reach his mouth without hopping?

He looked down at her, waiting expectantly as if he already knew what she would do next.

"I'd like to thank you for saving my life."

Chance dropped his hat as Ellie rose on her toes. She didn't have to hop, for he collected her in his arms and pulled her tight. She collided with the solid mass of his chest and was enveloped with the scent of oiled leather and bay rum. He cradled her head in one large palm, capturing her as he swept down on her like an eagle in freefall. Ellie closed her eyes.

The contact of his mouth to hers caused a shuddering jolt of sensation like dropping a stone into still water. What followed were the sinuous ripples that flowed through her, making it hard to catch her breath. His caresses tingled across her like a warm wind. As his lips moved over hers, parting them, Ellie felt herself falling backward, giving herself over to his strength and his control. As he held them both in that perfect moment, she lifted her arms to encircle his neck and allowed his muscular tongue to stroke hers.

He set her on her feet again, drawing away by slow degrees as she clung like a needy child. It was her recognition that she clutched at him that caused her finally to let go and step back.

Ellie felt a moment of utter embarrassment as she realized she had lost complete control of herself, and that Chance had been forced to pluck her off him as if she were a tick.

"Oh, my heavens," she said, her eyes wide with horror and her face burning hot as a kettle at full boil.

Chance stooped to retrieve his hat and then lifted it to his chest, glancing past her, down the hallway.

"Evening," he said to the couple just cresting the stairs.

She stared, slack-jawed, from the guests and back to him again as realization dawned. He'd heard them. Somehow, as she had lost her sense of everything in this world but him, Chance had been mindful enough to hear these guests coming and protect her reputation.

She knew she should be grateful, but for some reason his complete lack of involvement was more annoying than the recognition that she had just thrown herself at him. Was he so completely untouched by their encounter? But Chance must have had many women, just like all the Cahill men.

His father had picked Ruby, the apple of every man's eye, according to her father. And Quin had picked Addie K., and Bowie had picked Merritt, and Chance would choose an equally stunning woman, not someone that no one noticed at first or second glance.

He turned back to her, a silly smile on his face. Her irritation crumbled into humiliation. She wished she could disappear right now. But he kept his eye on her. She considered running.

"This room will be just fine, Miss Jenkins. I do thank you for seeing me up."

Ellie's ears prickled as her disgrace solidified to mortification.

The couple nodded as they passed. The Rawlingses, she recalled, from Corpus Christi, visiting for the wedding of their cousin's eldest daughter, Jane.

After they had passed, Chance placed the key back in her hand. When had he taken it?

"It's unlocked, in case you want to come up later and thank me some more. We'll close the door next time."

She had a good mind to slap his arrogant face.

"Chance Cahill, I am not some little…little… You should know better than to insult me like that."

His confident smile slipped. "Sorry, Squirt."

"And don't call me that. I'm only two years younger than you are."

"If you stood up to your mama this way, she wouldn't treat you like the help."

She aimed a finger at him and then recalled the last time she'd done that she'd nearly broken her neck on the woodpile. She lowered her weapon.

"You don't know anything about me, Chance. Not anymore."

"But I'd like to. My, I do like that fire in your eyes."

One look at Chance told her exactly what his words implied. He thought this all some little joke at her expense.

"I am not going to sneak into your room, Chance Cahill. In fact, I'm going to stay clear of you from now on, because I want a husband, not a reputation."

That stopped him. His brows shot up and his jaw clamped shut, turning his sensual smile into a grim line. An instant later he was scowling and she was smiling in satisfaction, feeling she had regained a tiny piece of her dignity as she stepped out to the center of the hall.

He came after her, holding the door frame as he swung out blocking her retreat. She halted. His annoyance was now masked behind a smooth, charming smile and that devilish glint in his eye. If she didn't know better she might have doubted she had gotten his goat.

She scowled at him, arms folded tight before her.

"But I smell real nice. Don't I?"

The man seemed determined to provoke her. Well, she simply would not allow it. She would not be his toy, nor would she be his source of amusement. Men as handsome as Chance did not pick girls as ordinary as her. So she forced a tenuous smile, wishing for a thimbleful of his pluck.

"Good evening, Mr. Cahill. Please let us know if there is anything else we can do to make your stay more comfortable."

"I can think of a couple of things right now."

She fumed at the speed with which he'd gained the upper hand again. Admitting defeat, she struggled for a dignity that she did not feel. She would have liked to call that a draw, but somehow felt Chance had the edge. Ellie managed to duck under his arm and hurry back to the safety of the ground floor and her pretty little cage. It seemed his reflexes were not all that quick. Was that because she'd been faster or because he didn't care enough to stop her?

Chance finished the last of his supper at Leanna's Place and sat back with a sigh. Cassie hovered at his elbow, a little too eager to please. These were Leanna's girls and he knew they were no longer in the business of taking a man upstairs, but he wasn't quite sure Cassie recalled that. His sister had been absolutely right about not staying here.

"So how is Ellie?" Leanna asked.

Chance dropped his knife and it clattered to the floor. Cassie had it before he could lean over the arm of his chair. They came up nose to nose.

"Thank you, Cassie. I think Chance is done now."

"We have cobbler." Cassie's smile seemed to offer something else entirely.

Chance loved cobbler. "No, thanks."

Leanna raised a brow. Cassie cleared the dishes and cast Chance one more brilliant smile before swaying back toward the kitchen. It was a wonder she didn't dislocate something.

"That girl has set her cap at you."

Chance rubbed his jaw, feeling the bristle of his whiskers already coming in. "You gotta pull her off me, Annie, or you'll have one less reformed dove."

"You wouldn't."

"Me? No. But what about her?"

"And don't change the subject. Is Ellie all right after the shooting?"

Why had Chance thought that Leanna knew about their kiss? He didn't know what to make of it himself. He'd kissed plenty of women, but that kiss had gone straight through him like a Comanche arrow with a barbed tip. If they hadn't been interrupted he might have laid her on that big, soft bed.

He had only been half joking when he'd told her the door would be unlocked. He winced as he recalled that dunderheaded comment. What kind of a thing was that to say to a proper gal like Ellie? And she had called him out on it, just as she should have.

He'd been around easy women too long. That was his only possible excuse.

He rubbed his hand over his jaw. "She's fine, I guess. Mother treats her bad."

Leanna pulled a face. "Oh, Minnie again. She thinks the world revolves around whether Ellie gets the right husband, instead of wanting her daughter to find someone who makes her happy."

"And she doesn't like being called Squirt anymore."

"Well, she's not ten years old, Chance, and really, she never did like it."

"But she isn't much bigger than when she was." He nursed his wounds with his coffee. "And she went after me like a snake in a horse pasture. Liked to stomp me to death."

"Ellie? I've never even heard her raise her voice. She's the most polite, quiet, endearing person in the entire town."

"Not to me she isn't."

"You have that effect on people."

"She said not everyone solves problems by running." Leanna went still. "That doesn't sound like Ellie." After another moment's consideration, she leaned half-across the table and narrowed her eyes on him. "What did you say to her?"

"Nothing. I just suggested she might not want to stay where she isn't appreciated."

"Chance, despite her mother's interference and all that has happened, Ellis is still my best friend. So if you hurt her I will pull out your intestines and tie them to a tree."

Leanna had read too many accounts of Indian abductions, but he knew she could use a knife because he'd taught her to throw one. Looking back, teaching her to fight like a Comanche might not have been the wisest of moves.

"I'm warning you, Chance."

So he was not going to mention the kiss to Leanna, then.

"What about what she said to me? You going to warn her off, too?"

"Certainly not. She's right. We've both been running. What you need is to find something that's worth staying for."

"You make about as much sense as Squirt."

"Don't call her that."

"She got a beau?"

Leanna positively beamed at him and he realized she assumed he had a healthy interest. Best dissuade her of that notion pronto. Even if he did think Ellie was more interesting than most females, as Ellie had so aptly pointed out, the only thing he could give her was a reputation.

"You askin'?" Her voice took on that flirty, vivacious tone he'd seen her use to great effect when she was younger. She'd had all the boys for miles around panting after her and every momma scheming how to make Leanna her daughter-in-law. Chance's spirits fell as he realized they didn't want her anymore. Did they even speak to her?

"I'm not asking for that reason. Lord, Annie, she's like a sister to me." His neck prickled at the lie and his insides began to tingle as he recalled the softness of her lips beneath his. Ellie was hot as a Mexican summer. He could hardly believe a proper little miss could kiss like that.

Leanna leaned in, thumping her elbows on the table and resting her chin on her laced fingers. "All right, then, smarty, why *are* you asking?"

"I heard Minnie say she thinks either Ira or Johny Fitzgerald would be good marriage material." Her face told him all he needed to know on how she felt about that. "Been a while since I seen those boys but I was concerned that they might still be the bullies I remember."

Leanna's spine stiffened. "Worse now than ever."

"Why aren't they on the cattle drive with their pa?"

"I'm not sure if their father has cut them off. But they seem to be across the tracks more than at the ranch."

"Maybe I'll take a stroll that way before bed."

"You be careful."

Chance stood and replaced his hat. "Thanks for supper, Annie."

"I wish you'd come over to the house."

"I get itchy indoors."

"Yet you're staying at the Royale?" She watched for a reaction.

Chance drew his hat low over his eyes. "Those Fitzgerald boys still running with Preston Van Slyck?"

Leanna went pale. He took her elbow and guided her back to her chair, then took a seat beside her.

"What? If he touched you, I—"

Leanna raised a hand to silence him. "I shot Preston a few weeks back, Chance. I killed him."

Chapter Seven

Chance shivered as if someone had just thrown a bucket of icy water over his head. His baby sister had killed a man.

"Why didn't anyone tell me?" One look at Leanna and his own pain dissolved into concern for her. Her pale face and huge blue eyes stopped him. Leanna had obviously been to hell and back since he'd seen her last.

"Annie?"

"He took Cabe and he shot my husband."

"But why?"

Leanna dropped her gaze to her lap and spoke to her hands. "Preston discovered we were trying to connect his father to Mama's and Papa's deaths and took Cabe to make me stop. Cleve went after Cabe."

Chance thought of a man ready to die to protect a child and his estimation of Cleve jumped.

"I got there after Cleve. Preston had a gun to my husband's head, so I used my rifle. Aim, hold your breath, let half of it out, squeeze. Just like you taught me." Leanna met his gaze.

He was afraid her haunted look would never leave him.

She seemed different now, reminding him of Bowie, with her cool stare. He'd been right, the experience had changed her. He felt as if he had lost his little baby sister and he wasn't sure he knew this woman at all.

"I think you saved our lives, Chance. If you hadn't taught me to shoot…"

"But I did and you remembered when it counted."

Leanna looked different without her bright smile and bubbly personality.

"So he's dead now," she said, spinning the ring on her index finger.

"The world is better without him. I know it and so do you. Don't you spend one second feeling remorseful."

Leanna began to cry. He thought to take her hand, give her a hug like Ma would have done. But he felt awkward and unsure.

"I see it, the entire thing, in my head," she said. "It plagues me."

"That happens. It will pass with time."

She looked up. "It will?"

"Yup," he lied.

She sighed, as if relieved, and wiped her eyes. He thought of her husband, shot protecting a child that wasn't even his.

Holden had done the right thing, but Chance still didn't know if he was the right man for his sister.

Leanna shook her dark head as if throwing off her melancholy and wiped beneath her eyes with her index fingers.

Chance made up his mind about something.

"I'd like to meet Cleve properly, Annie. I'll come to supper anytime you like."

Her smile returned. "Oh, Chance. It means so much

to me that you two get along. He's been a blessing, protecting me and Boodle and the girls. He's the love of my life and I want you two to be friends."

Chance nodded his willingness to try, even if he didn't really have friends. All he'd ever had was Leanna. Though Bowie and he had established a fragile truce. He wondered if it would last, because he knew he was about to do things that neither Bowie nor Leanna would like.

"What about his father, Willem? He been bothering you?"

"No. He has actually been in my place a few times. But I don't trust him. When Preston took Boodle, he told Cleve that his father keeps two sets of books and has been robbing us blind. Cleve said Preston was positively jubilant as he told him that the Cahills might own the town, but the Van Slycks were the ones getting rich."

"That's why Quin is calling for an audit."

"Yes." She looked surprised. "Did Bowie tell you?"

"Yeah, but he forgot to mention Preston." Chance leaned forward. "You still got your pistol?"

She nodded.

"Keep it close, Annie. I can't have anything happen to you."

She smiled and lifted a hand to his cheek. "Ah, you're going to make me cry again." She dropped her hand. "You need any money?"

He slid a hand in his pocket, feeling the scarce coins knock together. Damned if he'd take money from his little sister.

"Chance? I wouldn't even have this place if not for you."

"I brought in another bounty, Annie. I'm fine."

Now she looked sad again. "See you tomorrow for supper?"

"You bet."

"Be careful."

He grinned at her and then headed out the door.

Night had descended but the town was still full of light. Seemed no one went to bed early in this town, either.

Chance headed for the red-light district—bars, billiards and brothels. He didn't enter Pearl's Palace out of deference to Leanna's stance against prostitution, plus he didn't need a woman…or at least the kind you had to pay for. Monty's Dance Hall was lively. He ran into Ned Womack at the Black Diamond and was happy to accept a beer. Unfortunately, Ned, still scattered as buckshot, had forgotten his wallet, so Chance picked up the bill.

Womack, who was a neighbor to the 4C, was broad as a barn door with a misshapen nose and eyebrows that grew so thick and wiry they crept halfway up his forehead. He had recently lost his wife and told Chance that he had, as yet, been unsuccessful in finding a replacement. Chance could see that the big barrel of a man might be daunting to most women and wondered if his lack of a wife accounted for his disheveled appearance. He and Chance tried out the new billiard table and Chance decided to stir things up by telling him he was in town to sell his share of the 4C. It was a lie, but it gave Chance a reason to be here. He also said that he wouldn't speak to Leanna and that Bowie wouldn't speak to him. Nothing like a rift to bring the devil to his door. Ned liked to talk, so telling him was like posting a damned flyer. Word would get out. The two parted ways when Chance continued to Hell's Corner Saloon, the final establishment in the row.

He'd barely set foot in the place when Ira Fitzgerald slithered over to greet him. Chance didn't trust Ira and immediately looked for Ira's younger brother, Johny. He spotted him engaged in a game of cards at the table beside three men who Chance did not know and one he did—Glen Whitaker. Bowie's deputy seemed to be losing, judging from the tiny pile of chips before him and the crease in his brow.

Chance flicked his gaze back to Ira.

"Well, well, I heard you was back in town. Welcome home, Chance."

Ira hadn't changed much. He still had sandy-brown hair, bulging green eyes, a large nose and a sneer that seemed permanently fixed on his face. He'd filled out some, losing the lean frame that came from riding and roping all day.

"Ira, surprised you aren't on the drive."

"We have hired hands for that. Besides, I've had enough of eating dust for a lifetime. You, too, I expect."

Chance said nothing to that.

"Heard tell you brung in twelve men, all shot clean through the head."

"Is it that many?" Chance would have liked to join the card game, but he'd need to wait for his wire from Deadwood. Until then he had credit only at the hotel, and that thanks to Oscar.

"You going back to work at the 4C?" asked Ira, sticking his big nose where it didn't belong.

"No plans yet."

"What brings you home, then?"

"Following Annie, just like always."

"Oh, well, she sure did cause a stir, what with that

bastar—" Ira must have caught Chance's look because he reconsidered and tried again. "With the girls and all. She sure is a spitfire."

"See your brother's working on losing the family fortune." Chance nodded toward Johny, the younger, meaner brother. He still had that dangerous look in his eye. The boy was as erratic as the weather.

Ira glanced back at Johny. "Oh, he wins most nights, especially if Whitaker is playing. The man is a menace to hisself. So, you staying in town?"

"For now."

"Well, if you're looking for work you just got to ask."

Chance leaned in. "Need somebody killed, do you?"

Ira tried for a laugh and ended up rubbing his neck. "'Course not. Just we could use a man like you."

A man like him, a killer, a man people crossed the street to avoid walking past, is that what he meant?

"I'll think on it."

"Oh, sure." He clapped him on the shoulder.

Chance narrowed his eyes and Ira's hand slid away.

"Buy you a drink?"

"No, thanks."

"Well, then, I'll see you around."

Chance nodded. "Count on it."

Ira hesitated and gave him a long look and then headed off. Chance had the greatest respect for their father, Donald Fitzgerald, but he did not like his sons.

He'd come out tonight only to get his bearings in a town he barely recognized. Not one of these places had existed when he'd ridden out. But now the railroad had split the town into two sections, good and bad.

Which side did he fit on?

Chance was just about to leave when he spotted a

familiar face—Atherton, the blacksmith who used to shoe horses for the 4C.

"Why, Chance Cahill, that you?"

"Good to see you, Sidney. Still shoeing horses?"

He nodded. "It's a real honor to have you here. We been reading about you in the paper. How many men you brung in?"

"Some." And he could see the face of each and every one of them.

"Why, that's fine. First one's on me."

"Why, I thank you." This was the benefit of bounty hunting. Someone always wanted to buy him beer, but nothing was really free. They expected to hear tales of his bounty hunts and he didn't like talking about it.

Shooting a man was sometimes necessary, but it wasn't something to brag about or make your reputation on. Shooting was all he was good at and he'd turned that into a living. But he wasn't proud of it.

Atherton returned with his beer, but Chance could tell he'd told every man at the other end of the bar just who was drinking in Hell's Corner Saloon, because the men were gawking and whispering like old ladies. Chance knew what would happen next.

He had nearly finished his beer when three young bucks at the north end of the bar began making remarks about how they heard Chance shot his bounties in the back. He didn't bite. The comments got louder, harder to ignore. Sidney went to talk to them to no avail. Chance tried to figure which one would come over—the big one, the little one or the one wobbling on his feet. He guessed right; the little guy, the one with the most to prove, headed in his direction. He pulled in beside Chance, who had now spun so he was leaning back against the bar.

"Let's see how fast you are with them pistols," demanded the cowboy.

This is why he never stayed anywhere too long. They all came out like cockroaches at night—the young ones, the tough ones, the ones all looking to make their reputation by putting him in the ground. One day someone would succeed. But he had business first.

"You aiming to try to outdraw me or just want to see me shoot someone?"

"You don't look so tough."

"You go back to your friends now, son."

"I ain't your son. And I sure as hell don't take orders from a man who shoots fellers in the back."

He was spoiling for a fight. Chance considered his options. Despite what the boy thought, he was not a gunfighter and he had no stomach for killing a man purely because he was too stupid to know he looked death in the face.

"What are you looking at?" said the boy. He glanced back at his buddies, puffing up like a rooster strutting across the yard.

Chance looked to Bowie's deputy, expecting him to intervene. But he just sat there like a lump on a log studying his cards. Chance returned his attention to the boy.

"Last chance, boy. You run off now."

"Or what?"

"You want to see me pull these pistols? You first."

That would make it a fair fight. Bowie couldn't blame him, but he knew he still would.

The stupid kid went for his pistol. Chance's reaction was a blur.

Chapter Eight

The boy was slow as cold molasses. Chance had his pistol out before he'd even cleared leather.

The boy froze, fist clenched on the handle of the gun, the barrel still stuck half in his shiny new holster. His eyes grew wide now and the saloon was quiet as church on Easter Sunday, everyone waiting for him to kill this stupid kid.

Chance spun his Colt repeater so he held the barrel. "You wanted to see my pistol? Here it is." He hit the boy right between his raised eyebrows. His opponent dropped to his knees, clutching his forehead. Blood spurted between his clenched fingers.

Chance held his gun aloft and spoke to the room. "Anybody else want to see my pistols?"

Suddenly, Bowie's deputy sprang into action. Was the man a coward or just plain stupid? In a matter of minutes Whitaker had the cowboy and his friends herded out of the saloon.

Chance felt hollowed out inside, like a gourd scooped clean. To make matters worse, Johny Fitzgerald came over to congratulate Chance, slapping him on the back and laughing as if they were buddies. Somehow Chance thought it was for the benefit of their audience. But why would Johny want the customers here to think they were friends?

Chance refused Johny's offer to buy him a drink. He'd go thirsty before accepting anything from this man.

Johny didn't like that and tried to insist, but his eyes were cold and hard now. Chance leaned in, so as not to have every gawker in the bar hear his words and to be certain Johny did.

"I don't like you and you don't like me. You forget that?"

Johny forced a laugh as he stepped back. "Another time, then."

Chance watched him go back to his big brother. The men put their heads together. Chance decided he'd best call it a night. In his experience, nothing good ever happened in a bar after midnight. He headed out into the street and glanced up. He missed his bedroll and the night sky.

Chance made his way back along the row of warehouses and sidings. He crossed the railroad tracks, pausing at Leanna's Place. She'd told him that she was turning the gaming hall over to her girls. She wouldn't be there now. She'd be home with her husband and family.

So he turned his mind on why he was here. Quin and Bowie were after Willem Van Slyck, and if he was stealing money, they'd sort it out. But somehow he didn't figure that Van Slyck was the sniper. So who would be able to make a shot from seven hundred and fifty yards?

Seemed to Chance they were looking at a rancher or a hired gun. He thought he'd ride out to the ranches bordering the 4C tomorrow. That was Womack, Burnett and Fitzgerald. Womack knew his father well and the two had gotten on with no trouble, Chance thought. But appearances were sometimes deceiving. Both Womack and Fitzgerald had lost the bid for the railroad and each had been there at Wolf Grove the day his parents had died. Would that failure make either man angry enough to kill? Burnett was a former Texas Ranger who'd moved to the area since Chance had left. He might have the shooting ability, but he had no reason to do so, and from what Bowie said, he and Quin had become friends. Plus the man hadn't even known his parents.

Better swing by the 4C, as well. Two of the hands who'd been caught rustling and setting fires had worked there. Leanna said they'd claimed to be working alone, but really, what was a liar's word worth? There might be other spies there. Chance had thought that his father and mother had been liked by everyone, but he'd been wrong. Somebody had wanted them dead.

Their wagon had been wrecked on the way home from Wolf Grove at a place folks now called Ghost Canyon, practically on Burnett's land. He'd start there.

Ellie tried to disappear, which was difficult when seated at the breakfast table with her parents.

Since Chance Cahill was now under their roof, her mother felt it necessary to lecture.

Ellie wished she could escape to the hotel dining room, and would have if she'd had an inkling that her mother would be up this early.

"You stay clear of him, Ellen Louise. The very last

thing you need when looking for a husband is a scandal. Even the appearance of impropriety can be ruinous."

Ellie immediately thought of the kiss and how she had forgotten herself completely. She startled and lifted a piece of cold toast, spreading marmalade upon it with so much force she snapped it into two pieces.

Her mother's eyes narrowed as she lowered her teacup. "I know that look. What have you been up to?"

"Nothing. It's just that he's Annie's brother."

"You stay away from her, as well. That girl will ruin you just as surely. Unwed mother, now married to a gambler and nearly divorced. Her mother would roll right over if she knew."

When her mother was on a tear, Ellie found it best to just nod her head like a carriage horse.

Her father gave her a commiserating look over the rim of his coffee cup. Somehow today it wasn't enough to bolster Ellie and she could not manage to share his smile. They had been in this together for as long as Ellie could recall, trying to appease or steer around her mother.

"You might not be as pretty as Leanna Cahill, but I'm determined that you do a far sight better than she did."

Despite her mother's desires, Ellie did not aspire to catch a man of means, but rather to marry a man who noticed her, listened to her and most of all loved her. Now, at twenty-five, she had to admit that she might never meet such a man.

Her father finished his coffee. A sure sign he was abandoning ship. Ellie sighed. He rarely opposed his wife, preferring to cut and run until his wife had blown herself out. Yet, yesterday he had fought for Chance Cahill. Why wouldn't he do that for her?

Minnie wiped her mouth with the linen napkin and then returned it to her lap, but her eyes never left her daughter. "This girl needs a fire lit beneath her. I swear if given her choices she'd just wander off with a book somewhere. That's no way to attract a man."

Ellie thought of telling her that she was a girl no longer and that she would not allow her mother to dictate to her any longer. She straightened her spine, faced her mother and then took a bite of her toast.

She sighed. One day she'd do it. But not today.

"Are you even listening?" asked her mother. "I've never seen a girl who could daydream so. I asked if you've considered encouraging Dr. Lewis."

"No."

"Oh, for goodness' sake." She turned to Oscar. "She's going to let him get away the same as she did with Quin Cahill."

Ellie had always liked Quin, but had been only half-hearted in her attempts, which she didn't understand because marrying him would have given her what she wanted, wouldn't it?

"And Bowie used to take some of his meals here. You'd think you could have struck up a conversation that entailed more than, 'How are you today, Bowie?' You know, a little wit and flattery will go a long way."

Ellie looked at her plate. Bowie had tried to get Ellie to confide the name of the father of Leanna's child, which Ellie would not have revealed even if she had known it. She didn't like the look in his eyes. Bowie could be relentless and she'd been grateful when he'd announced his intention to become town marshal because her mother did not think a lawman a suitable husband. It had released Ellie from having to feign interest.

Maria brought in a small piece of folded paper. Oscar held out his hand, but Maria hesitated.

"It's for Miss Ellen."

Her mother motioned with her polished fingertips. "Give it to me."

Maria did as she was bid and then stepped back.

Minnie opened the page. Her scowl vanished and she pressed a hand to her bosom. "Why, it's your Dr. Lewis. He'd like to speak to you."

Maria made a strangling sound that caused all three to give her an inquisitive look.

Minnie handed over the paper. "Well, go on. See what he wants. And remember, wit and flattery."

Ellie lifted half of her toast and headed for the door.

"Did you see that?" her mother said from behind her. "She'll have crumbs all over her blouse."

Ellie left their private apartments, wolfing down the toast as she reached the corridor that led downstairs.

It seemed her mother was right. Dr. Lewis had taken a fancy to her. So now, instead of looking forward to a casual exchange, she had to find a way to become unsuitable.

She reached the lobby and looked about, but did not see Dr. Lewis. Instead, Chance Cahill stood by the cold fireplace with a suspiciously gleeful look upon his face.

He stepped forward to greet her.

"I'm meeting someone," she said.

Chance glanced down at the note. "I know. Lucky your mama doesn't recognize my handwriting."

"You!" she breathed.

Chance had her elbow and led her toward the door.

"I'm not going anywhere with you."

"You'd rather explain why you're back at breakfast?" She paused. "Chance, I'm a very bad liar."

"I remember. Got me a licking on more than one occasion."

"Well, if you were where you were supposed to be just once in your life, you wouldn't have had… I'm not having this conversation. I only mean to say that she'll find out, anyway."

"Maybe so. But by then it'll be too late." He set them in motion, out the front door and along the wide boardwalk.

"Too late for what? Where are you taking me?"

"To meet Bowie's girl for breakfast."

"I already know Merritt Dixon quite well."

"I was counting on it. You know everybody and don't have a bad word to say about a soul. So you'll run cover for me. Keep her from asking me too many questions and make me look good, just like you always did. Remember how you got me off the hook with Mrs. Wheeler?"

"Don't remind me." Ellie laughed at the memory despite herself. "Oh, you simply ruined her flower garden."

"It was my mother's birthday." Chance's smile faded.

Ellie felt his pain as if it were her own.

"Chance, I never got to see you after the funeral. You were already gone. I'm so sorry for your loss. They were such wonderful people and I miss them terribly."

Chance looked as if he were about to say something, but he stopped himself and then said only, "Thank you, Ellie."

"You don't need me to make a good impression with Merritt. I'm sure she'll welcome you unconditionally."

"There's some that wouldn't welcome me in their home."

"Well, Merritt isn't one of them. Really, you don't need me."

Chance paused and took her hand. His palm was warm, dry and calloused. She recalled the feel of his long fingers on her neck. The memory had her quivering like an aspic.

"You never did like meeting someone new."

"Can't stand parlors and teacups and flower arrangements. They give me hives."

She agreed with him, feeling much the same at times. "So you need me to do the conversing, is that right?"

He grinned. "You know me pretty well, don't you, Ellie?"

"I used to think so. I don't know who got me in more trouble, you or Annie."

"Annie. Definitely. Will you come?"

She drew a long breath, making him wait. But the truth was her mind was already made up.

"My mother will be so disappointed," she said.

Chance took off his hat and slapped it on his leg. "That's my girl."

Ellie's smile faltered. His girl? Why did that prospect make her pulse accelerate? If Chance Cahill had any roots he showed no inclination of putting them down. Yet he was the one who excited her and he was a very good kisser. Besides, he wasn't intending to court her. It was just breakfast with Merritt, running cover, as he called it.

"You'll owe me, Chance."

He placed a hand on his heart. "Anything."

They walked over to the Morning Glory Boardinghouse, a two-story pine home situated across from the Porter Hotel and right beside the new opera house. Chance guided Ellie up the steps and inside without even knocking. Ellie stopped upon the colorful rug as Chance added his hat to the coat tree just inside the entry as if he'd been there before, which she was certain he hadn't. He confirmed this by turning toward the cozy parlor to the right, instead of the dining room to his left. He paused to glance about at the empty room.

The aroma of coffee and fresh baked bread embraced her like an old friend. Ellie stepped into the dining room to find one of Merritt's boarders, Hank Wilson, lingering over a cup of Merritt's excellent coffee as he read the paper, perhaps one of the articles he, himself, had written.

"Are they expecting you?" whispered Ellie, not wishing to disturb the retired professor.

"Bowie asked me to supper, but I figured this would be less painful."

"I think Bowie might eat breakfast at the jail."

Chance made no reaction to this and she wondered if he knew this already. What was he up to this morning?

A woman bustled out of the kitchen, using her backside to open the swinging door, so that Ellie saw her profile first.

Merritt Dixon was petite with light brown hair caught up in a utilitarian bun, but that was all that was ordinary about her. Her figure was trim and lithe with an elegance in bearing that Ellie felt was altogether absent in her own composition. Merritt's skin glowed with good health; her cheeks were exactly the same color as a pink rose petal and she had the most stunning green eyes that Ellie had ever seen.

She had no trouble seeing the physical attraction Bowie might feel for Merritt and felt a pang of regret over her own shortcomings.

Merritt caught sight of Ellie and positively beamed

with pleasure. The woman was a beauty in any circumstance, but with a smile upon her lips she was stunning. Bowie was a lucky man.

She glanced at Chance to see his reaction, but he looked stone faced. This pleased her until she recalled how well Chance could hide his feelings when it suited him.

"Why, Ellie, this is a pleasant surprise. Have you had breakfast?"

"I'd love some coffee."

Her smile faltered. "I thought you drank tea."

"Only because my mother prefers me to."

Merritt's eyes flicked to Chance. "Who's this?" Even as she asked, Ellie could see Merritt working it out, noting the similarities and differences. Chance was as tall as Bowie, an inch shorter than Quin, with blue eyes somewhat paler than Bowie's and distinctly different from Quin's silver-gray ones.

"Merritt, this is Bowie's younger brother, Chance Cahill. Chance, this is your brother's fiancée, Merritt Dixon."

Merritt placed the platter she carried on the table as she rushed over to them, taking Chance in a hug that made his eyes bulge. He glanced toward Ellie for rescue but she merely giggled. Served him right.

Merritt stepped back to look him over. "Why, Bowie told me you'd arrived. I'm so happy to meet you at last. Well, come right in and sit a spell. I'll get you coffee and send someone over to see if Bowie can drop by."

Merritt took Chance by the arm and led him to the table, making introductions to the portly professor who had risen to take his leave, folding his paper and clamping it beneath his arm.

"Mr. Cahill, please meet Mr. Wilson, retired professor and occasional writer for our newspaper."

The professor shook Chance's hand and, before departing, threatened to do a story on him in something called the Meet Your Neighbor column. Some things were more frightening than death.

Their hostess retrieved two china cups from her sideboard and poured. "Perhaps I'll just swing by the jail and get Bowie."

Ellie lifted her hands. "Nonsense, I'll do it. Be back before the coffee's cold."

She had expected Chance to show some annoyance at her leaving him alone with Merritt. But he surprised her again by reaching for the cream and adding it to his coffee as if he had already forgotten all about her.

What was he up to?

Chance had never had a lick of trouble finding female company, nor did he share her awkwardness about the opposite gender. So why had he really brought her here?

Then she recalled that Chance never liked social gatherings or light conversation. He had ditched and run from every church social she could recall, acting more like a lone wolf than a member of a pack of four siblings. Ellie didn't understand it. As an only child she would have loved to take his place and have two fine big brothers to defend her and a sister to confide in. She was grateful to have been made welcome in their home for so many lovely years. He didn't know how lucky he was.

"I'll be right back," she said to no one in particular, and slipped out the door.

As it happened, she met Bowie heading toward Merritt's.

"Good morning, Bowie. I've just come to fetch you. Chance is at the Morning Glory and—"

Bowie didn't even slow down. "Well, that's a coincidence. I was coming to the hotel to kick him out of bed."

Ellie didn't like the sound of that but she hurried to keep up as he changed direction back toward Merritt's home.

"My younger brother is a busy little bee. After shooting that gambler, he headed over to Hell's Corner and dropped some would-be gun shark."

Ellie went cold. "He shot someone else?"

Chapter Nine

Chance held his coffee cup steady as Merritt Dixon poured with a confident hand. With any luck, Bowie wouldn't kick so much of a fuss with Merritt and Ellie present, at least that's what he was banking on. He sat uneasy in the ladder-back chair, feeling as out of place as a wrangler at a tea party.

Merritt introduced him to Jemima Little, a silver-haired streak-of-lightning who met him eye to eye from her place standing beside his chair. Merritt explained that the new cook had been hired to help with the boardinghouse so she could attend to wedding plans. Jemima had the professor's dirty dishes cleared before Chance even had time to stir his coffee. A moment later, the tiny widow returned holding a steaming plate that included a biscuit that smelled like home.

Chance eyed the older woman. His conversation skills were a little rusty, but he tried.

"Won't you sit with us, Miss Jemima?"

"Got lots to do."

Merritt disappeared into the kitchen, leaving him with Jemima.

Chance decided on a direct approach. "Bowie will be here in a minute and I clobbered some wet-behind-the-ears kid last night. When my brother gets here, I expect he'll tear into me like a hungry wolf. Unless you'd care to stay and defend me."

"Did he deserve that clobbering?"

"Yes, ma'am."

She patted his hand affectionately. "Well, you don't look like you need much defending, but I do enjoy a good shellacking, so I'll stay."

Chance kept his eye on the front door, unsure if he had gained an ally or just an audience.

He didn't have long to wait. A moment later, Bowie's silhouette filled the glass beyond the lace curtain. His brother opened the door without knocking, removed his hat and held the door for Ellie, who entered with her cheeks in high color. What had Bowie told her?

Merritt emerged from the kitchen with three more plates laden with eggs, bacon, biscuits and a generous serving of hash. She hadn't yet noticed Bowie.

"Chance, you like to step onto the porch with me?" asked Bowie, his eyes flashing blue fire.

Chance sat back in his chair between Jemima and Merritt, who now beamed at Bowie. His brother's gaze flicked to her and he was unable to maintain the grim countenance that he showed his brother. Who knew that Bowie had teeth and a lopsided grin? Chance felt better about bringing this to Merritt's doorstep already.

"Bowie," she said, her voice a kind of dreamy murmur.

Chance wondered what it would be like to have

someone look at him that way and decided he'd settle for just having someone glad to see him.

Merritt came forward and Bowie gave her a hug, drawing her tight against his side as if that was where she belonged.

Ellie stood awkwardly on his opposite side, forgotten by both Merritt and Bowie. But Chance noticed her and her stormy expression. So Bowie had spilled. That meant he wasn't opposed to airing their dirty laundry. A very bad sign. It looked like Jemima was right; he was about to get a shellacking.

Bowie released Merritt. "Chance? Outside."

"Well, brother, Miss Dixon here—"

"Oh, please call me Merritt."

Chance gave her a friendly smile and glanced back to see Bowie steaming.

"Merritt has just served me up a fine hot breakfast and I don't want it to get cold. Why don't you have a seat?"

"Have you eaten?" asked Merritt.

Bowie nodded.

"Coffee?" she asked, and at his nod she lifted the coffeepot, gave it a shake and then headed back to the kitchen.

Chance wondered how many miles a day she walked from one room to the next.

Bowie sat across from him, ignoring the food at his elbow. Chance rose to seat Ellie, smiling at her surprised expression.

"You sure you want to do this here?" said Bowie. "Running behind skirts will not protect you today."

Jemima cleared her throat and Chance thought she hid a smile behind the fist she now held to her mouth.

Chance nodded, knowing that Bowie was already holding back.

Bowie turned to Jemima. "Miz Little, did I ever tell you about the time Chance stole my older brother's horse?"

"I didn't have permission," Chance corrected.

"And it took a stone in the frog and turned up lame. Instead of taking the cowhiding he deserved, he ran to his ma. Seems Chance is still running."

"Here's your coffee," said Merritt, appearing from the kitchen with a steaming pot. She quickly retrieved a cup and saucer blooming with pink roses.

Chance was dying to see Bowie drink out of a vessel that had a grip so small his brother couldn't get his first knuckle through it. Bowie ignored the cup.

Merritt took her seat beside Bowie, but she now looked cautious and her smile had taken on a brittle quality.

"I heard from my deputy that you got into a fight last night at Hell's Corner."

"Did he tell you that the other guy drew first?"

"Doc Lewis said the man took nineteen stitches in his forehead."

"Or that he sat there like a bump on a log instead of doing his job? If he'd have gotten off his duff, I wouldn't have had to drop that saddle tramp. But he was too interested in his cards."

Bowie made a face. "I'll take that up with him. Right now we are talking about you."

"He came at me all horns and rattles. I was defending myself."

Bowie slapped his hands on the table, making the dishes jump and sloshing his coffee into pristine white cloth.

"Dang it, Chance. You been here one day and you killed a man and split another one's skull open. I got enough to do without you adding more work."

Chance kept his tone level. "He drew on me."

"Why were you over in the Badlands in the first place?"

"You know why."

Bowie glared, then lowered his voice. "Think you can get through a day without killing anyone?"

"Don't know. It's early yet."

There was a knock at the front door and Deputy Glen Whitaker stepped into the foyer.

"Marshal, I'm sorry to bother you, but I got Miguel Martinez's wife at the jail. She says her husband's gone missing."

Bowie glanced at Chance, who lifted both hands in surrender. "Wasn't me."

Bowie headed toward the door, pausing only to retrieve his hat. Chance followed. Bowie stopped. "I thought you wanted a hot breakfast."

"Changed my mind."

Bowie didn't move.

"I'm going," said Chance. "You can't stop me."

"I could shoot you."

"I wouldn't try that."

Bowie motioned with his head and the two set off. Chance paused to grab his hat and glance back to the women. "Ellie?"

"Go on, Chance."

He tipped his hat to the ladies. "Thanks for breakfast, Merritt. Pleasure to meet you."

Outside Bowie and Chance pulled ahead of his deputy.

"That wasn't right," said Bowie. "What you did back there. What kind of a first impression is that to make?"

Before Chance could speak Bowie was off again.

"And Ellie, why drag her into it? She never did anything to you. Now her mother is going to give her hell and why? Because you don't want to speak to me like a man."

Chance had heard enough. "I went to the Morning Glory so I could meet your fiancée."

"The invitation was for *dinner.*"

"And I brought Ellie to get her out of that hotel and away from her mother."

"Best thing you could do for that little gal is to steer clear of her."

"You, too? What the hell is so wrong with me that I can't take Ellie Jenkins out for breakfast?"

"Nothing I can see, except you're stubborn as a mule and dangerous as a snake. But you don't meet her mother's standards. Don't feel bad—I don't, either, though Minnie did throw Ellie under my nose a time or two before she realized I wasn't going back to the 4C."

That tidbit made Chance madder than a wet cat. He didn't pause to wonder why.

"You stay clear of her, Bowie."

His brother lifted his brows and gave Chance an incredulous look.

"Chance, I'm engaged. You can count on me keeping clear of Ellie Jenkins. Not sure the same can be said about you."

"What's that suppose to mean?"

"She's a nice girl, is all, and she's Annie's friend. There's plenty of good-time girls over on the other side of the tracks, but don't let Annie catch you. She's against good-time girls and thinks not a one of those ladies is there by choice."

"She's still trying to save the world."

Bowie gave a half smile. "She might just do it, too."

Chapter Ten

He and Bowie parted company after Chance had heard what Miguel's wife had to say, which wasn't much. It was suspicious, though, owing to the fact that his little sister had drowned the day before. They had searched the dock, spoken to the ferryman, Muddy Newton, by the river, but he was just waking up. They'd also spoken to Ace Keating at the saddle shop, for he sometimes purchased hides, but Miguel had vanished.

He headed back to the Royale past the new Town Square, craning his neck at the brick storefronts. A newspaper office? Chance couldn't believe his eyes. Where had all these people come from? There must be hundreds of them, going about their business, riding on roads that hadn't even existed when he left.

Back at the hotel, Chance found Ellie supervising the dining rooms, as usual. The light from the large room windows poured in on her, giving her brown hair a gilded halo. He stopped in his tracks to breathe in the sight of her unguarded and at ease. He thought about what he'd put her through at the Morning Glory and his usually dormant conscience panged him like a toothache.

All but two tables were empty, since it was too late for lunch and too early for supper. She turned at his approach, her welcoming smile fixed upon her face. It did not falter when she recognized him; in fact, it seemed to grow more genuine. That look of welcome, unfamiliar to him, made his stomach pitch. He slowed, growing cautious. He'd expected her to give him a sullen stare or the cold shoulder, but what she did surprised him greatly.

"There you are," she said as if she missed him and then, "Did you find Miguel?"

"No sign of him."

He felt even more off balance now, as if someone had tilted the floor beneath his feet. He recalled his manners this time and removed his hat, holding it awkwardly before him.

"Are you all right?"

"There wasn't any danger."

"I meant are you all right after what Bowie said to you. His words were harsh, I thought. After all, you've come back home to help him, have you not?"

The girl had a head on her shoulders, he'd give her that.

"Yes. But maybe he doesn't want my kind of help."

She nodded, her gentle smile warming him inside and out.

"Just what do you know about it?" he asked.

"Did you want to have something to eat? There's a very nice private table that's available."

"Your mama will skin you alive."

"Mother is off running errands. I haven't seen her since I returned this morning, unescorted."

Chance felt his ears tingle. He'd used her. She knew it, but instead of giving him hell, she forgave him.

Chance hesitated. "What about your father?"

"Chance, I am not thirteen years old. I do not need their permission to speak to you."

"Don't you?"

Her smile turned playful. "Let's say I think you're worth the trouble."

He didn't hesitate. "I'm not, though. You were right before. I got nothing to offer you."

"But you do keep things lively." She motioned into the dining room. "Right this way."

He followed her to a very nice room off the main dining area decorated with red velvet wallpaper, gilded chairs, a large round table and framed prints of locomotives, flanked by wall lamps with wide milky glass shades. Above the table hung a chandelier glowing with soft lamplight.

"Looks like the interior of a private Pullman car."

Ellie nodded. "Mother used just that as her inspiration, even contracted the lamps from the same manufacturer used by the Pullman Company." She motioned to one of the servers. "Please ask Sylvia to serve as hostess until I am finished here."

"Yes, Miss Jenkins."

Chance watched the woman scurry off. Ellie indicated a seat but Chance pulled out a chair for her first. She smiled up at him as he tucked her into the table.

"Have you eaten?" he asked.

"No, I was waiting for you."

The server returned and Ellie placed the order, checking with Chance as to his preferences and then she surprised him again by not launching into questions as Leanna or Bowie were wont to do. Instead, she filled him in on town happenings and told him all she knew about Quin's injury and his new wife, a woman Quin apparently called Boston, though her name was Adrianna McKnight. Ellie spoke highly of Addie K. and made Chance feel as if he knew her already. It sounded as if Boston and Quin's courtship had been stormy. The food arrived and Ellie told him about Merritt and how Bowie used to stay at the Morning Glory until they became engaged. Miss Dixon was not easily won, said Ellie, because her first husband had been a Texas Ranger and since she had been widowed she knew better than most women the dangers of loving a lawman.

Ellie made Merritt's choice to wed Bowie seem very brave and Chance felt he'd made a mistake bringing trouble to her home. Seemed Merritt had already had a full measure of trouble.

Chance sipped his coffee and tucked into a warm apple pie, the taste of cinnamon and baked apple glazing his tongue. He couldn't remember when he'd enjoyed a meal more. Ellie's company went down easy as cold spring water on a hot day. She both calmed and amused him. He didn't know how, but Ellie made him feel at home.

"Ellie, you're a fine hostess, you know that?"

"Oh, nonsense. My mother says I'm too shy and should speak to the customers more."

"You're not shy."

"Well, not with you. I know you, Chance. It's when I'm with someone new that I freeze up. I'm likely to swallow my own tongue as find something interesting to say."

"You're too hard on yourself. I think everything you

say is interesting. Of course, I've spent the better part of two years talking to my horse."

She laughed. The rich, rolling sound did something to his insides. "I hope I am a better conversationalist than all that. Though I'll wager your horse is a better listener."

"That's true." He watched Ellie enjoy the last bite of her pie and then scrape her fork over the sticky filling still on her plate. "Ellie, I thought you wanted privacy so you could grill me about what happened last night or what I learned about Miguel."

"I'd be happy to listen if you'd like to talk about it, but mostly I wanted to see you got fed. You didn't get a mouthful at Merritt's, thanks to Bowie."

"Bowie's right. I shouldn't have dragged her into it."

"She'll be your family soon. She'll be in it whether you like it or not."

That struck home. "I'll have a new sister."

Ellie nodded, but her smile seemed a little sad now. "You already do. Quin's wife, Addie K. Remember? I'm jealous, Chance. Your family is growing. I never had brothers and sisters, but I used to pretend I was a member of a big family."

"Is that what you'd like?"

"Oh, yes. I'd love to fill a house up with children." Her face took on a dreamy quality. "Someplace where I can see the stars and swim in the river and not have to talk all day to strangers."

Ellie liked to be outdoors and yet she spent nearly every waking hour inside this grand, gilded prison.

Chance felt a kick in his gut as he realized that he couldn't be the one she dreamed about. His job demanded that he move on, chasing the next dodger. It was all he knew now. If he didn't hunt bounties what would he do?

Chance tried to picture that house by the river and imagine what it would be like to be the kind of man Ellie Jenkins dreamed about.

Chance felt his stomach flip. Ellie wanted to be a mother. He could picture her with children. She'd be great at it. But he wouldn't be there with her. That much was certain.

Then his jaw clenched. The silence grew heavy. She nearly held her smile. "Everyone deserves to have a family."

"I don't," he said.

"Of course you do," she insisted.

Chance threw his napkin down. "Ellie, do you know why my father was driving that wagon with a busted wrist? Because I ran off that day. He asked me to drive, but I didn't want to go to Wolf Grove. I was so damn certain that Quin and Bowie would be back like they promised, I never considered they wouldn't make it."

"Oh, Chance. That's not your fault."

"It was. He asked me. I wasn't there."

"It was an accident."

Should he tell her the rest? He looked at her big, sympathetic eyes and knew he could trust her.

"But it wasn't, either. That's why we've come back. Quin found out they were murdered and he sent for us to help figure out what happened."

The shock faded from her face and she set her jaw, staring at him. "I knew something was going on." She made a fist and thumped it down determinedly on the table. "I just couldn't puzzle it out. But I knew."

"I'm here to find the ones who did this and make

them pay. In a funny way, this has brought us back together."

She leaned forward, her eyes now intent and focused. "I can help you. I hear things at the hotel. I swear I'm invisible sometimes. Folks just don't notice me."

He was about to ask her how she could believe she was invisible when she was the prettiest woman in the place, but instead he tried to find a way to let her down easy.

"I don't need help."

"Chance, I loved your parents like they were my own. Please let me do this."

She reached across the table, gripping his hand and squeezing his fingers. Her touch was warm and felt right somehow. He wanted to stroke the soft skin on the back of her hand, stroke the pale, fine hair on her bare forearm. Instead, he gave in.

"All right, Ellie. But you can't tell anyone. I'd be sorely pressed if I thought I'd put you in any danger."

She nodded, ready to keep his secrets, just as she always had.

"I won't tell a soul, Chance. I swear I won't."

"Won't tell a soul what?" asked Minnie from the doorway.

Ellie jumped an inch off her seat and then scrambled to her feet, but the evidence of her meal remained before her on the table, damning her.

"I just told Ellie that I'm afraid of scorpions. But if folks knew, it might hurt my reputation."

"I doubt that's possible." Her mother left the insult hanging in the air. "And as to scorpions, I find they are easily crushed beneath a boot heel." She narrowed her gaze on her daughter now. "Since when do you take meals with the guests?"

"He's not a guest, Mama. He's an old friend."

"Whom I have instructed you to avoid. How was your breakfast with Dr. Lewis?"

Ellie's face and neck flamed and she dropped her head.

"The note was from me, Mrs. Jenkins," said Chance, throwing himself on the sword for her.

Ellie gave him an appreciative smile.

"I see. Well, Mr. Cahill, my husband is permitting you to stay in our grand hotel, on credit, I might add, but let me be blunt. Are you planning on staying long in town?"

"Not long."

A tiny line formed between Ellie's brows. Would she be sorry to see him go?

"Are you planning to rejoin your elder brother on the 4C?"

Chance's expression turned stormy and the corner of his mouth ticked.

"No, ma'am."

"Then I will remind you that your stay does not include access to my only daughter. I do not want you seen in public escorting her and I most definitely don't want to find you hiding in shadowy corners again. Do you understand me?"

Ellie wasn't sure when this fine private room had become a shadowy corner, but she gripped the chair back, her fingers sinking deep into the upholstery and padding. She had a mind to tell her mother that she would not be bossed like a schoolgirl.

"And you, young lady, know better. Do you think this wild buck is interested in your charm or your pretty face?"

Ellie's chin sank to her chest as the comment sliced

into her, taking all the air from her lungs. Chance was on his feet now. He ignored her mother and spoke to her.

"Say the word and I'll take you out of here." His voice was quiet, but there was steel in his tone.

"And take her where?" asked Minnie. "To your sister's house of ill repute? Wouldn't that be fine?"

Ellie thought of how Leanna Cahill had thrown caution to the wind when she left her home and it had cost her dearly. Ellie was not nearly as outgoing, resourceful or adventurous as Leanna. If she walked out, where would she go?

"Annie runs a clean establishment," said Chance, his stance still relaxed, even if his jaw was not.

"I know what it is. Gambling, women and liquor."

"Ellie?" said Chance, making his offer again.

Chapter Eleven

Ellie met his gaze, seeing pity and compassion all bundled together in those blue eyes, and for one instant she actually considered going with him. But Chance wasn't offering to take charge of her, only to get her clear of her mother. Ellie looked away and gave her head a little shake.

Her mother made a purring sound of triumph. "I've raised her better than all that, Mr. Cahill." She turned to her daughter. "The fresh produce is being delivered. Go see to it."

Ellie folded her hands before her and slunk from the room, feeling a yellow streak forming down her back.

She hated how she felt, stupid and worthless and wrong. But if she really wanted to leave her parents' house with dignity, then she needed to guard her reputation. Didn't she? Running off with Chance Cahill would destroy all chance of respectability. If she wasn't a proper woman from a good family, then what was she?

She felt pulled in two directions at once. Half of her

wanted to be rebellious and independent and the other half always did what was expected. Both her parents wanted what was best for her. She knew this, but sometimes it was hard.

Ellie walked to the office and collected the correct ledger and a sharpened pencil. Then she made for the kitchen to take inventory of the arriving foodstuffs, as she always did.

She stood upon the back porch, protected from the harsh sun by the private balconies that faced the train tracks. The noon train had brought another bounty from California. A familiar voice interrupted her figuring.

"Where would you like the tomatoes?" It was Chance, holding a crate on his shoulder as if it weighed nothing.

Her delight was immediately stifled by her good sense. "Didn't you hear a word she said?" she whispered.

"I heard. I want to hear it from you. Plus you said you'd be willing to help. Like to take you up on it. But I don't feel right unless you know what you're getting into. So I need to explain a few things."

She glanced behind her. "Well, we can't speak here."

"Why'd you let her run you off?"

Ellie felt peeved at his clear disappointment. It seemed she was a disappointment to everyone.

"Because I don't have your sister's courage, or my mother's charm or your audacity."

Chance's eyes widened at that. Clearly, he'd expected sugar instead of vinegar. Ellie felt instantly remorseful.

"Thank you for sticking up for me. And for your offer."

"It still stands."

"Where would you take me, exactly?"

His grin was pure temptation. "Anywhere you like."

She rolled her eyes. "If only it were that simple."

"It is. You just set down that ledger and walk off the porch. Annie did it."

Ellie's spine stiffened at that. "And she was ruined as a result. Do you have the slightest idea of the scandal she caused or the way folks treat her?" Ellie clutched her ledger and shivered. "I'd never survive it."

"Guess she had her reasons. But she didn't let anyone tell her what to do. What about Merritt? She's on her own."

"She's a widow, a completely different situation, plus she's engaged to Bowie. She won't be on her own for very long."

"I don't like how they treat you."

"They put the clothes on my back and the roof over my head. I'm grateful to them for everything they have given me."

"I wouldn't take orders like that."

"That's very easy for you, Chance Cahill. You have a horse and can just disappear like a summer breeze. Or you can come and go where you like and when you like. A lady can't be seen in certain parts of town or with certain people. She has to guard her reputation or suffer the consequences."

"Looks like you've guarded it a little too well."

That jibe hit. She felt tears threatening and her throat burned like fire.

"Don't you presume to judge me, Chance Cahill! You know nothing of my life. A woman goes from her father's keeping to her husband's. Had I intended to marry before now? Yes, of course. But I have been unsuccessful in finding a suitable match and I don't need you to point out the fact, too."

"You're stronger than you think, Ellie. Best way to get what you want is to take it."

"If only it were that simple. But I fear I'll never find a man who can see me for who I am." She glared at him, eyes sparkling bright and lips pressed white with her ire. "Go ahead and laugh."

He didn't. He thumped the crate on the step.

"I see you, Ellie. And you're prettier than any girl in this town and a damn sight better looking than your peacock of a mother."

Ellie was so shocked she couldn't speak. No one had ever said she was prettier than her mother. Her mother was a great beauty. The belle of Atlanta for three seasons in a row.

"And you're smart and you're caring, and I've seen you take a stand when it comes to another person's trouble. You protected that woman yesterday and Annie told me you spoke to her in public when the rest of the town would have nothing to do with her."

That was true and both times her actions had cost her dearly. But she'd do it again.

She wanted to ask him if he really thought she was pretty. Instead, she hugged her ledger as if it were her only friend.

"Where can I meet you so that we can talk about my parents?" he asked.

"I have choir practice tomorrow evening at seven. I could meet you afterward."

Chance scowled. "You know it hurts my reputation to be seen in certain parts of town, too."

Ellie smiled.

He sighed. "Which church?"

* * *

Chance spent the afternoon poking around town, first speaking to any transplants he recognized from Wolf Grove and then to those who tended to know things, like undertakers, barbers and the clerks at the general store. He heard about old squabbles and much about his parents, but nothing that he recognized could help him.

At dusk he headed over to Leanna's home still thinking of what Ellie had told him about why she stayed. Ellie was a very conventional woman and probably knew best. He reminded himself that not all women were prone to spit in the devil's eye, like his sister. Ellie was too smart to run off with a reckless, irresponsible man like him. Plus she'd been in that hotel room yesterday and knew things about him even Leanna did not. Had called him to task on it, too. He smiled, recalling their first encounter. That showed sand. Still, he didn't like being told what to do. It often caused him to do it, anyway, just to be contrary. But he didn't want to cause Ellie trouble. He hoped that Ellie did find a suitable match, as she called it, and that the man recognized what a prize she was.

He wondered why Quin hadn't jumped at the chance to marry her. He sure missed the track, because Ellie would be the perfect rancher's wife. She was smart as a whip. Look at how she managed that restaurant and the kitchen and all the staff. Her parents didn't know how good they had it. Probably wouldn't know until she left the hotel. Why, they'd need to hire three people to replace her and they'd have to pay them, instead of getting the work for free.

Ellie had considered Bowie, as well. It burned Chance that he was always the last choice, the afterthought. Not that he was a choice at all or that he wanted a wife—no, thank you. But he didn't like being counted out of the contest before he'd even thrown his hat in the ring.

He was a dark horse and he liked it that way. He felt sorry for any woman who tried to rope him. Ellie was right. He had a fine horse and he could ride off on it anytime he pleased.

Or he could after he finished his business here.

Right now he had supper waiting.

Chance headed past the Royale toward Leanna's Place, feeling the unexplainable urge to stop in and see Ellie. She'd be there in the restaurant with a warm smile. He even made it halfway to the hotel before he recalled he'd decided to keep clear of her for both their sakes. He'd have to wait until tomorrow night to see her. He noticed the tug that thought caused in his guts, but he didn't understand it. Must be hungry, he decided.

He made it to Leanna's Place before realizing that he was expected at her home and had to turn around and pass the Royale again, craning his neck for a glimpse of Ellie, but he was disappointed again.

Leanna's home was in the residential part of town between the tracks and the river. He reached her door a few minutes later. The windows of Leanna's small clapboard house glowed a welcome against the darkness. It wasn't until after he rang the bell that he realized that it was very likely that Bowie had told Leanna about his breakfast appearance at the Morning Glory. His hunger must have addled his brain.

He was off the steps and hustling down the street when Leanna's voice stopped him.

"Chance, you coward, you get back here."

Yup. Bowie had told her.

Chance paused, wishing he had used more sense. But he knew when he'd been caught, so he retraced his steps, standing before her, hat in hand, waiting for her to rip into him like an eagle on a fish.

Leanna pressed her lips tight as her brows sank low over her pale eyes.

"What possible reason could you have to use Ellie like that?"

He tapped his hat against his holster, but decided silence was his best defense.

"Chance, if you hurt her, I'll castrate you like a bull."

He winced.

"What's *castrate?*" This voice came from behind Leanna's skirts. It was the freckle-faced boy from the saloon holding the wide leather collar of that huge dog. What was the boy's name again—Marvin, Milton?

"Never mind, Melvin. Go back to the table."

Melvin, that was it.

"Something sure smells good," said Chance, giving his sister a hopeful look.

Her frown seemed engraved on her face. At last she made a sweeping motion with the hand towel she held and Chance scooted past her.

"Wipe your feet."

"Yes, Ma," he joked, and then came up short.

His grin fell, her scowl faded.

The boy lost hold of his charge and the huge shaggy mutt barreled into Chance, buckling his knee and nearly taking him down.

"Melvin, get Stretch," said Leanna.

Melvin wrapped both arms about the dog's neck and the beast continued to sniff Chance as if he were dinner.

"Can Chance sit by me? Can he, Miss Leanna? Please!"

Leanna nodded and Melvin clasped Chance's hand. Chance blinked at the boy and then looked to Leanna for direction.

"Well, go on," she said.

Escorted by both boy and dog, Chance made his way to the dining room. Cleve stood as he came in and Chance hesitated.

"Chance, you remember Cleve…my husband?" said Leanna, letting her words vibrate with irritation.

"Sure do." Chance offered his hand. Cleve took it and gave him a rueful smile.

"Welcome to our home, sir." He motioned to an empty chair. "Please join us."

Chance looked at the bounty before them upon the table—butternut squash, fried potatoes, stewed tomatoes and a three-bean salad, along with a lovely rare cut of roast beef. His mouth began to water. His sister never liked the kitchen and so Chance could not fathom how she managed all this. He met her eye and she lifted a brow as if just daring him to ask the question on his mind. Then she walked to the kitchen door and poked her head in and answered his question.

"Dorothy, my brother has finally graced us with his presence."

He ignored the sarcasm as Dorothy hustled in with a place setting and napkin, plunking them down with enough force to let Chance know what she thought of him. He stuffed the end of the offered napkin into the front of his shirt and then accepted every dish passed his way. Leanna made an attempt at feeding the infant, who thwarted her every move by grabbing anything sent toward his mouth like a stage robber. Melvin kept Chance busy answering questions about bounty hunting until Leanna sent him off to wash his face and hands.

He protested but was lured to the kitchen for lemon meringue pie. The dog trailed Melvin like a monstrous shadow. Leanna followed, carrying a very sticky baby at her hip.

Chance frowned.

"Your sister is a good mama," said Cleve.

Chance had to agree. Leanna had grown up. She had become a responsible, brave and protective woman. Their mom would have been proud. Chance squeezed his fists beneath the table as he recognized that his mother was not here to see Leanna or enjoy her adopted children.

His sister returned alone, carrying two slices of pie.

"None for you?" asked Cleve, his dark brows lifted in concern.

She gave him a smile and a tiny shake of her head. Cleve continued to stare, but Leanna gave him a brilliant smile. Chance hoped Leanna wasn't trying to lose weight. Come to think of it, he hadn't seen Leanna eat during dinner. Had she had her meal earlier?

"You should have some," said Chance. "You are skinny as a picket fence post already."

Leanna ignored the comment and sat beside Cleve. He lifted her hand and kissed the back of it. Leanna flushed, then turned to Chance.

"Melvin idolizes you, you know? I've seen him practicing his draw and shoot technique with an imaginary gun."

That didn't sit right. Chance lowered his forkful of pie.

"Nothing glamorous about killing thieves and murderers."

"You're not an eight-year-old boy."

But he had been and he'd done just the same. He

hoped Melvin would be wiser than he had been, but he doubted it. Each man he'd killed had taken a piece of his soul until he wasn't sure he had one left. Now he felt changed by it all, damaged in some vital way.

Cleve noted the heavy silence and took over the conversation. He had a gift, Chance recognized, an easy charm and appeal that shone about him like a lantern's glow, falling on everyone in the room. Even the sour-faced cook seemed to like him and Chance was fairly certain she didn't like anyone.

From the kitchen came the cry of a baby. Chance had forgotten about him. Leanna stood, but Cleve was already on his feet.

"I'll take him. Give you two an opportunity to… reminisce."

Chance was suspicious that he'd just been thrown to the wolves. But it wasn't so. Leanna didn't say a word.

"Saw Ned Womack yesterday. Told him I was planning on selling my share of the 4C. Tomorrow I'm riding out to Burnett's spread and Fitzgerald's. Plan to tell them the same thing."

"Are you?"

Chance gave her an incredulous look.

"Well, then, you can tell Burnett the truth. He's related to Addie K. through his wife, Rosa, her cousin. And he wasn't even in the area when Mama and Papa died."

"If you trust him, I'll ask him for his help. Annie, I told Womack that I was ashamed of you and I'll do the same with Fitzgerald."

She squeezed his arm. "Are you?"

He shook his head. "Never been prouder of anyone in my life."

Her eyes turned watery. Cleve returned and Chance made his excuses. If he was going to perpetuate the appearance of a rift between them he needed to keep his distance.

She stood beside her husband on the threshold of the house they had made into a home. Chance paused to look back at the golden light pouring out the dining-room window. Leanna had a family of her own. Why did that make him so gloomy?

Chapter Twelve

Chance rode out to Burnett's place and met his new wife, Rosa, a blonde beauty with a New England accent. Burnett, a retired Texas Ranger, had purchased the horse ranch a few years back and Rosa ran a boutique alongside the prosperous new establishments beside the tracks. Burnett hadn't had any of the trouble with cut fences, brush fires or rustling that had occurred on the other three spreads.

He might have accredited the earlier attacks to rustlers if not for the fact that Bowie told him that Quin and his wife had discovered spies within their employees. The punchers were now in jail for committing the acts on Hobbs's orders. But who had sent Hobbs his?

Chance liked Burnett, despite his brusque, no-nonsense demeanor and the wolf he considered his dog. But Burnett didn't have much to offer in the way of leads. He said he didn't know anyone with exceptional shooting skills in the area, except himself. Most of the hands got plenty of practice shooting at coyotes and hares. But Burnett agreed that a shot taken from that distance would take an unusual marksman. Burnett had never met Earl or Ruby Cahill, but still offered his condolences and help.

"If you need another man, you be sure to ask."

They shook hands and Chance headed out to see the owner of the other adjoining property, Don Fitzgerald. That took him through the 4C, but he stayed away from the main house. Still, two of Quin's hands met him before he got too far along. He knew Ralph, who had ridden with him on two drives, and he was happy to see Chance again. They rode along until they reached the border between the two ranches and then turned their horses.

Chance continued on, finding Don Fitzgerald in the saddle as always, moving a herd down to the winter pasture. Seeing him gave Chance a hitch in his throat. From his back, he could have been Chance's father, Earl, watching over his men. Don had the same lean build and relaxed posture. His gloved hands were folded on the pommel and his rope and rifle were tied on the saddle. But his horse was a buckskin instead of a freckled roan. Chance shook off the memories.

Fitzgerald spotted Chance's approach and lifted a hand in salute. Chance reined in beside him. Don was still lean faced with hollow cheeks, keen, intent eyes, a wide nose with a distinct bump, a thick brown mustache that covered his upper lip and dark hair that brushed his collar.

If Don was surprised he didn't show it as he slid off his glove and extended his hand.

"Well, Chance, I wondered when you'd turn up. Glad to see you, boy."

"Then you're the only one."

He laughed. "Oh, don't be too hard on Bowie. He's

just like your pa. Everything all in black-and-white, while you and I, we see the colors in the world." He swept his hand ahead of him, showing off his land, then returned his attention to Chance.

"What brings you back?"

"Trying to get my share of the ranch. Time Quin broke the 4C up four ways."

His eyebrows tented. "That so? You aiming for land or cash?"

Chance didn't hesitate. "Cash. No offense, but I've eaten enough dust raised by beeves for a lifetime."

Don chuckled, but his eyes were shrewd. "You sound like my boys. They like town living. Can't understand it myself." He scratched the whiskers on his chin thoughtfully, then replaced his glove and crossed his hands over the pommel. "Don't think Quin will sell. But maybe you'd take your share of land instead and then sell it to me."

"I'd have to make a profit."

"Sure. That's understandable. If your brother is stubborn about it, and I think we both know he will be, you could talk to Slocum, your pa's attorney. He'll help you."

"Attorney? Quin's got my share of that money. I'm surprised they haven't built a special bank to hold it all. I mean to get it."

"As I said, I'd go for the land. You'll make more in the end."

Was it that Don knew Quin wouldn't sell to his neighbor directly or that he didn't want Quin making any big withdrawals from Van Slyck's bank? Was this the man he sought? His stomach tightened and he felt that muscle above his eye tick. He rubbed it away, as he tried to imagine Don Fitzgerald hiring the men who'd forced his parents' wagon off that bluff. He couldn't quite get his mind around it.

"I reckon that's so. I appreciate your advice and the offer."

Don tipped his head in a curt nod.

"You had any more trouble with rustling and cut fences?" asked Chance.

He sighed. "Seems there's always trouble. But it's not as bad as it was this spring. Why? They still hitting the 4C?"

"No. Seems quiet enough."

"Did Bowie tell you that we had a spy here? He was working with a puncher from the 4C."

"Bowie and I don't really talk."

"Well, that's a shame. But your sister's place is doing real good. I been there a time or two."

"Yup, though I don't know how she can lift her head up in public."

Don gave him a long stare and then said, "Don't be too hard on her, son. She's your sister, after all."

"Not anymore. I'm ashamed of her."

"You got a gal, Chance?"

"No, sir. And I don't aim to. I'm after my share and then I'm heading back to Deadwood. Now that's a lively town."

"Well, we'll miss you. You remember my offer. You want to sell, you come to me first, you hear?"

"You bet." Chance turned his horse and pressed his heels into Rip's broad sides.

He made it back to town just after dark.

Chance left Rip at the livery after buying a nose bag for his horse. He'd been looking forward to seeing Ellie all day, but it was too early, so he headed to the

Whistle Stop and spent his last two dollars on a meal before heading to the church.

Choir practice was underway and Chance paused outside, listening to the singing as he recalled his mother's battle to get him to attend services with mixed results. He realized he was thinking of his mother and smiling. The guilt rushed in. Ruby Cahill should be at choir practice instead of lying in an early grave. Chance's stomach roiled with his pain and rage.

He headed in, hanging back in the vestibule rather than entering the church proper, and peered in at the raised dais holding a group of four women and two men. Ellie stood in the middle wearing a stiff moss-green hat pinned to her bun. Her matching moss-green skirt and jacket were trimmed with a black flowing loop-de-loops pattern on her skirts and sleeves that seemed designed to blend in with the dark fabric. Chance decided that, unlike her mother, Ellie did not like to stand out. But she did. Trim and curvy and pretty as a song, Chance couldn't take his eyes off her.

Chance looked at the men. The older gent had a shining bald pate, fringed with gray hair long enough to brush his collar. Merritt's boarder, Professor Wilson, he realized. He glanced at the other gent, ginger hair, earnest face, brown eyes and a suit that said that he did all right for himself. Chance scowled at Dr. Lewis.

This man was on Minnie Jenkins's list of possible husbands. Chance didn't like him for the sole reason that Minnie did.

If Ellie chose him, she'd be stuck in town, but she could have the children she wanted. He should be happy for her. Lewis was a good man, kind and responsible. Instead, Chance found himself thinking of ways to put him down.

Now Chance faced a dilemma. He didn't care if anyone saw him with Ellie. But Ellie cared. With all the double dealings and the investigation, he'd become a dirty little secret and Wilson and Lewis both knew him on sight. Lewis would have to be a saphead not to offer to escort Ellie home. So, did he show himself or simply let Ellie believe he had stood her up?

Chance stepped far enough out of the corridor to be seen, but kept his hat low over his eyes. Ellie spotted him immediately, raising one hand from the hymnal in a salute. Her face brightened, as well. That change in her expression was an unexpected gift. It almost seemed that she'd been waiting for him and was as eager to see him as he was to see her. That showed a complete lack of good sense, but it pleased Chance unreasonably.

He stepped back out of sight, unsure if any of the others had spotted him because when he'd looked at Ellie, he'd clean forgotten everyone else in the room. He didn't understand it.

Chance rubbed his neck as he considered why he was sweating. He hadn't been so excited since the last time he'd had a chance to break horses at the 4C. It was the one kind of work he never tried to dodge.

But Ellie wasn't a horse and she sure the hell wasn't the kind of gal he went for. When the urge to be with a woman came over him, he generally liked them well-broke and well padded. Leanna would blister his ears, but he still found whores better company than a woman looking for a husband. Widows were also on his list. They had a more relaxed standard and knew what they liked. Though there was one in Dodge who liked Chance a little too much and had proposed that he stay and run her café. There was no surer way to see Chance's back than to ask him to stay.

He didn't want a wife and Ellie knew better than to pick him for a husband. Still, there was a spark between them. Chance cautioned himself. Sparks were dangerous. Especially when there was so much dry timber about.

The practice ended and Chance stepped into the darkest corner of the foyer beside a window so he could not be seen in silhouette. He'd had enough practice hunting outlaws to know how to lay low when it suited him.

Wilson reached the foyer with the other three women. None lingered before calling their farewells.

Ellie's laughter preceded her. Chance felt his mood darken. What the hell was he doing here, lurking in doorways like a lovesick calf? And what had Lewis said that was so all-fired funny? He didn't need her help badly enough to risk making a complete fool of himself. And what about Minnie's warning? Chance wasn't the kind to be bullied, but in this case Ellie's mother was absolutely correct. Being seen with Chance would only hurt her odds of finding a husband.

Ellie stepped into the foyer with Dr. Lewis. Chance set his jaw, positive he didn't want to hear their conversation.

"I'll see you home," said Lewis, not asking but just assuming she had no other choice.

Chance took a step in her direction, ready to challenge his claim, but then stopped himself. He had no claim. Lewis was a good catch with a promising practice in a booming town. Chance hated him.

Ellie hesitated and glanced about. Would she make some excuse to linger?

Chance's body tingled with the excitement he usually felt when on the hunt and closing in. His muscles tensed, preparing for whatever came.

"No. Thank you, Clancy. I believe I have an escort this evening."

She looked away from Dr. Lewis, missing the expression of astonishment that was followed instantly by annoyance. Chance savored the moment, a smile pulling at his lips.

Ellie had surprised Chance again. Was she wise, she would have linked arms with Lewis and left Chance in the dust. Instead, she glanced about for him.

"Chance?" she said.

He stepped from the shadows. Ellie rewarded him with a winning smile that lifted the corners of her pretty hazel eyes. Lewis retreated a step and then recovered himself.

"Oh, Mr. Cahill. I'm surprised to see you here."

"Surprised myself. Isn't my usual territory."

Lewis forced a tight smile, then replaced his brown felt hat with a brim hardly wide enough to keep the rain from his nose. He pressed down the crown with one hand and then nodded to Ellie.

"See you on Sunday, Ellie."

She gave him a bright smile and watched as he departed. She still had her back to Chance when the door swung closed, leaving them very much alone.

"That was foolish," he whispered.

She spun, her chin lifted in a defiant attitude that made him want to cup her jaw in his palm and kiss her again.

"He knows you're alone with me," said Chance, tipping back his hat and restraining himself. Images of kissing her made his heartbeat thrum, contradicting his outward self-control. Oh, he wanted her. Wanted to taste that mouth and press her lithe, small body to his.

"We're old friends. I told him that."

Chance laughed. "Old friends. Is that what we are?"

"Of course."

That took him down a peg. He was fantasizing about kissing her and unbuttoning her blouse and she was here to help an old friend.

Damn, that hurt. He wasn't use to much resistance from women and he wasn't used to being with women he had to resist.

He thought of what Leanna would do to him if he shamed Ellie.

"If Lewis is half the man I think he is, he's waiting outside."

"Oh, don't be silly. Why would he do that?"

"Because he's worried about leaving you alone with the likes of me."

"I don't think so."

"Bet you a dollar." Which he didn't have.

She cocked her head and considered his offer, then grinned and nodded, extending her little hand.

"All right. I accept."

He hesitated one more instant. Then he captured her hand with the speed of a snake strike and used it to pull her into his arms. She gave a little gasp before he kissed her.

Chapter Thirteen

Ellie stiffened as his mouth slanted over hers. Her shoulders rose as if she meant to fight. Chance ran his tongue along the full curve of her pouty upper lip and she gasped. Now his tongue skirted the sharp edge of her front teeth. The changes were subtle, just as she was. Ellie didn't suddenly give in and throw herself at him, but neither did she draw back and slap his face. Now, she wavered between resistance and surrender, capitulating, thawing like thin ice wrapped around a willow bough. By slow degrees her body became pliant. His tongue slid into her mouth, gliding over hers, and she gave a soft little moan that vibrated through him like a thunderclap. The sound was barely audible, but he knew then that she also wanted this and the thrill of her acceptance pulsed through him. She tipped her head, offering him admittance and he kissed her greedily.

Her tongue began to move, stroking over his. Ellie was a fast study, learning from their first kiss. How he wanted to teach her more, to be the one to show her just what it could be like between them.

He couldn't help himself from sliding one hand up her long neck and threading his fingers deep into the soft nest of her thick hair. His mouth demanded more and she withheld nothing. Her hands came up to knead the muscles of his chest like a cat's claws. His body quickened, making him feel dizzy as a boy spinning on a rope swing. What would he give to have those claws digging into his back as he thrust into her warm, wet body?

This time he groaned, a deep, dangerous growl of warning that he was nearing a threshold of control. Already his body was ready to take her. Ellie fueled a hunger in him, a burning thirst. He wanted to drink her in and gobble her down.

It was the jolt of need that revived him. He saw himself from the outside, even as he backed her into the shadowy corner by the window, pressing her up against the wall like some two-bit good-time girl. He had her or he could have her if he chose to be what everyone believed him to be. He couldn't do as he liked, because this was Ellie, who had offered him nothing but support.

And this was how he repaid her.

Chance broke away with a growl of frustration. Thank goodness for the darkness in this corner, so she could not see him panting, straining, fighting against himself not to do the unforgivable.

His voice sounded more snarl than speech. "I'm sorry."

"I'm not." Her voice had a breathy, airy quality that made the beast in him hungry for more.

He clenched his teeth, trying to clear his head, but instead breathed in the sweet fragrance of roses and vanilla. Ellie smelled like flowers. He groaned.

She stared up at him, her eyes all wide innocence. Red Riding Hood facing the wolf, too trusting to run. He ought to go out and shoot himself as a scoundrel. What the hell was he doing with Ellie Jenkins? She was a good girl and he was a killer.

"Do you still want that husband and kids?" he asked.

A line formed between her brows, but she nodded.

"Then let's get out of here." He offered his elbow automatically, recalling the rusty lessons his mother and father had drummed into him as a boy. She looped her arm in his, showing again that complete lack of self-preservation. But he liked the feel of her at his side, small, compact, her head just cresting his shoulder and the drab green hat tipped up so he could see the wisps of hair curling at her face and neck.

He held the door and she stepped out. He walked her down to the hotel, which was only at the corner.

"You owe me a dollar," he said.

"I don't owe it to you yet."

"There at three o'clock," he said, not turning his head.

On the right side of the wide porch in one of the many wicker chairs, still visible behind the large potted fern, sat Dr. Lewis.

"Pay up," said Chance.

Ellie glanced up at him, her lips puckered in a petulant look he'd not seen before. It made him want to kiss her again.

"I don't have the funds at present."

"Typical," he said in mock admonishment.

She lowered her voice. "You didn't tell me about your parents."

"Can't here."

"Which is why I suggested the church. It's quiet and private this time of night."

"Too quiet and too darn private."

Ellie looked away. She understood. He could tell by the starch in her spine as they crossed the street.

"Where, then?" she whispered.

"Damned if I know." He walked her up the front steps leading to the Château Royale's wide, welcoming porch.

Lewis extinguished his cigar and stood, removing his silly excuse for a hat.

"Doc, you think you could see Ellie in?"

"But…" she said, and then her words fell off.

Chance leaned forward, speaking so only she could hear. "He's the smart choice, Ellie, and you're a smart girl."

He pulled back to see her stiff with shock, her wide eyes looking up at him as if he had slapped her. Lewis stepped forward, still holding his hat like a damn fool.

"Where are you going?" asked Ellie.

He shrugged a shoulder. "Night's young."

"You're going across the tracks?"

Chance gave her a practiced devil-may-care smile that had gotten him into way too much trouble over the years. "That's where the fun is."

"Good night, then." She stepped away from him and up beside Lewis. It was the smartest thing she had done all evening.

Chance accepted her glower, understanding her objection to being cast off, but thinking how appealing she was, with her brows dipping low over her eyes and her nostrils flaring. If she had any sense she'd grab the man beside her and never let go.

Why had he kissed her again?

"Evening, you two. Don't do anything I wouldn't."
He winked. "That should leave a wide-open field."

Ellie gasped and Lewis set his jaw. Chance turned
his back and did what he did best—walked away.

Chance had wanted to spend most of the evening at
Leanna's Place, watching the comings and goings, but
since he was supposed to be at odds with his sister, he'd
had to skulk in the shadows. Still, he didn't return to
the Château Royale until late. He'd managed to make
it through the night without shooting anyone. Bowie
would be so proud. He had one foot on the steps when
a male voice stopped him.

"Chance? I'd like a word."

He turned to see Oscar Jenkins looking at him with
the same hazel eyes as his daughter, intent and intelligent. But unlike Ellie's, Oscar's eyes were unreadable.

He wouldn't blame Oscar for running him off. That's
what he'd do if a man like him came sniffing around
his daughter. What a thought, him with a daughter.

"Yes, sir."

Oscar motioned to his office. Chance preceded him,
grateful for the wide leather armchair that enveloped
him. Only after he'd sunk into the soft folds did he
recall that Oscar had not asked him to sit. His host said
nothing about his lack of manners as he leaned on the
arm of the opposite chair and folded his arms across
his chest.

"You sober?"

Chance narrowed his eyes, making no attempt to
hide his feelings at Jenkins's assumption. He was many
things, but drunk was not one of them.

Jenkins cocked his head. At last he nodded. "Why'd
you come back to town, son?"

Chance hesitated and then lied. "To sell my share of the 4C."

"That's what I'm hearing. Why now?"

He shrugged.

"You need money that bad, Chance, that you'd ignore your papa's wishes to keep the ranch intact?"

Chance hesitated, wondering if he could trust this man.

"What's on your mind, son?"

Oscar was an unlikely hotel owner. He looked more like what he was said to be, a privateer.

"You really run guns for the Confederacy?" asked Chance.

Oscar's mouth twitched upward. "Oh, more than guns."

"That give you the money for this place?"

He nodded. "I did all right."

"Your wife's from a wealthy family, too?"

"They were, before the war took it all. Why do you think she settled for an old salt like me? I'm ten years her senior and I wasn't handsome, even then."

They were silent again.

"That about it, son?"

Chance wanted to ask him if he could make a shot from seven hundred and fifty yards out. Instead, he nodded.

"Then let me speak my mind. I like you, Chance. Always have. I'd even favor you as a suitor for my daughter if you'd set your mind on it. But if your intentions are not honorable, then you best not trifle with her. Is that understood?"

Chance didn't know what shocked him more, the threat or that Oscar would actually consider him as a suitor.

* * *

Chance's kiss had kept Ellie up most of the night. She'd half expected him to come to collect his wager. Silly idea, as he'd certainly forgotten all about her the minute he'd turned her over to Dr. Lewis.

She patted the pocket of her dress, feeling the large one-dollar coin there within the folds. Despite her stern admonition to herself, she found her gaze wandering to the stairs, watching for Chance.

He appeared before nine, which was a wonder because she knew from her father that he had not returned until after three in the morning. He grinned at her and her insides jumped and sizzled like butter on a hot griddle.

"Got a minute?" He didn't wait for a reply but grasped her elbow and guided her again to the back porch, now awash with morning sunlight and the comings and goings of staff. He drew her to the far end, where the wood was stacked in neat rows. Here they were blocked from view from the guests leaving and arriving at the depot by the wall dividing the service entrance from the second guest entrance. Once tucked from sight, he released her and leaned back against the rail.

"Lewis get you in all right?" he asked.

"He did."

"He kiss you?"

"That's none of your business, Chance Cahill."

Oh, he didn't like that answer, judging from the glint in his narrowing blue eyes. Well, fine. Chance had kissed her twice and then pushed her into the arms of another man. What did he expect?

"You regret it?" he asked.

"What?"

The corners of his mouth turned up and he regarded her through sleepy eyes as he stared at her mouth, sending her heart knocking against her ribs. Still, she held herself with a gratifying outward calm that was only skin-deep.

"I don't seem the worse for wear."

He took a step in her direction but this time she moved to evade.

"You can't kiss me again, Chance."

His expression turned speculative and then devilish, as if taking up the challenge. "Can't I?"

"You told me last night that Clancy was the wiser choice."

He returned to his resting place and folded his arms over his broad chest, his eyes narrowing on her. Did he think he could just kiss her whenever and wherever he liked?

"So he is. I got nothing to recommend me, except that I'm a good kisser."

She could not hold her veneer of detachment while looking into those eyes. Ellie turned to look out at the tracks.

"We're alone, Chance. What is it you wanted to say?" She cast a look back over her shoulder at him.

His playfulness dissolved and his face turned sober. "I trust you, Ellie, and so does Annie. But I'm worried. I don't want you harmed for helping us."

She dropped all bravado and gently touched his forearm earnestly for a moment.

"I will do all I can to help, Chance. I'll take the risk."

His eyes looked troubled as he proceeded in very short order to turn her world upside down, describing the murder of his parents, the telegram from his brother and all that Bowie and Leanna had told him since his return, including their suspicion that Tobias Hobbs had been hired by the same man who killed their father. Ellie felt ill.

She'd thought Quin had been shot by rustlers. She had not even been aware of all Merritt had endured. She shivered as Chance told her that Bowie's fiancée had been held as a living shield, preventing Bowie from firing, but not the unknown gunman who did not care if he killed her in order to get to Hobbs. She sagged against the rail trying to understand how anyone could do such a thing.

"But they were such good people," she said at last, bewildered and still feeling quite ill.

Chance lay a hand on her forearm, bringing her back to the here and now. "Ellie, aren't you related to Van Slyck?"

"You don't think he had anything to do with it."

He didn't answer. He did.

"Preston was my second cousin. My mother and Willem are first cousins on her mother's side. Papa gave him the venture capital to start his bank. He owes everything to my father. He did something, didn't he?"

Chance's expression remained guarded.

She met his steady gaze, chewing on her bottom lip, torn between the need to tell Chance all she knew and the fear of betraying Leanna.

"What else, Ellie? Spit it out."

"Talk in town is that Preston was Cabe's father." Ellie braced for the explosion, but Chance only nodded.

"That makes sense. But he's not. I know that much."

Ellie let her relief out in a long breath. "But why then did he threaten the baby?"

"Because Annie was poking around in his father's

business and interfering with the whores. Preston wanted her to stop."

Ellie absorbed this. She felt frightened now, more so than before. She wasn't afraid for herself, but for her mother. What if her cousin was behind this? Her mother hated scandals and something like this would devastate her. She held her hands over her throat now, afraid to ask her next question. "Why was she poking around?"

Chance hesitated only a moment. "Because one of the gunmen mentioned Van Slyck before he died."

Ellie gasped, feeling physically ill. "Which one?"

"We don't know, but one of them is involved. What else do you know about the family?"

Ellie searched her mind. "Willem's wife left him after his store failed back in Virginia. Just dropped off his son and disappeared. My mother said he should have known better than to marry a girl from South Carolina. Mother also says they were poor as church mice, nearly starved after the war. They sent a desperate letter to her and she sent the funds to bring him and his son to Texas. That's all I know, really."

"He's not poor now."

"Papa says it's hard for folks who have lost everything. They're always afraid another storm will take it all." Ellie looked away. She'd always felt that her mother's fixation on Ellie marrying wealth seemed grounded in her troubled past. The bright, expensive clothing and the grand surroundings seemed like a defense against the world she no longer trusted. "My father indulges my mother greatly, because he understands how it is with her."

"Are they close, your mother and her cousin?"

"I heard her say recently that now that her cousin

can do without her help, he has forgotten what she did for him."

He turned sideways, straddling the rail as if it were a horse and leaning forward on his hands, making the muscles of his arms bulge against the blue cotton of his shirt.

"Is your father a good shot?"

Ellie stilled at this question and was about to spring to her father's defense. She felt her ears tingle as she stared at Chance. Was he really asking her to betray her parents?

"No. He says he prefers cannons to guns. He doesn't even carry a sidearm."

He nodded. "Sorry to ask."

She inclined her head, accepting this.

"Anyone else?"

"Not specifically. But I did tell everyone who'd listen that I'm back to force Quin to sell the 4C."

Ellie pursed her lips and scowled. "That was not what your father wanted."

Chance smiled at her. "I'm not selling, Ellie. Just stirring the pot."

Her relief was instantaneous. "Oh. I'm glad to hear it."

Chance swung his long leg over the rail and stood. "Thanks for listening, Ellie."

"I'll do more than that. I'll tell you everything I hear. Annie and I used to pretend to be spies. We were very good. We spied on you and your brothers."

He quirked one brow. "This isn't a game, Ellie. It's serious, deadly serious. So you promise me that you will only listen. Just tell me what you overhear, but don't ask any questions."

Ellie thought of Quin, Merritt and Leanna and nodded. "No questions."

Chapter Fourteen

Chance spent a late night in the red-light district watching the two sons of Don Fitzgerald from the street. His work chasing bounties had taught him patience and he stuck with them until they headed home at dawn, sure they hadn't ever seen him.

He was on his way to his own bed when he found the ferryman, Muddy, lying precariously between the tracks. He scooped him off before the noon train ended his days. Chance helped up the old drunk and kept him from falling.

"That you, Chance?"

Muddy stared up at him with bloodshot eyes, his cheeks and nose a river of threadlike purple veins and burst blood vessels. Chance wondered why a man would drink that hard for that long. Maybe for the same reason he hunted outlaws.

Chance detoured to the river, seeing Muddy to his ferry before leaving him to sleep it off. He'd already turned to go when Muddy called to him.

"You know that wagon accident? The one that took your folks?"

He stilled and took a step back. Something in Muddy's voice, the strain, brought Chance to alert. "Yeah?"

"They was…" He looked at Chance and then shook himself. He glanced around, as if searching for his parents' ghosts. Now his words were rushed as if he had to hurry to get them out. "They was real good people, Chance. And I miss them."

Chance swallowed the lump rising in his throat and nodded. Not trusting his words.

"You look like him, like your dad. Anyone tell you that?"

"See you around, Newt," said Chance, and left him behind, needing to get away, feeling the darkness closing in again, just as it had every time he recalled that day.

By the time he reached his bed the sun was well up. He drew the curtains and collapsed facedown on the mattress. It seemed only a moment later that some woodpecker came rapping on his door.

He lifted his head from his pillow, wishing he had worn his guns to bed so he could shoot whoever was knocking.

"It's open!"

The door creaked and Ellie stood in the gap, pretty as a songbird. Chance flipped over and dragged himself to sit on the edge of the mattress, happy he'd left on his drawers.

Her eyes rounded at the sight of him tangled up in the sheets. She stared at his chest, a long, direct stare that made Chance's skin tingle and his muscles bunch. If she knew what was good for her, she'd clear out. But she didn't. By slow degrees, her eyes shifted to meet his. By then her face was flushed and his mouth had gone dry. Chance grabbed his shirt and shrugged it on. It didn't help. Tension crackled between them like heat lightning.

"Did I wake you?" Her voice quavered.

"Just from a sound sleep."

"I'm so sorry. I didn't expect to find you still in bed."

"Up late. What time is it?"

"Nearly five in the afternoon." She glanced down the hall.

He took the opportunity to tug on his trousers and then came out to meet her in the hall as he worked on the buttons on his shirt.

Ellie turned back to face him. "Oh. There you are. Well, I learned something that might prove valuable. I discovered that your father was not the only one who courted your mom."

Chance leaned against the frame. "Didn't know that."

"Yes, but then your father showed up and shortly afterward they were engaged. I understand the other suitor did not take the news well. Both my parents recall it distinctly."

"Who, Ellie?"

"Don Fitzgerald."

Chance retraced his steps, finished dressing and splashed some water on his face.

"Bowie needs to hear that." He reached for his hat. On his way out the door, he paused, drew her in and kissed her hard and quick. "Thanks."

Ellie blinked up at him as he set on his hat. "You're welcome."

He headed for the jail but on reaching his destination he found Bowie's lazy deputy making use of one of the chairs on the porch as he read the newspaper.

"Oh, Bowie is at dinner over at Miz Dixon's place," said Whitaker.

The thought of going to see Merritt after what he'd pulled left him cold. So he had a choice—wait at the jail or go find Leanna.

"Tell Bowie I'm at Leanna's Place and I need to speak to him."

"You want me to tell him what it's about?"

"No."

He found Leanna at her gambling hall and told her what Ellie had found out.

"Oh, Chance, if anything happens to her, I swear I will never speak to you again."

"She came to me."

"Of course she did. She's my dearest friend. She'll do whatever she can to help us. But you shouldn't have accepted."

"The gal's a bloodhound and I'm glad she is on our side." He thought of Ellie standing in the hall staring at him and licked his bottom lip. When he glanced at Leanna it was to find her brows dipping dangerously over her clear blue eyes.

"I know that look and don't you dare. She's my friend."

"I didn't. I just…" His words trailed off. If he told Leanna how Ellie made him feel, she'd use that little pistol he bought on him.

"Just what? Are you planning on courting her?"

"Don't be stupid."

"Then stay away from her."

Her father had said much the same. They were both right and that aggravated him to no end.

"You sound just like Quin now."

She sat back at the insult. They had both been lorded

over by their elder brother for years and she did not cotton on to his implication.

"If you pursue her without honorable intentions, then you're just like Preston Van Slyck."

That blow stung, for he knew that Preston's favorite sport had been luring innocent girls from good families into a liaison, making false promises and then taking particular delight at their pain as they lost everything.

They glared at each other over the table. He'd counted on Leanna more times than he could remember and he'd gotten her out of more than one scrape, defended her from bullies and boys who she wanted chased off. But where Ellie was concerned, Leanna was no longer in his corner.

Bowie stomped in at that moment, sweeping the room with his cool gaze. From the depth of his brother's glower Chance speculated that his addled deputy had not waited for his brother to return from supper but had taken the initiative to drag him from it. Bowie found Leanna first and she indicated Chance's location with an inclination of her head. Her expression said, *You deal with him.*

Chance was now bruising for a fight. He stood to meet Bowie as he stomped across the saloon.

"This had better be good," Bowie said.

Why could he and Bowie never get along? Too close in age or was it that Bowie thought those few years gave him the right to boss Chance? That had always resulted in Chance telling Bowie where to go, but still they kept coming to the same old dance.

"What the hell do you think you're doing?" asked Bowie.

Chance's face felt hot and his fists were bunched at

his sides. Before he could ask Bowie to sit, Bowie was at him again.

"Do you know what you're putting me through? Are you really going to make me arrest my own brother?"

"I didn't know calling you from supper was illegal."

"I got a man outside says you drew your gun on him."

Chance came to his feet. "What?"

"Are you drunk?"

"No!"

Bowie stepped forward, leaned in and sniffed. Chance's temper flared, knowing that if it were anyone else the marshal would listen to what he had to say. But not his brother. Bowie had already made up his mind. Chance knew it from the ticking at his left eye and the set of his jaw. Bowie was dug in deep.

"It was a mistake your coming back. You need to clear out." That was Bowie, putting his job before his family again.

"I'm not going anywhere."

"You're leaving. Sooner is better." Bowie spun and walked away as if that settled the matter.

"Hold on now," tried Chance.

Bowie didn't turn as he spoke. "I've got to see about the complaint and hope I don't have to arrest you."

Chance tried again. "Bowie!"

Bowie kept walking. Something bubbled up inside Chance, molten and icy all at once. A lifetime of being ignored and bossed around wrestled its way out. And suddenly he couldn't take it anymore, not from Bowie. If Bowie wouldn't listen, well, by God, he'd make him listen.

Before he knew what he was doing, Chance had lifted the chair he'd been sitting on, swung it with one hand and thrown it like a Comanche spear. The chair sailed across the room. Someone screamed. Bowie spun and watched as the chair crashed through Leanna's custom-made stained-glass window.

Bowie's jaw dropped as shards of brightly colored glass showered down like a broken rainbow. Both brothers turned to Leanna to see her face flame. She lifted her fists to her temples and shrieked.

"Out! Both of you! Get out of my place!"

Bowie made his escape first, trailed closely by Chance, who followed at a run. Chance thought he and Bowie were as tough as any man in Texas, but not tough enough to face Leanna. They fled like mule deer before a wildcat.

In the street they paused, side by side, staring at the light now streaming through the gap where the window had been. The framing remained across the breach, bent and twisted, holding the chair like a huge leaden spider's web.

"You know I have to arrest you," said Bowie, his voice now conversational.

"That ought to keep Annie from killing me."

Bowie motioned with his head. "Come on."

Chance went along with Bowie to jail, hoping Leanna couldn't get at him there.

"Where'd she get the window?" asked Chance.

"She hired some artist from St. Louis."

Chance hung his head.

"Bowie, I never drew my gun tonight."

The window seemed to have calmed Bowie and he nodded. "I'll get to the bottom of it. But for now, I can't treat you any different than anyone else."

Whitaker, his deputy, met them at the jail and did a

poor job of hiding his shock as Bowie led Chance to a cell, took his guns and locked him up.

"What are the charges?" asked Whitaker.

"Disturbing the peace, for now," said Bowie.

Bowie leaned against the doorjamb, folded his arms and stared at Chance. He didn't look mad anymore, just disappointed. Suddenly, he looked exactly like their father.

"I don't even recognize you anymore."

"I'm trying to help."

"Well, then, stop trying."

"I still have something to tell you."

"Later," said Bowie, and left him with his deputy, who at least offered him coffee. Chance could not believe he was going to spend the night in jail. It seemed like hours before his brother returned with a judge.

"That's him," said Bowie.

The judge stared at Chance and nodded. "So you're the wild one. I've heard about you. I'm setting bail at a hundred dollars. You pay up and you can go. You are also paying damages for the window. Understand?"

He nodded.

"I'm only doing this because Bowie said you won't run. You got any money?"

Chance glanced at Bowie, not wanting him to know, but there was no helping it. He shook his head. He noticed Bowie's eyes widen. Funny to be from the wealthiest family this side of Texas and be flat broke. But Quin had kept his word and poured all revenues back into the ranch, as he'd promised. Leanna had told him that Quin had made two more land purchases since they'd left. The 4C was bigger than ever, but it seemed there was none left for bail. Chance glared at Bowie, feeling the defiance flowing cold as spring runoff.

"Then I guess you'll be sleeping here," said the judge.

Chance glanced at Bowie. He looked him right in the eye and shook his head. "Not me, brother. I'm still so mad I could spit. And if I were you, I'd steer clear of Annie for the next, oh, I don't know, six months."

"I still want to talk to you."

But Bowie left him again. Chance drank more coffee and thought about what Ellie had told him. From somewhere far off he heard a train whistle; he listened to the hum of the rails as a train passed through.

Leanna came in and for one moment Chance thought that she was there to spring him. But for once, it seemed, Leanna had had enough.

"Earl Thomas Cahill, you had no right to do that to my window."

It was odd to hear his given name. Everyone had called him Chance for as long as he could remember. He had been named after his father but spent a lifetime knowing he would never be his match. They should have named Quin after him.

"I'm sorry, Annie. I just… I couldn't get him to listen. He never listens."

"Maybe if you stopped shooting folks and breaking things, he'd have less paperwork and more time to chat." She aimed a finger at him. "You're paying for that window."

Leanna turned her back and headed out.

"Wait a minute. Aren't you going to spring me?"

She made a sound that he recognized was not good. He gripped the bars as Leanna sashayed out the door.

Chapter Fifteen

Chance had a long time to ponder the evening's happenings and in the end two things plagued him. The first was the image of Leanna's window shattering into a million sharp fragments of glass. The second disturbed him even more. It was Ellie, digging up the past. He'd forgotten to ask how she had learned Don had courted his mom and that troubled him. He just felt in his gut that she'd broken her word and asked questions. Leanna had been right, of course. Ellie would do anything to help them and he should have known better than to drag her into this mess.

Bowie returned, still looking troubled but no longer livid. He drew up a stool and leaned forward, elbows on knees, hands clasped together like a man about to pray.

His deputy hung in the doorway, leaning against the frame. Bowie glanced toward him. "Give us a minute, Glen."

His deputy started, and then made apologies as he disappeared.

"I just finished talking to the drifter who said you pointed a gun at him, and his friend who said he'd witnessed you do the same."

Chance sat on the narrow wooden bed frame, which was bolted to the wall, one hand wrapped about the cold steel of the bars.

"Bowie, I never..." His words trailed off as Bowie lifted a hand.

"I'll get to the point. They were saddle bums passing through, yet I found a ten-dollar gold piece on each. They couldn't account for them until I threatened to arrest and throw them in a cell with you. They said some man at Hell's Corner had paid them each to slander you. Either they don't know his name or they aren't saying. They've left town at my request."

"I told you."

Bowie nodded. "Looks like someone wants us at odds. So I suggest we let them think they've accomplished that."

"Shouldn't be too hard. You just treat me like you always do. That ought to convince anyone."

Bowie made a face. Was that chagrin? Chance watched his brother. He seemed to be struggling.

"I don't much approve of bounty hunters. Hurts me to see you in that line. But it's your life, Chance. I just think you could do better."

"So, you ready to listen to what I have to say now?"

Bowie nodded and Chance repeated what Ellie had turned up. When he finished, Bowie said, "If Don harbored ill will, I never saw it. Plus that was a long time ago."

"Still, it's something." He paused. "There's more. I went out to speak to Fitzgerald."

Bowie drew close. "What about?"

Chance motioned him close. Bowie leaned in and Chance repeated his story that he had come back to get his share of the land and sell it. Bowie listened; his eyebrows descended lower and lower over his intent blue eyes.

"So he thinks you're here to collect your inheritance?"

Chance told Bowie that he'd conveyed the same thing to Womack on his first night in town and he had made no offer, but Fitzgerald had shown real interest.

"Both Womack and Fitzgerald put in proposals for the depot. Either one might hold a grudge," said Bowie.

Chance related Fitzgerald's offer to buy him out and his suggestion that Chance see Slocum.

"That's Pa's old attorney. Quin still uses him."

"Might want to think on that," said Chance. "Why would Fitzgerald recommend I use the same lawyer as my brother? Isn't that a conflict of interest?"

"Sure is." Bowie pushed off the bars. "I better go talk to Slocum."

Chance stood, hands now both on the bars. "I'll go with you."

"We're at odds. Remember. Besides, I can't run an investigation if you keep me so tied up I can't get clear of the jail."

"Yeah, but you said that charge was false."

"I arrested you for disturbing the peace. That charge is genuine."

"I can go places you can't, Bowie. You need me."

That stopped him. Chance knew the look. He was considering it. "Maybe."

"Maybe nothing. You have to abide by the law."

"So do you."

"No, Bowie. I don't. No one expects me to and I won't get caught."

"If you do, I'll have to treat you like anyone else."

"I know that. And, Bowie?"

He lifted his eyebrows and waited.

"If I find him first, I'm killing him."

For once Bowie made no argument. Instead, he turned and walked away.

Chance had settled in for the night, dragging the thin, scratchy gray blanket across his chest and lying on the cot. The blanket smelled musty as a wet dog. He tried to rest, but his mind was uneasy. Was Ellie safe?

Chance closed his eyes and recalled the curve of her neck and how the long curling wisps of her hair danced around her face in the evening breeze. He felt his body becoming aroused.

"Damn it," he whispered, and then shouted, "Whitaker!"

The deputy appeared a moment later.

"Get me a chunk of wood. I want to do some whittling." Carving always settled him.

"You can't have a knife in there."

"Well, I got one." More than one, he thought. "You gonna take it from me?"

The man's eyes widened. "Nope."

"Then get me some wood."

"How big?"

Chance held his hands about six inches apart and then used his thumb and forefinger to indicate the height.

Whitaker left, returning a moment later with a branch from the stove box that he fed through the bars.

He hovered as Chance reached in his pocket, his

fingertips brushing soft cotton fabric. He absorbed the pang of sorrow as he withdrew his mother's handkerchief carefully folded about his father's pocket knife. He removed the knife, refolded the cloth, then set to work.

Chance used his thumbnail to flip open the longest blade and began to shave off the bark. He felt his father most closely when he worked on wood. His dad had taught him how to hold a knife and how to carve. The connection endured. When stressed, Chance didn't reach for a drink. He reached for a stick.

Whitaker stared from the doorway. "What are you making?"

He didn't know yet. But it would come to him as he worked. It always did.

"A spear to stab you to death. Now git."

But he didn't. Chance wondered if he was losing his touch or if the bars between them had given Whitaker a spine. He glanced up at the man.

"If I bring you a bucket will you use it for the shavings? Otherwise, Bowie will skin me faster than you can skin that stick."

Chance stopped whittling and looked up at the deputy. "Why do you work for him if he's such a tyrant?"

"Oh, pay's decent and I get meals. Mostly it's quiet." Whitaker rubbed his neck and gave Chance a melancholy look. "Mostly."

Chance studied the man and then nodded. "I'll use a bucket."

The deputy opened the cell. If Chance wanted to escape, here was his opportunity. Instead, he accepted the bucket and sat back down. Chance decided on a bird, a little brown bird that didn't look like much but had a song like nobody's business. He had the entire thing carved, when Whitaker appeared.

"It's a bird!"

The man was bright as tarnished silver.

"Your bail's posted, so you can go."

Chance perked up. He closed the blade and returned it to the handkerchief before tucking the bundle back in his pocket.

Leanna had forgiven him faster than he'd expected. He would have laid money that she'd leave him for the night, if he had any money, that is.

He tucked the bird into his vest pocket and stood, holding the bars, looking toward the exit, his fist tightening on the cold iron as she appeared.

His savior was not Leanna, but Ellie Jenkins.

"Ellie! What are you doing here?" Chance didn't know if he should be elated or angry. His heart didn't, either, for it began beating in his eardrums like hoofbeats. A smile spread across his face as he recalled belatedly where he was and his ears began to prickle with shame. Ellie had seen him caged like an animal. His smile died with his joy.

"She sprung you. Paid cash." Whitaker turned the lock and swung open the door. "Guess you're in her custody."

Chance stood just inside the open door, unsure now. Ellie said nothing, just regarded him with those deep hazel eyes, masking her emotions completely.

Chance went for a bravado he didn't feel.

"Just can't go a day without seeing me," he said, and then realized his mistake as Ellie's face went pink and she glanced at Glen Whitaker, who was suddenly very busy with his keys. When had he become such an inconsiderate boor?

He shut his trap one sentence too late.

Whitaker held the door. Chance handed over the bucket. "You have a good evening," said Whitaker.

Chance glanced out at the gray world beyond his window. "Is it still evening?"

"Nope," came the answer.

In the main office, he collected his gun belt and pistols, then followed Ellie out of the jail, succeeding in getting his holster buckled as they reached the street. Had it been Quin or Bowie or Leanna, they would have lit into him the minute they were clear of outsiders, but not Ellie. She kept herself to herself.

"Well, say something," he begged.

She paused to regard him. It was a struggle not to fidget beneath her steady stare.

"So," she said. "How did your meeting go with Bowie?"

He grinned, enjoying her humor, so unexpected and so different from his family.

"Could have gone better."

He could not believe his ears. Was she giggling?

"Ellie?" The exasperation rang clear in his voice.

"Well, Chance, it is funny. You went to see the marshal and ended up in jail. Things between you haven't changed much in all this time."

They hadn't and he didn't appreciate her laughing at him. She forced away her smile, trying for a straight face, but her eyes continued to dance merrily and the corners of her mouth tugged upward.

"How did you know?"

"Nothing happens in town that folks don't talk about at the hotel. I went downstairs early as always and the breakfast cook told me." Ellie's mirth dissolved and her expression turned sad. "I heard about the window.

Annie was so proud of it. I think she chose the horses to represent her brothers, each of you at the 4C, in an ideal that never really existed. Just, perhaps, the way she would have liked it to be."

Chance threw up his hands. "Well, now I feel even worse."

Ellie roused him from his dark musings with a gentle touch and her quiet voice. "I'm sorry."

He nodded. "I told Bowie what you said. Took a while because he kept shutting me down, just like always." He was so glad to see her safe, but still worried about what Leanna had said. "Ellie, how'd you find out about my ma and Don Fitzgerald?"

"I just asked my father…" Her words fell off.

"A question?" he finished, scowling.

"Oh, Chance, he's my father."

"But you promised."

She said nothing to this, but her mouth went small and tight.

"Ellie I can't have anything happen to you. I'd never forgive myself."

She seemed not to have heard him for she continued on. "I think Ned Womack is having financial trouble. I know Quin tried to buy him out a while back but he refused to sell, for what reason I don't know. Yesterday, he and Mr. Stokes had a heated discussion outside the general store. Ned refused to settle up his credit there and he's just back from Dodge. He should have plenty of money from cattle sales."

"Ellie." His voice turned threatening.

She sighed. "All right. No more questions. But I overheard Ned and Ace. Truly. Now tell me what happened last night."

He repeated what Bowie had said and their agreement to continue the appearance of a rift.

"But why?"

He told her about the drifters and the setup and how Bowie had figured it out faster than a streak of lightning.

"He is very quick," Ellie admitted.

Now Chance felt the nasty coiling snake of jealousy winding through his guts. What did that mean—that Bowie was smarter than him, as well?

"But how will you meet with Bowie if you are supposed to present a facade of ill will?"

He loved the way she strung words together. It was like listening to poetry.

"Hadn't discussed that."

"Well, perhaps I could be your liaison."

"No!" He spoke too quick and too loud. She paused in the street. But he faced her, lips pressed tight. He knew that Ellie had once set her sights on Bowie and that Leanna had always supported her friend's ambitions. Even with Bowie engaged, it hurt him to think of Ellie mooning after his brother.

Her smile was mysterious, feline and seductive as hell. Who was this woman? She turned to face him and lifted a hand to his cheek, stroking him as if he was her pet. Her hand fell away, but her gaze continued to hold him captive. Had she and Leanna even considered him as a candidate or had they counted him out like everyone else had?

"I wasn't going to see Bowie directly. But I do see Merritt Dixon quite frequently. She is a gem and Bowie is so lucky to have her. I know she'll make a perfect wife. I told you about her former husband—the ranger?

Killed in the line of duty. I believe it was one of the reasons that she rejected Bowie initially."

"What were the others?" Chance would dearly love to have a list of Bowie's faults, because from where he stood, his big brother didn't have any, unless you counted his lack of faith that Chance could do anything right.

"I believe she did not want to come second to her husband's profession again."

That made Chance think of his eldest brother. Quin lived for that ranch, had been married to it body and soul for as long as Chance could remember.

"But he convinced her somehow. I think it's very romantic."

There was that voice again. Chance set them in motion and didn't stop until they had entered the hotel lobby. The lanky fellow with an Adam's apple the size of a peach pit stared at Ellie from behind the desk, lifting an eyebrow as he saw Chance's hand on her elbow. Chance nearly drew it back, but pride wouldn't let him. Instead, he narrowed his gaze on the man, who became suddenly very interested in the registry on the desk.

"He going to cause you trouble?" asked Chance, indicating the clerk with a lifting of his chin.

"He might." She didn't even pause as she said it. "But I'd imagine that by noon everyone in town will know that I bailed you out."

"Then why didn't you go in first and I could have come in later?"

"Two reasons. First, I do not approve of sneaking about like a child, and second, I'm escorting you to your room so you don't get into any more mischief."

The mischief he wanted to get into could be handled very neatly in his room, if Ellie would step inside with him. Chance's heart began that painful thumping, sending blood south. He frowned. Now he'd have to do the right thing and chase her off, when the truth was he wanted Ellie in his bed. She should have left him in jail. That way she'd be safe from him. As it was, she'd have to rely on his conscience, which was unpredictable at best.

"I thought you did as you were told."

"If that were true, Leanna would no longer be my friend and I would certainly not be speaking to the black sheep of the Cahill family."

Ellie had a plain way of speaking that he admired. Most women talked nonsense or in circles and he didn't know what was in their heads half the time.

They mounted the stairs side by side.

"Why'd you bail me out?" he asked.

"Because I care about you." She said it in such a matter-of-fact voice that he wasn't sure if she meant she had feelings for him or that they were friends. They *were* friends, of course, but recently his musings toward Ellie involved seeing her naked in his bed.

"Well, tonight you cared about a hundred dollars' worth."

"Ninty-nine. I owed you a dollar."

Chance paused to stare at her, that calming smile on her face and the devil glinting in her eyes. She was equally sweet and sassy, intelligent and unbelievably naive. Unless she knew exactly what she was doing?

That thought raised his hopes.

She did not stop her slow climb, but she tucked in her chin in a way that always meant she was up to no good and she gave him that sly smile with a quick shifting of her eyes. The more Chance thought back, the more he recalled that Ellie had not only joined him and Leanna in their mischief, the ideas had often been hers to begin with. What was she up to now?

She stopped before his door. Ellie turned and he captured her upper arms and drew her in. Her back contacted his broken door, which creaked open.

"Why did you bail me, Ellie? The truth this time."

She met his gaze. "So you could kiss me good-night, of course."

That idea went through him like a burning Comanche arrow, right to his guts, spreading flames south like a brush fire. This gal did have a way of stirring him up. He wanted to kiss her, too. But he didn't want to cause her more trouble and he didn't like being her last choice. He released her and stepped back. She stepped forward.

"It's nearly morning," he said.

She smiled.

"Clancy paid me a call last evening."

"Who?" said Chance.

"Dr. Lewis."

Now he was chewing rawhide again. Seemed he wasn't her only interest and she was sure certain to let him know.

"Chance, does that bother you?"

He should say that the man was a decent sort and would make a good husband but instead he said, "He smells like rubbing alcohol and cod liver oil."

Ellie giggled. Chance saw nothing funny.

She lifted a hand, palm up, and swept the air, motioning at nothing in particular. "This will all be mine someday."

"You'll be rich," Chance realized aloud.

"And I aim to sell it and buy a ranch."

"What do you know about ranching? You lived in town your whole life."

She faced him, with chin lowered and eyes flashing. "My whole life is not over yet and I think I could find someone who knew ranching."

The way she said that made him lift both eyebrows. Ellie didn't often show that piss-and-vinegar attitude. But it was sure there now.

He lowered his chin and said what was on his mind. "I understand from Leanna that your mother favored Quin for your husband."

"As did every mother in the county. He owns half of Texas."

Chance felt the resentment roll. Each of them owned a share of the 4C. But Chance had forfeited his legacy when he had ridden away. He didn't regret his decision, until right this instant. But sometimes he wished he had land again instead of just blowing over it like tumbleweed. That wasn't going to happen anytime soon.

"What about you?" he asked. "Did you favor him?"

"I didn't discourage him, I suppose. But he wasn't my first choice."

He wanted to ask who was but was certain she'd say Bowie, so he said, "Why not?"

"He's a little too…self-contained."

"What's that mean exactly?"

"He doesn't seem to need anyone or anything. Please don't misunderstand me. That changed when he met his wife and he loves Addie K. with his whole heart. He'll be a strong, dependable husband. But he doesn't seem to need much help."

"Been that way long as I can recall."

They shared a nod.

Suddenly his mouth was as dry as cotton.

"Bowie?" he asked, and braced himself.

"Is engaged, but before that my mother pushed me at him every chance she got until she discovered he was not going back to the 4C. I was relieved. Now mind, I think that Merritt is very fortunate to have him. He's protective to the point of being fierce. Still, Bowie is a very driven man and attractive—or he would be if he ever smiled."

"Too serious?" asked Chance.

"Grim," said Ellie, and tucked her chin to smile that secret smile.

"Grim?"

"I can't see him pretending to be a horse with a small child on his back or making faces at a fussing baby. Still, he might surprise me."

Chance felt a hitch in his stomach. "Ellie, can you see me doing those things?"

She gave him a barely perceptible nod.

Chance was feeling more optimistic now. He found he could swallow.

"What about me?" he asked.

"You're impulsive, demonstrative, childish—"

"Ellie! I meant the good stuff."

"Oh," she said, and then giggled. She clasped his hand, giving it a squeeze, and then released him. "You're kind, faithful."

He interrupted again. "Faithful? You make me sound like a hound."

"I know you gave your bounties to Leanna. And she needed them. What would have become of her without your help? So yes, faithful. And I knew you before your parents passed, so I also see in you all the things I'm not—playful, whimsical, funny, lively, daring and joyful. All traits I hope to see again in you."

Chance reached in his vest pockets to resist the urge to grasp her hand. He touched the warm carved bird nestled there and drew it out, offering it to her.

"What's this?" She lifted it to study the carving by the light of the nearby lamp. "Why, it's a little wren!"

"Prettiest song on the prairie. I made it for you." He realized that he had been thinking of her all along. The little brown bird that went unnoticed until it sang.

"Thank you, Chance!"

She tucked the gift into the folds of her skirt. Then she lifted her hands and pressed them to his chest. Suddenly, he couldn't move.

Chance felt a cold sensation down his spine, like an icicle skittering on frozen ground. Chance had a nose for mischief and a way of always ending up in the center of it, and Ellie, he realized, was the one who had often led him right into trouble. It seemed Ellie was more like him than anyone knew.

"Ellie? What are you up to?"

She stepped back into the darkness of his room and then turned to him, a perfect welcoming smile that touched her lips.

"Chance, I don't want to be invisible anymore." Ellie lifted her trembling fingers and began to unbutton her blouse. She kept her eyes pinned on his. "I know you can see me, Chance. You're the only one who can."

Chapter Sixteen

Ellie could not believe her audacity. Had she actually entered a man's room? Scandalous and exciting enough to make it hard to catch her breath. She hadn't felt this alive since she'd sat behind Chance, arms looped about his waist as he rode a half-wild horse when they were children. She wondered if he recalled the day as plainly as she.

Chance did not seem certain, either, judging by the way he lowered his chin and glanced about as if someone might happen down the hall at any moment. The room was nearly dark, except for the light from the kerosene lamps in the hall, turned low. She glanced about her familiar surroundings, knowing each room in the hotel intimately, but was still unable to see the chairs, washstand, armoire. But she could see the foot rail of the large double bed. His gaze followed hers and then returned to her.

"Ellie, you best go," he said.

She would go in a moment. And sometime soon—a day, a week, a month—Chance would go, as well. She held no delusions about that. He was not rooted like Quin, or devoted like Bowie or steadfast like Leanna. But despite all that, she wasn't quite ready to see his back.

The sensible thing was to walk out. Why didn't she?

"Ellie, you can't stay here." His voice held strain. Was he fighting to do the right thing? Just her luck that his conscience only extended as far as her.

"Where is the boy I knew who used to spit in the eye of the devil?" she asked, stepping closer until she stood toe to toe and had to tip her head to meet his troubled gaze.

"He's right here, standing next to the man who doesn't want to shame you."

Ellie felt her heart ache. He did still care for her, then, but was it the caring of a man for his woman or the concern for his sister's friend? She prayed that she was not about to make an utter fool of herself.

She looked up into those ghostly blue eyes, gray now in the poor light.

"Do you know what you're doing, Ellie?"

She took both his hands. "Choosing the only Cahill man I ever wanted."

His intake of breath was sharp and his eyes rounded.

"But, Ellie, I'm not staying."

"I know that." At worst, he would leave her behind. At best, he'd take her along.

"Then why? You could have Doc Lewis and those kids."

She moved in to rest her head on his shoulder, nestling against his big, warm body, breathing in his scent. "Until you came home, I'd forgotten how it used to be, how *I* used to be. Back then I did as I pleased and paid for it afterward, like you. Somewhere along the way I stopped being willing to pay the price. But you never have stopped, Chance. You've always taken the risks and accepted the consequences."

"I don't want that for you." His arms came around her, holding her tight, as if trying to protect her from herself. "I don't want to be the cause of your hurt."

"You brought me back to life, Chance, and have shown me something that makes me willing to take a risk."

"What's that?"

"You."

She felt his chest rise in a long steady breath that he released into a sigh.

"Leanna wanted you to marry Bowie."

"She did. But she never asked me who I wanted."

"Ellie, I'll ruin you."

She hesitated, drawing back to look up at him. His jaw was set and his muscles bulged. He'd dug his heels in.

She stroked his cheek, thrilling at the coarse stubble that abraded her hand. She let her fingers dance over the corded muscle at his throat and felt his Adam's apple bob as her hand swept down to rest over his thrumming heart.

"Kiss me," she whispered, then threaded her hands through his hair and pulled.

He resisted a moment and then drew her in.

Ellie again felt the flutter deep inside her and then a falling sensation as Chance molded her to his body. She opened her mouth eagerly now, pressing their lips together as his tongue danced with hers. His arms tightened about her, so she could barely draw breath. Still, it wasn't close enough. She gripped her fist in his dark hair and pulled him closer. His hat fell to the floor as his hands slid down her back, over her corset stays and to her waist. He locked his hands there, at the narrowest part of her, as he carefully pushed her back.

Was he trying to put her aside? She clung tighter, not ready for the kiss to end. But Chance was stronger and easily brought them apart. She made a very unladylike lunge at him, but he captured her wrists and held them pinned before her in a game she recognized from childhood. But in that version he'd be preparing to lift her and throw her into the river, squealing like a piglet.

She struggled a moment and then gave up, lifting her face to meet his gaze. His eyes no longer looked blue. In this light they were gunmetal-gray and narrowed to a dangerous glint.

"You got your kiss, Ellie. We go on and I think you know how it will end."

He released her and stepped back. She stepped forward.

He aimed a finger at her. "You stay clear of me, Ellie, or you'll regret it."

His finger hovered before her nose. She licked it.

Chance gasped and drew his hand back, clutching it with his finger still raised like a gun and staring at it as if she'd burned him.

"All right, then. You asked for it."

He stalked forward. The predatory look in his eye made her body jump as a thrumming pulse of blood pounded in her ears, her chest and down deep at the junction of her legs.

Chance advanced and she felt a jolt of fear at his expression as he snatched her wrist and yanked. She slapped full against his side. With a move, quick as drawing his pistol, he scooped her up in his arms like a groom carrying his bride, only he didn't carry her.

He threw her a distance of five feet through the air so she landed with a bounce on the bed.

Then he followed, his strides long, his expression dark. He stood on one foot, drew off his boot with an angry swipe and dropped it with a thud. A moment later it was followed by its mate. His hands moved to his hips, releasing the buckle to his gun belt and then the boot knife strapped to his calf.

Ellie found herself inching back. She didn't recognize this dangerous, frightening man. She had wanted Chance even knowing she'd never keep him, but she didn't want this.

He had his vest off. Next came his shirt. Ellie watched in cold fascination at the ripple of muscle and the play of light across his ribs and torso. He was broad at the shoulder and tapered at the waist, lean in the hips, and his hand was now at the buckle of his belt. He walked to the table beside the bed, padding silently on bare feet, and struck a match, lighting the lamp resting upon the table. A moment later he had the door shut and had shoved a chair under the doorknob, locking out the world beyond. Then he turned to face her.

"Undress," he said.

She didn't. Instead, she clutched a pillow before herself, thinking it meager protection against a man like Chance.

He rested one knee on the bed and leaned over her, his hands now flanking her head as she rolled to her back. His arms were locked straight and the muscles bunched, showing the long ropes of veins beneath skin that was sprinkled with dark hair. He hung suspended above her in the golden glow of the lamp, motionless save for his breathing. She stared up at the dark curling hair on his torso, the gleam of healthy tanned skin and the flat brown nipples. She lifted the pillow up to cover her mouth, as she looked into the dangerous eyes of Chance Cahill, the bounty hunter. In that moment she knew what those outlaws had seen and what they had felt during the last moments of their lives because she felt it now, the same cold terror and certainty that there would be no escape.

"Is this what you want from me, Ellie?" he growled.

She shook her head in adamant refusal. He gave her a cold smile and a little snort.

"I didn't think so." He pushed off the bed, looming over her now, gazing down. And then he made a mistake. Just before he turned away, he let slip his cold, murderous exterior and gazed at her with a look of pure tenderness and she knew she had been duped. He'd been trying to frighten her, chase her off, protect her even from herself. And it had nearly worked.

He sat on the edge of the bed and scooped up one boot. She reached for him, coming at him from behind, circling his waist beneath his shirt, feeling the warm flesh and crisp hairs dusting his belly. She pressed her cheek to his.

"It won't work, Chance."

He stiffened, turning to stone beneath that warm, velvet skin. She stroked him, feeling the muscles of his stomach twitch at her passing. He grasped her wrist to stop her.

"Ellie. I'm trying to do what's right."

"Running," she whispered.

"Yes. Now get out of here before someone sees you."

Her chin began to tremble and her voice quavered. "I don't know why you push away everyone who cares about you. You can't keep the world forever at arm's length, Chance."

His chin sank to his chest.

"Is it really better to be alone?" said Ellie.

"Compared to what? Having the people you love die on you? Yeah, I'd say better."

Ellie held on to him, wrapping her arms about his torso and locking them together, refusing to let him go.

"I never thought I'd see you run from me, Chance Cahill."

He turned his head, glancing back at her. "I run all the time. I ran from my responsibilities at the 4C. I ran from my brothers after the funeral. I'm a good runner, Ellie. Let me go and I'll show you just how good."

She lowered her head against his warm skin. "No."

The muscles of his back stiffened. "You'll regret it."

"That's what everyone keeps telling me, but my body is humming for you, Chance. Don't make me beg."

He dropped the boot.

Chance knew his bluff had failed. It was a rare thing. Men couldn't see through him; women, either. How had she? Ellie knew him better than most, but he didn't know a female alive who wouldn't have been scared to hysterics by the stunt he'd just pulled.

Ellie turned up the lamp's wick and stood on the opposite side of the bed now. His body jumped and twitched with the need to take her. If he picked up his gear and ran for the door she couldn't stop him.

He stood immobile as Ellie regarded him steadily. She unbuttoned the last of her blouse and Chance knew he was finished. His conscience drowned in a roaring surge of blood and desire.

Chance stripped out of his shirt and dropped it with the rest. When he set himself in motion, it was toward Ellie, not away.

His fingers were nimble and quick. He made short work of the tiny pearl buttons and then swept the gauzy fabric over her pale shoulders. Ellie was small, reaching only to his chin and she was so narrow he could span her waist with his two large hands. He kissed her on the bare shoulder and worried he was too big to rest on top of her.

Chance turned her so that she faced the full-length oval looking glass on the opposite side of his room. Ellie gasped as she saw their reflection. She, small and light, he, tall and dark—they were a mismatched team, yet when he held her nothing had ever felt so right.

He found the hook and eyelets at her hip and released her skirt. She stepped out of it with her gaze still pinned on him. He knew that look. Ellie on a dare. Ellie released from her mother's grip and roaming over the 4C, Ellie free to do as she pleased.

He pulled the ribbon fastening her first petticoat, the satin ribbon slipping between his fingers. The ruffled skirt fell to her ankles as did the next. Her bloomers billowed out about her. Chance needed to see those legs. He recalled them as strong and remembered the flash of white as she ran through the timber by the river, smooth slippery calves sticking in the air as she performed a handstand on the muddy bottom of the river. He bent to kiss her neck. Her head dropped back and she leaned against him, her chest rising and falling, the swell of her breasts exaggerated by the cinching corset. He could pluck them from the chemise like picking ripe fruit.

His hand splayed across her stomach, inching north to free her from the confines of whalebone stricture. He held her warm, tender flesh in his hand as he kissed her neck and then moved to the shell of her ear. He was rewarded when Ellie groaned and arched against him.

He glanced to the mirror to find her eyes still pinned on his. She had lifted her arm to caress his head as he nuzzled along her soft neck. She was slim and pale and lithe as a dancer. Her gaze now flicked to his hand, cupping her breast. He squeezed and she gasped as her eyes fluttered closed.

Chance slid his hands away and she made a throaty sound of protest. But she would have to be patient for a few moments.

"I want to see you naked, Ellie."

She turned to bury her face against his chest. He watched himself unlace her corset strings until the stiff garment gaped and dropped to the floor. He bent before her to roll down her stockings and unlace her shoes. Then he placed a hand at each hip and drew down her bloomers, glancing to the mirror to marvel at the round curve of her bottom and the twin dimples just above them. He stroked the soft curve of her backside and Ellie rocked from side to side as he rose to stand before her. Whether intentionally or accidentally, she pressed briefly against his erection. This caused Chance to grit his teeth as he struggled to keep from taking her hard and fast. He wanted to lift her up and then lower her down on top of him. He wanted to bend her over the bedrails and plunge into her from behind. He wanted her on her back, gazing up at him as he touched her wet, velvet flesh and rocked deep within her.

Instead, he drew down the delicate ribbon straps of her chemise. Ellie's hands looped about his neck but she leaned back to give him access to the buttons that closed the last barrier between them. He glanced in the mirror. Her back was a map of small red lines where the wrinkled chemise had been pressed into her soft flesh by the restrictive corset. Chance rubbed her back, trying to erase the marks as she hummed in approval. He drew her close, whispering to her.

"You're so beautiful, Ellie. Turn around now. Let me see you."

She pressed her face against him and lifted a hand to cover her eyes as if ashamed of the perfection of her body. If she were his, he would spend every night telling her how lovely, how appealing, how sensual, he found her.

He spun her slowly. She didn't resist or use her hands to cover herself as he expected. Instead, she looped her arms about his neck and stared up at him, watching him as he admired their reflections. Her breasts were small and round as apples, her nipples pale pink and drawn into perfect buds. Her torso was so narrow that he could see his own ribs on each side of hers. Her stomach was flat, save the slight rounding above her sex. He stared at the triangle of dark curls. Unable to resist, he slid his hand over her hip and down into that nest of hair. She whimpered and stiffened as his fingers slipped between her legs, but she did not shy at his touch.

She was his, only his. For reasons he would never fathom, Ellie had chosen him. He vowed to do all he could to make her glad.

He drew her back against the warmth of his body, rubbing himself against the temptation of her backside as he stroked her soft, wet flesh.

"Look at us, Ellie."

She opened her eyes and stared transfixed at their reflection, rocking in rhythm to some secret music that only their bodies knew. Her mouth dropped open and her breathing grew erratic. She pressed back against him, closing her eyes as he moved his slick fingers faster, using both hands now, entering her with two fingers as he stroked her with the others. She shook her head no and bit her lower lip. Her body flushed and she seemed to glow from within with a soft light.

From deep in her throat came a low animal cry. Chance held her about the waist with one hand as he petted her with the other. Ellie arched against him, while deep inside her body, he felt the rolling contraction. How he longed to be inside her.

She went slack, but he held her, dipping to scoop her up in his arms. His first thought was to run with her, back to his horse, away from this place.

But instead he laid her on his bed and stripped out of his trousers and drawers. She roused herself now, opening her eyes, and reached for him as he slid a knee between her legs. She glanced down between them and her eyes went wide. Chance hesitated, feeling something was wrong. But she spread her legs for him without his urging, so he poised himself above her.

She gave him a funny little smile and the smallest of nods before he slipped slowly into her warm, liquid folds and straight into the barrier he had feared and anticipated. Chance pulled back.

Ellie was a virgin.

Chapter Seventeen

Chance gritted his teeth, poised above her, battling between what he wanted and what he needed to do.

At last he pulled out, but he'd gone too far, waited too long and so he bucked like a wild horse against her stomach once, twice and then felt the hot rush of release, even as she cried out in surprise at the warm fluid that spilled between them.

Chance lowered himself against her. "I'm sorry, Ellie. I couldn't wait."

"But, but," she stammered. "I thought…"

"Hush a moment."

She did as he asked, but lay immobile as a rabbit hiding from a fox, only the rapid drum of her heart hammering between them. Chance rolled clear and off the bed. He snatched up his drawers and tugged them on, then strode over to the washbasin, pouring water from the pitcher and bringing back a damp cloth for her.

He returned to find Ellie curled on her side, covering herself with her upraised knee and her arms crossed over her chest. Rather than modest, the picture she presented was one of the most provocative he'd ever witnessed. He found everything about her appealing, except for her shame. Her disgrace scorched him like hot iron. She wouldn't look at him and he thought she was trying to disappear.

Since he'd come home, he couldn't think of other women because he wanted Ellie so badly, but he had no right to do this. Now he had one more thing to regret, one more mistake he couldn't live down.

"Ellie?"

She could not meet his eyes.

He sat beside her on the bed and washed her stomach as best he could while she covered her eyes with her hand. Then he threw the towel at the basin. He stooped to retrieve her chemise and voluminous bloomers. She snatched them from him, holding them before her like a curtain.

Chance drew on his shirt and sat beside her on the bed. His heart felt so heavy. And then he knew why.

Suddenly they were strangers again, awkward, silent, regretful. He wished he could go back to the instant before he'd kissed her. He'd push her back into the hall and slam the door in her face.

Or would he just do it all over again? Chance hung his head. He didn't know what was right anymore. He only knew that hurting her was like peeling off his own skin.

He couldn't go back. The past two years had taught him that much. All he could do was live with this whole new set of bad decisions.

"Is there something wrong with me?" Ellie's voice held a quavering tone of anguish that ripped into him like the claws of a cougar.

"I just don't feel right about taking what should be your husband's."

She rocked up to sit on the bed, behind him, facing away as if trying again to disappear. Her words were muffled by the fabric she held before her face. "But I wanted you."

"You've more sense than this, Ellie. I know you have. You don't want me. I'll only do you harm. I already have."

That made her cry. He held her, stroked her head as she sobbed, wishing he were back in jail. Anything would be better than making Ellie cry.

"I'm going." He stood.

Ellie wouldn't look at him. But he looked at her, a good long look at what he'd done. Most of the pins had come loose from her hair, which now fell over her shoulders in thick ocean waves of lustrous brown silk. Her shoulders jumped with each shaky breath and that white cotton was not working to gag her sobs. Chance had thought that his heart could only break once, but he'd been wrong. Ellie's tears shattered it all over again.

Likely she was just recognizing that she'd made the worst mistake of her life.

Chance drew on his holsters and tied them around his thighs. He tugged on his boots and set his hat low over his eyes. A pink shaft of sunlight poured over the windowsill, flooding the room with a rosy glow that only darkened his mood.

He removed the chair from beneath the knob and paused to glance back. "Ellie?"

"Please, Chance, just go."

If only she had said that half an hour ago, he thought as he opened the door to find the sneaky desk clerk standing in the hall craning his long neck to see into

Chance's room. He grabbed him by the throat and shoved him to the opposite wall.

"What are you doing?"

"Nothing," he squeaked.

Behind him the cursed door swung open, revealing Ellie wrapped only in a bedsheet, staring out at them with wide eyes.

It took Ellie some time to compose herself. She had thrown caution to the wind and that wind had blown her right off her feet.

She washed her face, fixed her hair and dressed. She was usually downstairs before six, but this morning she would be late. Neither of her parents would notice, of course, but she did not like sneaking about like a thief in her own home. Ah, but it wasn't her home, not really. It was her parents' home and she still lived here, well past the time when most women her age set out to start their own family. And now she knew why she was still here. It was not because she couldn't land Quin or Bowie or Johny Fitzgerald or Ned Womack or Clancy Lewis. It was because she had not *wanted* to land them, not any of them. The realization froze her to the spot. She stared out of the window at the railroad tracks, now shining pink in the dawn light, and recognized that all this time she had been waiting for Chance Cahill.

Somewhere deep inside herself, she had always known that this would happen. It was why she'd never dared to tell him. Now she could no longer pretend that she didn't have feelings for Chance. He knew and the knowing had only served to drive him off.

Had she expected that throwing herself at him would suddenly make him realize he could not do without her? Yes. She had. Yet, he'd been away for two years and never written her a single letter. Still, somewhere in her lonely heart she allowed herself to pretend he secretly cared for her, as well.

If she had an ounce of sense she'd marry Dr. Lewis.

She walked downstairs on wooden legs, planning to speak to Mr. Hoppock, the clerk who had spent the better part of his six-month employment at the Royale mooning after her and who, today, had seen her naked in a man's room. She knew that he could ruin her reputation with a word.

No, she realized, she had done that quite handily herself and she would not chase after the clerk to try and silence him. Instead, she would be like Chance and accept the consequences of her actions.

Ellie passed in a fog through her duties with the staff. Her father appeared before nine, seeking her out and regarding her a long silent moment.

"Ellie? Your mother and I would like to speak with you."

The consequences, it seemed, had arrived more swiftly than she had expected.

How did a girl as pure as snow learn to kiss like that? Chance wondered.

But it wasn't the kiss. It was Ellie. He couldn't get her out of his head, couldn't get enough of her, couldn't get clear of her fast enough.

Taking a woman now, even one as perfect as Ellie, was a real bad idea. The Cahills had enemies and he was about to go after them with both barrels. An association with him would put a target right on Ellie's back. They'd already shot Merritt and murdered his mother. Killing women was nothing to them. And if that wasn't reason enough, the idea of telling Ellie how he really felt scared the tar out of him.

He knew she liked his company, but so did a lot of women. They were attracted to his image and the danger surrounding him. But that wasn't him. Did Ellie know that?

He left the Château Royale in predawn light and headed to the livery, spending time with Rip until the sun was well up, then he headed over to Merritt Dixon's boardinghouse again, but this time he went by way of the back door. It was still on the early side for a visit, but he wanted to see Bowie without everyone in town knowing about it and Merritt could fetch him. In all the excitement last night, he'd forgotten to tell Bowie what he'd seen the other night when he followed Ira and Johny.

He cupped his hands around his eyes and peered through the glass, spying a small woman cracking eggs into a large green ceramic bowl. Her clothes were spotless and her hair was pulled into a neat bun, and though her hair was silver-gray, her motions were quick and expert. He recalled that this was Merritt's cook, Jemima. He rapped on the glass with his knuckles. Jemima stilled, then turned, lifting an eyebrow in his direction. But one look at him and she dropped the two halves of the eggshell into the bowl. She did not let him in, but scurried out of sight. He added *spry* to her list of attributes.

A moment later Bowie stormed into the kitchen with a hand on the grip of his pistol. Bowie spotted his brother and dropped his hand from his gun, but not the look of aggravation on his face.

Bowie tugged open the door.

"Chance, you scared the heck out of Jemima."

"Well, I'm sorry. Can I come in or not?"

Bowie stepped aside and made a sweep of his hand that was decidedly hostile.

The marshal preceded him. "It's just my idiot brother, Jemima."

The woman stood between Merritt and Leanna, clutching a chair back. Her face had lost the cheery glow in favor of a grayish tinge. Chance worried she might faint.

Merritt patted the older woman's hand. "One more for breakfast please, Jemima."

The woman advanced but kept her back to the wall as she scooted through the swinging door.

"That was fairly thoughtless," said Leanna.

"Well, how am I supposed to appear not to speak to either of you and still speak to you?" he asked.

"You keep this up and you won't have to act," said Bowie.

"It's all right," said Merritt.

"No, it's not," said Bowie.

Cleve intervened, drawing out a chair. "Chance, why don't you sit here beside your sister?"

Bowie and Chance glared a moment and then Chance took the offered seat. Bowie settled into the one opposite and beside Merritt.

"You do have a knack," whispered Bowie, and then flinched and said, "Ow."

He glanced to his fiancée, who was lifting a coffeepot and giving no indication that she knew why Bowie was now rubbing his shin.

Chance was surprised to find Leanna and Cleve here. They had the baby, Cabe, with them but Melvin was mercifully at school. After a few moments of one-sided conversation, led by Cleve again, Leanna joined in.

Cleve did have a knack for making his sister laugh, and when she did, she lit up the room. Cleve even took that baby on his lap and fed him toast dipped in a saucer of milk. That seemed to make Leanna happy, too. Chance didn't understand how Cleve could act as if that boy was his. It would kill Chance if his wife brought home another man's child.

But wasn't that what many widows did? He pondered that as he feasted on a first-class breakfast. The biscuits were nearly as good as his mother's.

He kept glancing from Leanna to Bowie, listening to them laugh. Bowie, laughing. He couldn't believe his ears, and the way his brother looked at Merritt made Chance envious and sick all at once.

This was what it was like, he realized, the way it had been at his parents' table all those years ago and the way it would be at Leanna's and Bowie's and Quin's in the future. He looked about him, glimpsing the kind of happiness that a man could have if he were fearless enough to stay in one place and put down roots. If he were brave enough to let himself feel something again. Chance had been dead inside for so long, he didn't know how to come back to the land of the living. He wasn't sure until now that he wanted to.

He tried to picture Ellie fussing over him as Leanna did over Cleve or having her look at him the way Merritt did at Bowie when he wasn't looking. But he stopped himself. That life was never going to happen—not to him, anyway.

He was strong enough for dying, just not brave enough for living.

Bowie waited until Merritt left the room before speaking to Chance directly. "We found Miguel floating in the river this morning with a knife in his back."

"You know who killed him?"

Bowie shook his head.

Chance drew his chair closer to the table. His brother leaned in, closing the gap between them.

"I followed the Fitzgerald boys the other night. Saw something real interesting."

Bowie folded his big hands before him, obviously interested.

"They're shaking down the business owners over there."

It was Leanna who spoke first, thumping a fist on the table and making her cup and saucer rattle. "I knew it!"

Bowie glanced at her. "Did you, now? Then why is this the first I'm hearing of it."

"I didn't have any proof."

Chance spoke. "Now you do. I'm an eyewitness."

"But I can't use you. We're not supposed to be speaking."

"Quin could do it."

Bowie's expression turned cautious. "Was he there?"

"No, but I'll just tell him what I—"

Bowie threw himself back in his chair. "No. We don't do things like that here."

"Fine. Then you wait for Quin to rope in the banker, but my money is on Fitzgerald or Womack."

"Which one?" asked Leanna.

Chance gave her a look and pressed his lips together.

"Well?" said Bowie.

"I'm not sure yet."

The brothers faced off, only this time Chance found himself in the unusual position of trying unsuccessfully to get Bowie to do something instead of the other way around.

He didn't like it.

It was Cleve who again acted as arbitrator. "I could follow Ira and Johny tonight. Meanwhile, Chance could give you the names of the owners who he saw pay out and you could go speak to them. If one or more of the gentlemen can be convinced to do the right thing, well…" He gave a shrug.

Both Bowie and Chance gaped at him and Leanna beamed at her husband.

Chance gave Bowie the names of the men he'd seen paying the Fitzgerald boys off.

"You speak to Slocum yet?" asked Chance.

Bowie shook his head. "Waiting for office hours."

Someone knocked at the front door. Chance stood, placing his napkin on the table in his preparation to leave. Merritt returned from the kitchen.

"Thank you for the fine breakfast, Miz Dixon."

She smiled. "I thought I asked you to call me Merritt."

"Yes, ma'am. I don't want to be seen with Bowie. You understand."

She asked Jemima to see him out, but before he could clear the back steps, Bowie was there calling him back.

"Think you better come in here."

He returned to the dining room to find Ellie, weeping onto Leanna's shoulder.

"What happened?" he asked.

Leanna leveled a killer look in his direction. "Ellie has left the hotel."

"I'm not going back," said Ellie.

"Why?" asked Chance.

Ellie lifted her head to stare at him and so did everyone else in the room.

Chapter Eighteen

Leanna led Ellie from the hall into Merritt's cozy parlor and sat with her on a settee facing the large fireplace. Merritt joined them instantly, taking the seat adjacent, while Bowie and Chance shifted nervously in the doorway glancing at each other and then back to the women.

Bowie fled first. "Maybe I best go find Slocum."

Merritt glanced up and gave a barely perceptible nod. Was that the way it was now? Bowie needed her permission to leave the room. Chance vowed to never let himself get into such a situation. Then he looked at Ellie and called himself a liar.

Cleve appeared with Jemima a moment later carrying a flowered teapot. What in the world was happening to the men in this family? Jemima deposited a tray of toast and jam, then left without a word.

Cleve and Leanna began a completely silent exchange that was incomprehensible to Chance, the upshot being that Chance ended up alone in the room with the three women.

He recognized he'd landed in dangerous territory and he edged toward the hall when Leanna snared him like a jackrabbit.

"Where are you going?" she asked.

He widened his eyes, thinking, *Anywhere but here.*

She gave him a tight little shake of her head and a warning glare.

Likely this was his fault. He looked at Ellie, hiding her face in her hands as she wept, and felt lower than dust. He backed up into the hall, sitting on the small bench that butted up against the stairs.

Over the course of the next ten minutes, Leanna succeeded in getting the story out of Ellie. She had argued with her mother about bailing Chance out and allowing the doctor to court her. But if her parents didn't know about their evening together, why was she defying them? She'd lived her whole adult life with their rules and the constraints of a woman in search of a husband. Or she had, until he'd arrived and confused her to the point where she didn't know what was best. But he did.

"Well, you are certainly free to stay with me," said Leanna.

Chance realized Leanna was picking up another stray. It dawned on him that he might also fit into that category. That irritated him more than a burdock under a saddle blanket. But Ellie had two parents and a home and, according to her, that was where she belonged.

"Or here," said Merritt. "I have two vacant rooms just now."

Chance didn't like the idea of Ellie being bossed, but he didn't like seeing her run, either. Running wasn't like her. Ellie stayed and endured like granite.

"She should go back home," he said.

All the women stared at him. Then Merritt and

Leanna exchanged looks. Were all women able to converse without speaking? A man didn't stand a chance against them.

"She is not!" said Leanna, pulling Ellie closer.

He looked at Ellie. "You waited all this time for the right man. You put up with your ma and now you got a man, a good one, like you wanted, and you ran out. I don't understand."

Ellie drew away from Leanna. He stood and met her halfway.

"Just because I want a husband, it does not mean that I will marry anything in pants."

"Well, who asked you to? But running out isn't going to solve anything. Lewis is a good man. If you don't want the doc, then who do you want?"

The silence in the room was deafening. As she looked up at him, for just a moment, he thought she would say, "You." He held his breath, afraid for the first time since his parents' deaths. Afraid she'd want him. Afraid she wouldn't.

"I haven't decided," she said. "Maybe I'll just run off with the first man I meet. Isn't that what you suggested?"

He had said that to her. But that was before he knew what she wanted. Instead, she was running, and whether she said so or not, he knew he was the cause.

He released his breath and grabbed Ellie's wrist.

"What are you doing?" she cried.

"Bringing you back to your father."

Ellie used her other hand to tug at her wrist, but Chance pulled her along. He ignored Leanna's and Merritt's cries of protest. They didn't know what was best for Ellie and suddenly Ellie didn't, either. But he did.

Ellie needed to be under her parents' roof, not causing a scandal like Leanna.

He stopped at the door and faced them both.

"She's not a widow, Merritt, so she can't do as she likes." He held the woman's gaze a moment and then he faced his sister. "And she's not like you, Annie, and you don't want her to be."

Both women pulled up short as if they'd hit a barbed wire fence, invisible to all but them. They didn't look happy, but they made no further protest as he drew Ellie through the door and down the front steps of the Morning Glory Boardinghouse.

So much for using the back door.

Ellie had to trot to keep pace with him, but once he set his teeth on the bit there was no turning back. Ellie was living under her parents' roof until she was properly wedded.

She dug her heels in when they reached the hotel and Chance had to choose between carrying her or stopping. Either one would cause talk, judging from the looks of the guests on the porch who had now ceased rocking and conversing in favor of the drama they sensed would play out before them.

"Stop," she said.

He did. But he kept his focus on the elaborate front door, not fifteen feet from them. He could toss her over his shoulder like a sack of corn and be in before she could even holler.

"Why are you doing this?" she asked. "You're the one who said I was crazy to stay."

He looked at her at last, her bewildered expression and the parting of her perfect mouth. Damn, he wanted to kiss her again.

"That was before you told me that a proper woman goes from her father's keeping to her husband's."

Ellie dropped her gaze to the dusty street.

"And you *are* a proper lady." Chance glanced around, knowing what he must do. This was his fault. He had confused her, drawn her off her path. It was his job to set her feet back on that trail again. He'd tried last night, but had obviously failed. And although it killed him to think of her with that doctor, he would not be the one to destroy her dreams.

"Marry Lewis, Ellie."

Her voice dropped to a whisper. "He doesn't make me feel like you do."

That comment burned him. Why the hell did he have to take her to his bed and why the hell did he want to do so again?

His voice was low, barely a growl. "That was a mistake. You know it, Ellie. Put it behind you. If you're to have a future, it's not with me."

She looked up at him, the tears welling again. He would have preferred she shoot him in the guts, but it felt as if she already had.

"Come on." He took her elbow and guided her up the steps, glaring at the two men sharing a spittoon. "What are you gawking at? You never seen a lady escorted home?"

They startled and looked away. Chance stomped up the steps, fit to be tied. He knew this was the right thing, but it grated like coarse sandpaper.

He wished he could be the kind of man she needed, instead of the kind she wanted.

Inside the lobby he slowed and cast her a glance. She walked with her chin high, holding her shredded dignity.

"I'm too far gone to be respectable, Ellie."

"Don't speak to me."

Chance glared at the receptionist behind the desk, a doughy little man with jowls like a hog and beady eyes set behind wired spectacles.

"Where's Mr. Jenkins?"

The man wobbled badly, holding one hand over his heart as if to check that it was still beating. Then he pointed toward Oscar's office, located beyond the reception desk.

"Tell him I have his daughter."

Ellie tried to regain custody of her arm, but he only tightened his grip. He didn't like it, but for once in his life he was going to do the right thing.

Oscar appeared a moment later. His gaze flicked from Chance to his daughter and then back to him. He didn't say a word but simply motioned them inside.

Chance explained where he had found Ellie and that he thought it best to bring her back to their safekeeping. Ellie said nothing, just stood, grim as a pallbearer.

Chance glanced at her. She looked so little, standing like a child called before the teacher. But she had a toughness, too. He could see it in the way she drew back her shoulders and in the way she now refused to look at him.

Jenkins leaned back against his desk, folding his arms in a relaxed sort of way that might have put Chance at ease if Ellie was not now glaring at him.

"Thank you for looking out for Ellie."

"That isn't hard to do."

Oscar lifted an eyebrow at him. "Yes, I can see that."

He pushed off the desk and patted Chance on the shoulder, giving his neck a little squeeze as he guided him toward the door.

"We just received an invitation to the wedding. We're very excited to attend."

Chance's step faltered. He wanted to get the heck out of here, but he paused to take the bait.

"What wedding?"

"Why, your brother's. Bowie and Merritt. Just a month away. I'm sure you're staying for that. Merritt is inviting the entire town, I think. Not like Quin. I swear that man could hardly stop working long enough to go to the church and say, 'I do.' And Leanna, well, we feared she would heap scandal onto scandal when she threw that new husband out almost as soon as they were wed."

What was he saying? Leanna and Cleve had separated? His sister had failed to mention that.

They reached the door after a short journey that seemed to take an eternity.

"My wife is mortified of scandal, though she forgets the stir our engagement caused." Another clap on the back. "Why, Chance, soon you'll be the only Cahill who isn't married."

With that, Jenkins cut him adrift like a ship he had looted and scuttled.

Ellie waited for her father to return to his office, standing formally instead of taking her usual place by the potbellied stove.

Her temper took time to reach a boil but once there it rolled for a good long while before cooling. Right now the target of her ire was walking out on her yet again. And the most irritating part of all was that he had told her that he would.

"That boy is loaded with potential," said her father,

looking after the man that made Ellie's stomach quiver and her teeth gnash.

She turned her attention back to her father. He'd put her off balance again. She'd expected either a gentle talking to or the warm welcome of his open arms. But his hands remained clasped behind his back and his eyes had that devilish twinkle that never failed to make her mother giddy as a new foal. Despite their bickering, her parents did enjoy private time. That was obvious from the amount of time they spent in their rooms.

What was it that he saw in Chance that was invisible to all others?

"Mother hates him."

"He scares her. She wants you to have a stable man. A quiet man. One you can run like you do that restaurant. Clancy Lewis is that sort of man. He's predictable, conscientious and a very good healer. What she doesn't want is for you to take a risk on a half-wild stallion with wanderlust. But we aren't talking about what your mother wants. I'd like to know what *you* want."

"He told me flatly that he's not staying and has no interest in settling down."

Her father laughed. "Ellen, did you tell him you love him?"

She sucked in a breath. Was it so obvious?

"What is it that you see in him that no one else does?"

Her father gave her that lopsided grin. "Myself." He patted Ellie's arm and guided her to the overstuffed leather chairs before the stove. All heart-to-heart conversations between them took place in these chairs that Oscar had insisted moved with them from the old hotel, despite his wife's protests.

"He's nothing like you, Papa. He's reckless with his life and takes terrible risks. It's as if he were lost."

"Just like me, before I met your ma. I drifted the Atlantic Coast, rootless as seaweed." He placed his elbows on his knees and folded his hands between them. "The reason I was so good at bringing supplies around those blockades was because I lost all my family in that damned war and I didn't care if I lived or died."

Ellie looked at her father, the familiar lines of his face and the deep brown of his eyes, and tried to imagine him there as a young man, fighting the Yankees.

"Only I was lucky. I had an enemy to fight, while Chance has been fighting himself. I don't know how he's survived it. He's stronger than I was."

"Papa?"

He tore himself from his thoughts, regarding her.

"What did she do? Mama, I mean?"

There was a fire in his eyes as he looked back, recalling something. A slow smile spread across his face.

"She ran off with me. You understand the difference? I didn't run off with her, *she* ran off with me. I went back to the *Elizabeth* and set sail and that night I found her in my cabin, dressed in a…" He motioned to his chest and then stopped himself. "Well, I'm only human."

Shock left her momentarily mute. Ellie could not get her mind around her mother's daring. But then she realized she had done nearly the same thing and Chance had still set her aside. She flushed.

"But she came from a good family."

"And her father was still alive then. He tried to shoot me, but she stopped him, too. She was having me and that was that. And look at me now, roots deep and strong."

Ellie didn't want to broach her final concern but she did. "But you fight."

"Yes. That's true. Your mother is not easy to live with and I do drive her to distraction. But that is because she is a passionate woman." He gave Ellie's chin a little squeeze between his thumb and the curve of his index finger. "Like you."

Ellie blinked at him, shocked at her father's confidence.

"Your ma settled me. You could do that for Chance Cahill."

"But how?"

"Oh, you'll think of something, something brave and bold and not at all safe. That's what Minnie did."

She nodded. "He keeps pushing me away."

"Trying to keep you safe. Push back. If you don't know how to run around a man's blockades, then you're no daughter of mine."

"Yes, sir."

"Ellen Louise, you've done the sensible thing all your life. Now's the time to follow your heart."

"What if I do that and he still turns me down?"

"What if you don't and you never know?"

"But, Papa, he doesn't care about me."

"He does."

"How do you know that?"

"Because he brought you back to me."

Chance was already in a bad mood when he left Ellie and it didn't get any better when he ran into Glen Whitaker. Bowie had sent his deputy over with the wire for the five-hundred-dollar bounty he'd earned before leaving Deadwood. The money meant that he had no more excuse to stay at the Royale.

Chance collected the bounty at the telegraph office and returned to the hotel to settle up with the desk clerk. He collected his things and headed out. He knew he needed to get out of this hotel. She was too damned accessible here and his need for her seemed to grow like a hunger the longer he was parted from her.

It was past time to leave town because he was getting foolish notions. He was recalling the pleasures of having a home and being a part of a family, even when they drove him crazy most days. He had to clear out before Ellie did something foolish, like try to take up with a no-good bounty hunter who would break her heart as sure as he had broken everything else he loved.

He moved down the street, away from the fashionable part of town, across the railroad tracks, and checked into the Hobart Hotel because he knew she couldn't follow him here. From his second-floor room, he could see the new depot and, beyond it, the back of the Royale. When he realized he was staring at the kitchen entrance and hoping for a glimpse of Ellie, he turned away. Chance draped his saddlebags over the foot rail, pausing to consider that everything he owned fitted into those two pouches. What did he have to offer Ellie, anyway? Nothing—that was what. Even if he wanted to stay, which he didn't, he had gained nothing in two years but a bad reputation.

Chapter Nineteen

It took Bowie a day to browbeat, cajole and otherwise wrangle up three proprietors willing to sign statements against the Fitzgerald boys. But today he had them.

Bowie arrested Ira and Johny as soon as they dismounted, taking them to the jail only to find one of the two cells occupied by Muddy, who was sleeping one off yet again. He tried to rouse the old drunk but failing he ordered his deputy to take him over to the morgue.

"His snoring won't bother anyone over there."

Bowie locked away his prisoners and then helped Whitaker haul Muddy out and set him on a plank in the back of the morgue. Maybe he'd learn a lesson, because if he didn't lay off the bug juice, this was sure where he'd end up.

Bowie stepped onto the street and immediately saw a familiar bloodred bay at the hitching post. Cactus, his brother Quin's horse, looked thin after the long cattle drive.

He found Quin waiting in his office, filling the room, as he always did, without even trying. For more than half his life, Bowie had been trying to measure up to the high-water mark set by Quin. It had had them at odds most of their lives. Things had changed for the worse when Bowie had left the ranch and then for the better when Quin had got married. His wife, Addie K., was a firebrand, but it was by her request that Quin had called the family together when he discovered their parents' deaths was no accident.

Quin wore polished stovepipe black boots, a black suit with a waistcoat and a spotless white shirt collared with a lanyard tie. He reminded Bowie of their father, who would never be seen in town in work clothes, either. He was shaven, his hair well groomed, and holding his hat that sported a new band of silver conchas. Beside Quin stood a short, bald man with watery eyes and a weak chin that his full mustache did not completely obscure. He held a brown bowler derby in his pale hands with a briefcase. Bank examiner, Bowie decided.

Bowie shook hands with his brother and welcomed him home. His big brother was more tanned than usual from his drive to Dodge. Big and broad, he now was nearly as thin as his horse.

"Didn't Addie K. feed you on that drive?"

Quin gave him a rare smile. His new wife had insisted on going along, saying that half the cattle were hers and she wasn't going to let Quin have all the fun.

Bowie knew better. Drives were not fun. They were grueling, cold, wet, hot and dusty. And that was on a good day.

"Heard Chance is back," said Quin.

Bowie nodded. "Broke Leanna's big picture window."

He knew that, too, judging from the complete lack of surprise on Quin's face.

"Heard you arrested him."

Bowie nodded.

"That must have been satisfying."

"Not as much as you would think."

Bowie knew the two had not spoken since the three of them had ridden from their childhood home. He didn't expect it to go easy during their reunion and thought he might better sit this one out at the jail.

"He also shot a gambler and bloodied some young hammer-fanner."

Quin rubbed the back of his neck. "I can't decide if he finds trouble or it finds him." He glanced back toward the hall leading to the cells. "I also heard that he's here to get his share of the 4C."

Something about the way Quin said that, without the usual fire in his eye, confused Bowie. Of course Quin knew Leanna had left his telegram back in Deadwood. So he must also know why Chance had come home.

Bowie glanced at the stranger beside Quin and played along. "I heard that."

"I'm not breaking up the ranch."

"Didn't expect you to. Chance is talking about seeing an attorney."

"Let him." He glanced toward the back. "You got prisoners?"

Bowie nodded. He didn't know this examiner so he said no more.

"Thought I heard someone moving back there. Assumed it might just be Muddy." He waited, fishing, his brows lifted expectantly, but Bowie said nothing.

Quin turned to the examiner. "Could you give us a minute?"

The man nodded and stepped out to the porch. "I'll be waiting."

Quin turned to Glen Whitaker. "You, too."

Glen looked about to object, but instead glanced to his boss for help and got the signal to do as he was told.

He stomped out like a child who didn't get his way. Bowie closed the door leading to the jail cells, sealing off his prisoners.

"Who you got back there?" asked Quin.

"Johny and Ira Fitzgerald, charged with extortion for shaking down the businesses on the other side of the rails. Protection money, the owners called it."

Quin lifted his eyebrows. "Not really surprised."

"You talk to Chance?"

Bowie nodded. "You know he isn't back for his share."

"I know it." Quin pressed his lips together in a gesture Bowie recognized spelled trouble.

"What's wrong?" asked Bowie.

"Chance had Ellen Jenkins in his room at the Royale last night."

"What! How the hell do you know that?"

"Everyone knows. It's all over town. I wasn't even off my horse when Sam Brody trotted up to tell me and then Ace Keating over at the saddle shop told me."

"Her father finds out and there'll be hell to pay," said Bowie.

"Her mother scares me more. That woman runs Oscar like I run cattle."

"What are we going to do?" asked Bowie.

Quin clapped him on the shoulder. "Don't know about you, brother. But I plan to hunker down."

"Easy for you. You're not marshal."

"Might think on resigning before you have to arrest him again."

"One more thing," said Bowie, telling Quin that he'd been to visit their attorney, Slocum. "I pressed him and got a bad feeling he's hiding something. He seemed scared clean through."

"Of what?"

"Not sure yet." Bowie retrieved his hat. "You ready?"

Quin nodded. They headed out, pausing on the porch to find Glen and the examiner in conversation. It seemed Glen was doing his level-best to discover the man's business.

"Glen?" Bowie spoke to his deputy. "Stay here. I expect Don Fitzgerald to come for his boys. Tell him I can't release them until they see the judge and bail is set. Might be later this afternoon."

Glen looked nervous, but he nodded his understanding. "I'll come get you when he turns up."

"No. Don't leave him alone with the prisoners. Send someone for me or wait until I get back."

"Oh, right. I'll send someone for you, then."

Quin gave Bowie a look of concern and Bowie shook his head.

They only made it to the front porch when Muddy, the ferryman, staggered out of the morgue and onto the street, looking pale and wide-eyed. His gaze darted frantically about and landed on the marshal.

"Oh, hell," muttered Bowie.

"Marshal, I'm risen from the dead!"

"You look it," said Quin.

"I seen the light, Marshal. I turned myself over a new leaf and I got something to say to you both."

Bowie gave him a vexed look. Muddy took up too damn much of his time. And if he didn't quit sleeping in the jail, Bowie would have to start charging him rent. "You can't sleep here. I got the Fitzgerald boys in there. One in each cell."

Muddy's mouth snapped shut. He hunkered down, seeming to shrink back to his usual height.

"Who you got in there?"

"Ira and Johny."

Muddy held his dirty hands in twin fists before his mouth.

"What is it you got to say, Newt?" asked Quin.

He glanced at them and then back down the street. "I need a drink."

Bowie snorted, watching the man hustle in the opposite direction. "So much for his new leaf."

"The man is a public menace. I don't know how he gets that ferry across the river."

"It's tied to the other side."

"Right."

"Pa liked him," said Bowie. "And he wasn't always like this."

The two headed in the opposite direction, falling into step, leaving the bank examiner to scurry after them. Bowie told Quin everything he could squeeze into the time they had during the short walk from his jail to the bank.

Halfway down the street Bowie spotted Ellie Jenkins, walking beside the tanner, Jose Martinez, both hustling straight for him. He and Quin exchanged looks.

"Two of his girls work as maids at the Royale," said Bowie.

"Still an odd pair," said Quin.

Ellie paused before them, her cheeks flushed from her haste.

"Hello, Ellie," said Bowie, tipping his hat.

"Ellen," said Quin, doing the same.

"Welcome back, Quin. How is Addie K.?"

"Fine."

Ellie made a face and Bowie knew she never liked Quin's version of conversation. Quin was stingy with words, as if they were in limited supply. Except around Addie K. and then Bowie had seen him gush like a fountain.

"Please send her my regards."

He nodded for answer, and Ellie dismissed him, pinning her unusual eyes on him.

"Marshal, Jose tells me that you have arrested Johny and Ira Fitzgerald. Is this true?"

Bowie gave a nod. Perhaps Chance had brought him another witness and sent Ellie because he and Chance were supposed to appear at odds.

Ellie translated for Jose. The tanner began speaking, looking at Bowie, whose Spanish was not as good as it might be. Bowie caught his son's name and Fitzgerald, but Jose was in a hurry and his words strung together like laundry flapping on a clothesline.

Ellie translated. "He wishes me to tell you that he witnessed Johny Fitzgerald kill his son. He stabbed him in the back with a knife."

Jose burst into tears and began to speak again. Ellie repeated his words. "He says that when he threatened to stop tanning the stolen cattle, they killed his little girl and now they have killed his eldest son. He's already sent his entire family to Mexico for their safety and says he wants justice more than he wants life."

Ellie offered Jose the handkerchief tucked in her sleeve.

"He'll have to testify," said Bowie.

She nodded. "He knows that."

"I'll need him to make a written statement, but I'm on business now and my deputy doesn't speak Spanish any better than I do."

"I can do it," said Ellie. "I'll write what he tells me and he can sign it. Would you like it in Spanish or English?"

The men exchanged a look.

"English," said Bowie. "Glen will show you what to do and he'll help with the statement."

"When we've finished, can we go?"

"Best ask him to wait. But you're free to leave."

Ellie nodded. "Fine."

Bowie offered his hand to the tanner. "Thank you, Mr. Martinez. I'll see you get justice."

The men shook hands. Bowie had just turned to go when she stopped him again.

"Chance has moved out of the Château Royale. Do you know where he has gone?"

Bowie knew but he wasn't inclined to tell her. He loved his brother, but Chance was all wrong for Ellie. He made a stab at talking sense into her, but she shut him down. If what Quin heard was right, might be too late to help either one of them.

Bowie debated and then said, "He's at Hobart's."

He wondered if she had the backbone to go after him. Proper ladies did not venture into that side of town, even in broad daylight.

"Thank you," she said, and guided Jose, still wiping his streaming eyes, into the jail.

Quin watched her go. "I think I underestimated that gal."

Chance watched the exchange between Bowie and Ellie from a safe distance. It had been a rough morning.

He'd already blackened a man's eye for mentioning Ellie to him. His question left no doubt that the clerk who'd seen Ellie in his room had, indeed, flapped his gums to the entire town. His return of Ellie to her father had been too little, too late to protect her reputation and had merely added grist for the mill. Poor Ellie.

He'd ruined her, after all. Now that his daughter's name was being dragged through the mud, Oscar Jenkins would come after him. Whether sooner or later, he doubted that Mr. Jenkins would have a shotgun, unless he wanted to use it to run him off.

But he wasn't going just yet.

He watched his brothers approach with the short dandy clutching his bowler and briefcase as he trotted to keep stride with Quin and Bowie. This could only be the bank examiner. Chance's gaze flicked to his oldest brother. Quin looked tough as rawhide and forbidding as the badlands, just as he remembered him. Bowie held the expression of a man dragging a wagonload of responsibilities. Damn, his brothers made a menacing duo. He almost felt sorry for Van Slyck.

Chance stepped out and both brothers pulled up short. Judging by the looks on their faces, he was as welcome as a spring blizzard.

"Sleep well?" asked Quin.

Chance screwed his mouth up and glared.

"You know there are a good deal of available women over yonder. So it is inconceivable to me that you would do something so brainless as sleep with Ellen Jenkins."

"When you going to stop trying to run my life?"

"When you do just one thing that isn't boneheaded."

Chance stepped forward and Quin leaned in. Chance wanted nothing better than to knock Quin down, a feat at which he'd never succeeded. Bloodying his brother's lip would sure feel satisfying, though he knew full well that he'd be bloodied himself in the process. But hurting someone, especially himself, seemed for the moment like just the right thing to do. He clenched his fist. Quin's mouth lifted in a grim smile. Oh, he'd been looking forward to this, too.

Bowie stepped between them.

"We got business." He motioned with his head toward the examiner, now clutching his briefcase before him like a barricade.

"Right," said Quin, from between clenched teeth.

Chance fell in beside Bowie and the three made their way to the bank in angry silence. Their appearance there caused a stir. The Cahill brothers were together again and looking like they were gunning for bear. Several customers decided that their business could most definitely wait and hurried for the egress. Others dallied, curious to see what would happen next.

Their comments and speculation reached Chance as they passed.

"Quin is here to withdraw his money."

"Are they splitting up the ranch?"

The bank owner, Willem Van Slyck, came to greet them. His sharp, intent eyes belied his welcoming smile. His hair had continued to retreat on his forehead and was more silver than Chance recalled and he thought the gold-rimmed spectacles were new. His clothes were impeccable, clean and well tailored as always. He wore black shoes with heels that clicked on the floor as he made his way toward them. If his son's death weighed upon him, it did not show in his face.

"Well, welcome home, Quin. I hope you had a successful trip." The red beneath his eyes and the dark circles pointed to a man who spent his days studying ledgers. The tightness of his fancy silk vest and the thick rope of a gold pocket watch chain pointed to his success in business. The man had prospered. Chance wondered if he had prospered a little too much.

Van Slyck offered his hand. Quin snubbed him. Van Slyck's face reddened as he dropped his hand to his side. Chance noticed the sheen of sweat glowing on his forehead.

"This is Jeffery Collier. He's up from Austin to examine your books."

Chance noticed the widening of Van Slyck's eyes before the forced smile emerged again, if a little more slowly than before.

"But your own attorney, Mr. Slocum, examines the books twice a year. Perhaps I should call him?"

"Slocum's not our attorney any longer," said Bowie.

That information rattled Van Slyck enough for him to remove his handkerchief from his jacket and dab his brow.

"The books," said Quin.

"It will take me a little time to gather them."

"Are you refusing to let him examine your books?" asked Bowie, resting a hand with practiced casualness on the grip of his gun, as if he were leaning on a bar rail rather than a deadly weapon.

"Of course not. You are well within your rights." He motioned them toward his office, then paused. "But it is an unnecessary expense. Everything is quite in order, as you know."

"No trouble," said Quin, pushing past him.

"Mr. Elliot!" shouted Van Slyck.

A clerk hurried out from behind the barred area reserved for tellers. The two conversed and Elliot headed for the exit. Chance stepped before him.

"Nope," he said, and pointed back to the cage.

The teller and Van Slyck exchanged looks, but the man retreated. Chance decided to spend his time watching the entrance for trouble, because as Quin and Bowie both reminded him, finding trouble was what he did best.

It seemed hours, but it was actually still before noon when the examiner found inconsistencies and things began to unravel. Bowie had cleared the bank of all customers save the three of them, the examiner and Van Slyck. Chance watched the door and Van Slyck in turns. Trouble came first from the bank owner. He moved his hand by infinitesimal degrees toward the front pocket of his vest. From the way his hand moved and the amount of sweat on his upper lip, Chance didn't think he was checking the time. He glanced to Bowie, who was watching the front door, and then to Quin, who was looking at a broad ledger with Mr. Collier.

Just as he feared, Van Slyck drew out a small pistol from his vest, clutching it to his chest. It was the kind favored by dandies and riverboat gamblers for its size, appearing like a toy but deadly at close range for one shot.

With three of them there, each with a pistol and Chance with two, plus a boot knife that he could throw accurately from fifteen feet, he didn't think the man planned to shoot his way out. That left only one reason to draw his gun; he planned to take the coward's way out.

Van Slyck inched the gun up his body, cradling it like a baby. Chance reached for his gun, then paused, recalling Bowie's admonishment. Plus, if he winged him, he might just get an infection and die, anyway.

They needed him alive. Chance lifted the wooden chair before the desk and threw it at Van Slyck with enough force to knock the second-most prominent citizen in Cahill Crossing to the floor. The chair skidded off him. Van Slyck yelled and dropped his gun. Chance kicked it toward Bowie, who had his gun drawn. Bowie holstered his pistol and stooped to retrieve the tiny gun. His eyes met Chance, who waited for another admonishment.

"Good work, Chance."

His jaw dropped open. Then he glanced to Quin, who stared in silence a moment and then flicked his attention back to the books, dismissing Chance without so much as a nod.

Bowie grabbed Van Slyck from the floor. Chance noted with satisfaction that the banker's nose was bleeding all over his pretty vest and he was cradling his right arm. His brother took the precaution of checking the man for weapons and then offered him to Chance, by the collar. Bowie righted the chair. Chance pushed him into it.

The man began to blubber and bawl like a branded calf. And the words started flowing with the tears. He'd tell them everything, be their witness for clemency.

Bowie didn't agree. "I'll ask the judge for leniency if you tell us everything and I mean right now."

"Clemency," he begged.

"No."

Van Slyck's head sank to his chest and his shoulders slumped in defeat.

"Who?" he asked.

"Don Fitzgerald. That's where I put the money. Into his accounts. I had to hide it somewhere and he came to me." His face lifted, showing red-rimmed eyes and snot running with the blood. He was the perfect picture of a man caught. "He hates you. All of you, for stealing the railroad depot. Said more than once it should have been his." He turned to Quin. "And he's got your attorney, Slocum, in his pocket. Looking the other way when he collects the rents."

"Why would Slocum do that?" asked Quin. "He was a friend of my father."

"I don't know. But Don got to him. He's got a knack for finding a man's weaknesses. He found mine."

"Which is?" asked Chance.

"Money." He lifted his head and his eyes had turned lethal. "And revenge for what your sister did."

There was no need to ask what he meant. Leanna had shot and killed his only son. Obviously the circumstances slipped Van Slyck's mind, because she had acted in defense of her husband and the child.

"Don wants to be cattle king, badly enough to see all competition removed."

Quin blinked in shock.

"Do you understand? He doesn't just want a share. He wants to break you and bury you."

Chance stepped forward, wondering if Van Slyck meant what he thought he meant.

Van Slyck wiped his nose and his fine linen handkerchief came away crimson. But his expression was no longer filled with fear. In fact, there seemed to be a nasty smile flickering on his thick lips.

Chance decided to wipe that grin from his bloody face, so he squeezed the banker's shoulder, pressing hard enough to get the man's attention. The banker winced and writhed.

"The rest of it."

"Don hired Hobbs to murder them." His voice was a gasp, his words a running stream as he hurried to get it out. "Hobbs hired Vernon Pettit to do the killing. He took on the other two, Allen and Bream, on his own. Hobbs told them to make it look like an accident. But Pettit found out who he had killed and got greedy, went to you to try to work a deal." Van Slyck looked to Quin. "Information for money, right?"

Quin inclined his head.

"Hobbs killed Pettit to shut him up."

Chance released him and he sank forward, cradling his shoulder and arm.

"Who killed Hobbs?"

The banker didn't even lift his head. "I think my arm is broken."

"Who?" demanded Bowie.

"Fitzgerald, again. Hobbs was the only connection between them. When he saw Hobbs talking to Bowie, he shot him."

"How'd he make that shot? It was seven hundred and fifty yards. I measured it," said Bowie.

"Sharpshooter for Alabama in the War Between the States," muttered the banker. "Praise our glorious republic."

Chance wondered if they would ever live down that damned war.

The room fell silent. They had the name of the man who had planned it all. Not just the money, but the killing. Their neighbor, a man they had all respected and welcomed into their homes, a man who had never given any indication of the hatred he harbored in his heart.

"You'll testify to this," Bowie asked.

Van Slyck nodded, whimpering now.

"Testify, hell," said Chance, and turned toward

the door. "I'm going to shoot that murdering brand-blotter—"

Both Quin and Bowie moved to block his departure.

"You can't go off the handle," said Bowie.

"Don't be stupid," said Quin.

Chance felt all the familiar friction scraping between them.

"You're not taking him alive. Tell me you know that?"

Quin and Bowie exchanged a grim stare.

"A man who will shoot his own men and kill women…he's willing to do anything," said Chance.

"I know," said Bowie. "But I'll take him alive if I'm able. I'm entitled to see them put a rope around his neck and watch him kick."

"Hang him like a dog," agreed Quin.

Chance hesitated, still in favor of shooting him in the forehead.

"What do you think Leanna would want?" asked Bowie.

It was a low blow and his brother knew it.

"We can take him if we work together," said Quin.

Chance kicked the wicker trash basket so hard that it flew up and struck the window across the room.

"Tarnation!"

Quin tracked the basket as it fell to the floor and then looked back to Chance.

"That mean yes?" he asked.

Chance drew a long breath, filling his lungs with stuffy air that smelled of ink and ledgers.

"Yes," he growled.

The sounds of shouting reached them in the office. Bowie went to the door. Beyond they could see Ace Keating, owner of the saddle and boot shop, loping toward them at a quick trot. He was a big man and brawny. Chance didn't know until that minute that he was so spry. His shop was just past the jail and his appearance and his relative haste set Bowie on alert.

"Marshal, I heard shots at the jail. Then I saw Ira and Johny ride off on two of my customers' horses."

And this was why Chance preferred a bullet. His captives didn't run.

Bowie took charge.

"Ace, find Dr. Lewis. Tell him to come quick." He glanced to Quin. "You come with me." Then he turned to Chance. "Stay with Van Slyck."

No, he would not be left behind on this. "I'm coming."

Chance started toward them. Bowie strong-armed him hard enough to get his attention and bring him to a stop.

"No. You won't. You'll guard him." He motioned a thumb at the banker still sitting in the chair Chance had thrown at him. "He's our only witness. Without him, we have no case against Fitzgerald. Do this. It's important." Bowie's voice was still a command, but his eyes pleaded for Chance to do as he was told, just this once.

Chance nodded his consent. Bowie slapped him on the shoulder and took off toward the street. Chance watched him go. Van Slyck began to rise from his chair.

Chance drew his pistols. "I will shoot you where you stand."

The banker took a seat.

Chapter Twenty

Both Quin and Bowie flanked the open door of the jail, pistols drawn. From within, Bowie heard a moaning.

"Glen?"

Another groan. Bowie stepped over the threshold to find Jose Martinez's body sprawled on his back, blood soaking his shirt.

Quin stepped in behind him. "Hell's bells!"

Bowie stooped to lay a hand on the man's torso, looking at the bullet hole. There was no heartbeat.

"I promised him that he'd get justice," he said, his voice mournful.

Quin stepped over Jose, heading toward the holding area. "Then we best see that he does."

They found the cell doors open and his deputy sitting propped up against the bars. There was a three-inch gash on his forehead, sending a fountain of blood down his face and neck.

"They took my gun," muttered Glen, his eyes half out of focus and glassy as two black buttons. "Took my gun."

"Okay, Glen. Doc's coming."

Quin made a face. "How'd you get close enough to let them take your gun?"

Glen closed his eyes and groaned. "I'm gonna be sick."

Quin spoke to Bowie now, ignoring the prostrate deputy. "They get to Fitzgerald and he'll know everything that they do."

Bowie took a bandanna from his pocket and pressed the folded square to Glen's head.

"Hold that," he told his deputy. Then he faced Quin. "I have to sequester Van Slyck."

"What?"

"Hide him. I'm not losing this witness, too."

Glen held the bloody bandage. "What's Van Slyck got to do with it?"

Bowie ignored his deputy. "We need to stow him somewhere safe."

"Your jail isn't safe?" asked Quin.

"Not if Fitzgerald brings an army," said Bowie, ignoring Whitaker. "We need to hide Van Slyck so nobody can find him."

"The 4C?" asked Quin.

Bowie shook his head. "Too far and too many ways in and out. What about Leanna's Place?"

Quin and Bowie both shook their heads at that. They would not bring this to their sister's door.

"Merritt's boardinghouse," asked Quin.

Bowie's "no" was emphatic.

"A hotel. We can put him under a false name," suggested Quin.

"The Royale has the most number of rooms."

Quin gave him a look and Bowie thought of Chance.

Despite his denial, Ellie meant something to his brother and so he wouldn't place her in jeopardy, either.

"That's out," said Bowie. "What about the Hobart Hotel? Chance has a room there."

Quin chewed on that a while. Hobart's was on the wrong side of the tracks, beside the billiard hall. "Never think to look there. But we'll have to sneak him in."

"And guard him until we can bring in Don Fitzgerald."

"Don Fitzgerald!" cried Glen.

"How do we aim to do that, exactly?" asked Quin.

Chance was about out of patience. All the action was going on at the jail and here he sat guarding a thief who'd failed to shoot himself when he'd had the opportunity.

"They hang people for embezzlement?" he asked Collier, the bank examiner, who lifted his nose from the ledger and peered at him over his half-moon reading glasses.

"Unfortunately not." Then he glanced at Van Slyck. "But they should." He spoke to Van Slyck now. "Where is the second set of books, the ones with the actual rents collected?"

Chance allowed Van Slyck to rise to open a false front in his desk, in which he had secreted two worn black ledgers. This had clearly been going on for some time. Mr. Collier now had both sets and turned to comparing them line by line. Chance thought his head would explode from boredom. Damn Bowie and his orders, anyway.

After another decade had come and gone, Collier spoke. "It appears that he was collecting rents from properties and land not deeded to the railroad." He glanced at Chance. "Those privately owned by your father and now jointly by the four remaining heirs, and then made the appearance of depositing these funds into the three accounts set up by your elder brother two years past, but, in fact, he was placing most of this revenue into the coffers of Don Fitzgerald. Plus, the actual figures of rent collected was more than he recorded in any of these accounts, so not only was he stealing from your family, he was stealing from his partner."

"Did you say three accounts?"

"Yes. One opened in each of your names in April of 1880. Here it is, one for each of his siblings—Bowie, Leanna and you, Mr. Cahill. Sizable accounts." He pointed at the ledger. "Or they will be once we recover the money that's owed."

April. That was the month after the funeral, Chance realized.

"He said he was pouring all the money he made back into the 4C."

"And so he has," said Collier, pointing to a line on the ledger that looked like any other. "Here. So much so that he has made two sizable additions to the acreage." Collier moved his finger. "And here."

Chance leaned in and looked at the figure before Collier's index finger.

"Your share," said Collier.

Fifteen thousand dollars. Enough to buy land. Enough to put down roots.

"And he took no share for himself. That's odd. He is entitled to a share."

Chance felt his resentment slide away with his bitterness until he felt a tenderness squeeze his heart. Quin, his big brother, hadn't abandoned any of them when they had abandoned him. Instead, he had done his best to look out for them all, just as he always had.

Collier was studying the ledgers. He stiffened and shot another glare at Van Slyck. "You had to scramble to cover the land purchases, didn't you?" He pointed at the books. "Here and here, you transferred monies out of Fitzgerald's accounts at the same time the purchases were made. I imagine that he and his accomplices would have tried very hard to see Quin didn't purchase any more property, because if the money was not available, your brother would have recognized that something was amiss."

Chance put it together. "The rustling, the brush fires and the shootings. You were trying to keep him busy so he didn't buy any more land."

Van Slyck nodded with the slowness of a man exhausted. "And trying to remove the witnesses to the wagon accident. Those men, Pettit and Allen, they weren't happy with their share once they discovered just who they had killed. I told Fitzgerald to get Hobbs to pay them off instead of running them off, but he wouldn't do it. You get what you pay for, I always say."

"And I'll see that you pay for this," promised Chance.

Van Slyck dropped his chin once more and the bean counter continued his hunt. Chance kept guard and watched the door, visible from the owner's offices. Bowie returned, and from the expression on his face, Chance knew the news was bad.

Quin parted ways with Bowie outside the jail.

Bowie was going right, toward the doctor's offices with his deputy and then on to the bank to ask Chance to hide Van Slyck in his room at Hobart's. Both hoped that Chance would consent to this task, but you never knew with him.

Quin had left, heading to Leanna's gaming hall, but as he turned the last corner, he found Leanna hurrying down the street in his direction, gripping the hand of the ferryman. Beside her, Cleve stretched his long legs to keep pace. Quin recognized the posture and the determined set of her jaw. Leanna was up about something. It was just how she'd looked when she'd suggested they break up the 4C. How he wished he could go back to that day. Looking back he saw himself as a scared kid, stepping into very big shoes and trying to bully his way through. And he'd stumbled ever since, especially with Leanna.

Things were still strained, although they were better. Misunderstandings had led him to believe she had caused a town scandal and she still wouldn't tell him who the father of her baby was. He assumed it was Cleve, though he didn't know for certain.

She'd spotted him now. But instead of slowing, she broke into a graceful run, forcing her husband to break into a lope. Quin met her halfway.

"You're back!"

Was that relief he saw in her eyes? She released Muddy and threw herself into Quin's arms. She hadn't done that in years. Quin closed his arms about her and his eyes slipped shut at the sweetness of having his little sister back.

He pulled her gently away, so he could see her face.

"We found out who it is, Leanna. The man who planned the murder was—"

"Don Fitzgerald," she said, finishing his sentence.

"How did you—?"

"Newt." She motioned toward the ferryman. "He fell

asleep in the jail and woke up in the morgue, for some reason." She gave him a hard stare and Quin couldn't meet her gaze. "It scared him and got him thinking. Right, Newt? Go on, tell him."

The ferryman had obviously been crying because his face was wet and his eyes puffy and sore looking.

"He won't yell at me. Will you, Mr. Cahill?"

Quin frowned. Why would he yell at an old drunk?

"He was there that day at Ghost Canyon," said Leanna. "He was on foot and that was as far as he'd gotten the night before. The shots woke him. He saw three men attack our folks. They clubbed Papa and sent the wagon over with Mama still alive." Now Leanna was weeping. "Newt described everything, right down to the color dress Mama was wearing and what was in the wagon. He crawled down there to check on them... but..."

Quin gathered her up in his arms again. "Okay, Annie. I understand."

Quin handed Leanna off to Cleve and then reached out to grab Muddy, but Leanna dashed his hand down.

"No." She turned to Newt, sobbing now.

"She wasn't dead," he whispered. "So one of them climbed down and hit her with a rock. I seen them, but they didn't see me. I heard them say Don Fitzgerald would be worth a fortune now, and they could hit him up for more, because the town would be his now that Ruby and Earl were dead. But the railroad never changed its mind." Cleve was holding Leanna now. Quin felt as if he might throw up.

"Why didn't you say something?" he asked Muddy.

"Scared. Booze blind and scared, most days since that one."

Now that Quin thought back he realized how much

worse Muddy's drinking had become after his parents had passed.

"I just can't take that to my grave. That Don Fitzgerald needs to pay for what he done and I'm not scared no more."

Quin turned to Cleve. "Who else knows?"

"Nobody but us."

"Can you keep him out of sight?"

Cleve nodded, drawing his wife to his side. She still clung, but the sobs had lessened.

"What's wrong, Quin?"

He told them. "Chance is guarding Van Slyck and I need you two to guard Newt. Don's boys escaped and are slapping leather back to his spread. They killed Jose Martinez because he witnessed them murdering his son. He was at the jail giving a statement to Bowie's deputy."

"Is Whitaker dead?" asked Leanna.

"No, just cracked him on the head."

Leanna pursed her lips, her brow now knit in confusion. "Why didn't they shoot Glen?"

"What?"

"They killed Jose, because he was a witness. Now Glen is a witness to them killing Jose. That's still a murder. So, why didn't they kill him, too?"

Quin felt as if river water was pouring down his back and his skin went prickly with fear.

"He's in on it," he whispered. "That's how they got out."

Quin turned tail and ran back the way he had come.

Quin reached the jail, out of breath and scared clean through. He hadn't been this frightened since he'd found out his wife was kidnapped. But now it was Bowie who was in danger and his brother didn't even know it. His own deputy had betrayed him.

Quin charged in through the jail's front door to find Bowie with Druckman, the undertaker, who knelt beside Jose's corpse.

Quin sagged with relief. Seeing Bowie unharmed took away the terror and he could draw breath again.

"Where's Whitaker?" Quin asked, his gun still out and ready at his side.

"What the hell, Quin?"

"Where?"

"At Doc Lewis's office having his head stitched."

"Come on," said Quin.

Bowie fell in with him as Quin told his brother what Leanna had said.

"I don't believe it," said Bowie, but his voice held a note of pain that told Quin that he just might.

They reached the doctor's office and charged up the steps. "That's why he didn't back Chance when that kid drew on him. I thought Whitaker was just stupid."

"He was on the payroll," said Quin, reaching for the knob.

Bowie drew up short, a stunned look on his face. "He knows about Van Slyck. He knows we're stowing him at Hobart's. Chance is there and he doesn't realize."

The two stood, stilled by indecision.

Quin pushed open the door. "We'll check the doc's first."

Chapter Twenty-One

Chance approached the second floor of the Hobart Hotel, gripping Van Slyck's arm. The banker was now wearing Bowie's duster, Bowie's green kerchief and a wide-brimmed black hat that belonged to one of the bank tellers.

The smell of stale beer clung to the sticky stairs that no one had bothered to wash. The second-floor hallway contained eight rooms, four on each side. The four-pane window at the end of the hall gave little light.

Someone stood before his door. He pushed Van Slyck behind him and drew his guns. The figure stepped away from the wall, and he saw she was small and female. As she moved in his direction, Chance recognized her quick, methodical step.

"Ellie?" Chance holstered his gun. "You shouldn't be on this side of town."

"I had to speak to you." Her gaze flicked past him and then she did a double take, her confusion clear from her wrinkled brow. "Mr. Van Slyck?"

Chance reached his room and opened the door, pushing Van Slyck inside.

"Move and I shoot you," he growled at Van Slyck.

Van Slyck didn't move. Ellie hovered in the hall.

"Sit," Chance ordered Van Slyck, and waited while he complied. Then he turned to her. "Get out of here before someone sees you."

Her chin began to tremble. "It doesn't matter. They know, everyone knows, that I was in your room."

He stilled at the prickling warning blanketing his back. The rumors had reached her already. Chance met her eyes and saw the shame there.

Chance hung on the hooks of a devil's choice. Marry Ellie or leave her behind. He wanted to do what was right, but either way seemed wrong for Ellie.

Chance heard the pounding of footsteps coming up the stairs. Ellie paused and looked back. Chance pulled his guns. But it was Glen Whitaker, Bowie's deputy, who appeared. Chance holstered his pistols.

"What?" he asked.

"Bowie said I'm to guard him. He sent me to fetch you."

"Why?"

"Something about going after those two prisoners."

Chance stepped aside and allowed Glen to move past him into the room. Then he glanced at Ellie, who was peering at Whitaker. The look on her face and the odd expression brought Chance's attention back to the deputy, who had stopped with one hand on the open door. Something was wrong.

"There's blood on his neck. And he's shaking." Ellie tugged at Chance's arm and whispered, "Look at his head."

Chance glanced at the trickle of blood escaping from beneath the deputy's dusty brown hat.

"What the hell?"

Glen slammed the door in Chance's face.

"No," screamed Van Slyck.

Chance drew his gun and kicked open the door at the same instant he heard the shot. The door flew off the hinges to reveal Whitaker, his gun drawn and smoking. Van Slyck crumpled to the floor as the deputy swung the pistol in their direction.

Chance acted on instinct, everything slowing as it always did in that last critical moment, but instead of reaching for his gun, he reached for Ellie. His dive carried them past the doorway and into the hall. He covered her with his body as the rush of fear crashed over him like a thunderclap. The second shot sounded, striking the adjoining door, followed by a third. Chance imagined Ellie, there in that exact place only an instant earlier, and felt his insides ice over. Chance sprang to his feet, his hands still pressing Ellie to the floor.

"Stay down."

"You, too!"

But he didn't. He crouched beside the door, gun drawn and the pistol upright as he prepared to fire. The sound of feet pounding on the stairs caused him to turn. Bowie and Quin, crested the stairs, coming at a full run.

"In there," said Chance. He took one quick glance into the room and found it empty except for the body of Van Slyck. "Gone!"

Bowie charged past him and into the room. Quin followed.

"Out the window," yelled Bowie, firing a shot.

Quin poked his head out, as well, both brothers

firing at their fleeing target. Chance felt dizzy and sat beside Ellie, dragging her against him as he stared after his brothers. Bowie crawled out on the roof. Chance glanced at Ellie, looking her over.

"You all right?" he asked.

She nodded, but her white face said otherwise. That was twice now that connection to him had brought her into the middle of gunplay.

"He's mounted. Go after him!" Bowie yelled, and he and Quin charged back out the way they had come, taking the stairs at a run and disappearing from sight.

Chance staggered to his feet. Ellie sat, drawing her knees to her chest.

He pulled her up, cradling her close, not sure if he was trembling or if it was her. Her heart beat fast as a sparrow's.

"What just happened?" she asked.

He squeezed his eyes shut against the rush of gratitude. Ellie was safe. "I don't know."

She peered up at him with those big soulful gray-green eyes. "You didn't draw."

"I know. I don't know what happened."

Her eyes widened as if she beheld something wonderful. "You avoided danger instead of charging into it. Chance, you saved me again. Only this time without risking your life."

That's not what happened. Because of him, Ellie had almost been shot. It only proved what he'd been saying all along. He was no damn good for her. Her ridiculous hat now lay on her back, tethered by the black ribbon beneath her chin. He cradled her beautiful head in his hand, feeling so damned lucky he hadn't got her killed.

He couldn't bear it if anything happened to this woman. Despite all his admonitions and denials she had somehow wheedled her way into his heart. He stilled, pressing her close to his chest, and dropped his cheek to the top of her head, letting the relief wash him clean.

Gunfire sounded in the street.

Bowie's voice reached him from the window.

"Chance!"

He raised his head, recalling his duty to his brothers, to his family, to his parents. He set Ellie aside and he followed Bowie and Quin, just like always.

He scrambled out of the window and crouched on the roof. Both his brothers standing side by side, looking up at him. Bowie had thrown his hat.

"Whitaker?" asked Chance.

Quin shook his head.

"Is Van Slyck dead?" called Bowie.

Chance recalled the banker now, ducked back into the room and rolled the body, curled like a dead spider on the floor. The former embezzler sprawled out upon his back. Whitaker's bullet had left a hole over his heart that still oozed blood.

Chance returned to the window. "Dead. You going after him?"

Bowie collected his hat. "Eventually. Who was that with you?"

Chance looked at the crowd gathering below and then back at Ellie. "Nobody."

Ellie narrowed her eyes on him.

Chance drew back into the room. "We have to get you out of here."

"If you are thinking of my reputation, it's already gone."

"Come on." He didn't wait for her reply as he took her out the back.

Chance managed to get Ellie over to the proper side

of town and to the Château Royale, by way of the service entrance. He stopped when they reached the porch and Ellie halted beside him.

"Where are you going?" she asked, concern etching a line between her dark brows as she reached for him.

He dodged her hand, drawing back. Her mouth gaped in surprise as her arms dropped limp to her sides. She looked at him as if he'd kicked her. Chance knew what he had to do.

"Back to my brothers. And you keep clear of me. You understand? You keep following me like a stray cat and you're gonna get shot."

Her chin began to tremble, but he held on to the last shreds of his resolve. He'd keep her safe, no matter what it cost him. Chance aimed a finger at her pretty nose.

"I mean it, Ellie. Stay away."

Chance spun on his boot heels and left her behind. It was for her own damn good. For a smart girl, she sure had a knack for finding trouble. His blood still coursed cold as seawater when he thought of that bullet missing her by inches.

He retraced his steps and didn't stop until he reached Hobart's. There he found the hotel owner, Jonathan Hobart, and Bowie and Quin and Druckman, the undertaker, who was wrapping Van Slyck in a sheet.

"Here he is," said Bowie at Chance's appearance. "I told you he didn't go after them alone."

The comment told him exactly how crazy both his brothers believed he was. It stopped him, because he recognized that the day he'd ridden into town, he would have done just that. But now he questioned his actions, his reflexes and his desire. Why had he gone for Ellie instead of his gun?

And then it came to him, illuminated like the silver

edges of a cloud before the sun. If he had taken the shot, Whitaker would be dead, but Ellie might have been hit by the deputy's bullet. And he couldn't have let that happen because he loved her.

Him, a roving bounty hunter with a death wish, had somehow fallen in love with a woman who dreamed of putting down roots so deep they would nourish generations. Ellie was an oak and he was a tumbleweed.

"What's wrong, Chance? You sick?" asked Bowie.

Yes, he thought. But he shook his head, denying that the world now tipped beneath his feet so dangerously that he thought he might fall off.

The hotel owner looked none too pleased to see one of his bedsheets stolen from the mattress.

"You're paying for that," he said to the undertaker.

"Mr. Van Slyck was a leading citizen. I'm certain his estate can cover the cost of a sheet."

Chance and Quin exchanged knowing looks. Van Slyck's estate was not as healthy as everyone believed, but neither felt compelled to say so aloud. All that would come out in the wash.

"What are we going to do?" asked Chance.

"Get our men together," said Bowie. "And then go after them."

Chance had been prepared to go after their parents' murderer. But he had planned to go alone. Bowie and Quin had families now and women who loved them.

"I don't fancy riding out after them only to get picked off along the way. Fitzgerald has plenty of men and they'll do as he tells them. Plus, he knows every inch of that ranch," said Quin. "For all you know he has an armory of weapons and men just waiting."

"I'll go out and see," said Chance.

"No," said both brothers simultaneously.

"I'm the only one with no woman. Makes sense."

Quin made a sound in his throat. "You got a woman. You just haven't claimed her as you should."

Quin was still bossing him. Only this time he was right. He should claim her and would if he believed he could do right by Ellie, which he didn't. "You leave her out of this."

"How? She's in it, brother. You put her there."

"Ellie needs a man with roots."

Quin gave a half shrug. "That could be you."

"I'm not coming back to the 4C."

"Who asked you to? But you ought to marry Ellen."

Chance should be riding out to the Fitzgerald spread, guns blazing. Instead, he wondered what it would be like to marry Ellie. He knew they were good in bed, but that didn't mean he'd be a good husband. He looked at his brothers. Quin had married. Bowie was about to. Did they ever get scared right down to their heels that they'd be a disappointment as a husband? That they wouldn't be able to provide for a wife and children?

He regarded them closely. Quin, serious and confident. Bowie, brave and just. Both were exactly the sort of men that a woman would want. Could he be like them?

"We might be able to take them if we wait for darkness," said Quin. "I could get my boys from the 4C."

"No," said Bowie. "I'm not going to start a land war. We're riding out to his place and arresting him and if he won't come in, well, we'll have to make him."

Chance knew something of this. His time chasing outlaws had taught him a few things.

"First, there's not a chance in hell they'll let you arrest them," said Chance. "Ira and Johny are wanted for murder and know they will hang. Even if they kill us all, they'll be tracked down by bounty hunters and brought in eventually. That means they have to run and it only makes sense that they'll run for Mexico."

"Don doesn't know we have a witness linking him to Ma's and Pa's deaths. He might think he's shored up all his fences," said Quin.

"Which means we have a choice," said Bowie. "Right now, he can deny any knowledge of what Van Slyck was up to, claim ignorance of the use of his accounts to hold the money Van Slyck embezzled. He'll say that he was as much in the dark as we were. He thinks he's clear."

"That doesn't mean he'll be willing to hand over his boys."

"No. He'll help them."

"So we need a party to go after the boys and one to take Fitzgerald."

"Or we could tell him we have a witness," said Quin.

Bowie scowled. "You tell him and his back is to the wall. He'll come at us with everything he's got."

Quin gave a cold smile. "Exactly."

Bowie and Chance exchanged a look.

"If we tell him, he'll run," said Bowie.

Quin looked at Chance. "That examiner say whether or not Fitzgerald actually has our money?"

"Don doesn't have it," said Chance. "It's in his accounts at the bank."

Bowie's crystal eyes narrowed. "They'll come for it. They'll bring the fight to us."

"They have to," said Chance.

"We best get ready, then."

All three brothers nodded, in agreement at last.

"But we don't have a witness against Don," said Bowie.

This time it was Quin who smiled. "Yes. We do."

Chapter Twenty-Two

Late that afternoon, Bowie decided to give the Fitzgeralds a chance to surrender without bloodshed. He sent two representatives, Dr. Lewis in his carriage, drawn by his black trotter, accompanied by Ace Keating, the owner of the saddle shop, riding beside him on a muscular bay gelding. Both men had a vested interest in the town but no argument with Don and his boys. They carried with them a letter from Bowie, in which he advised them that he had a witness to Earl's and Ruby's murders and that if all three came in, he'd guarantee their safety and a trial in a location other than Cahill Crossing.

Bowie, Leanna, Quin and Chance all watched their emissaries until they passed Town Square and turned toward Fort Ridge, knowing that the men would reach Fitzgerald's ranch in less than an hour.

"Will they be all right?" asked Leanna.

"Yes," said Bowie.

"You think they'll come in?" she asked.

"I do," he said. "But not to surrender."

* * *

Don Fitzgerald eyed the dust coming up the road. He'd given his men orders that nobody get close to the house, yet that was definitely a buggy heading his way with several of his boys as escorts.

He sent his sons and Whitaker inside to wait until he knew who it was. He hoped it was Bowie. He would just love to shoot that sanctimonious son of a gun between the eyes. But it wasn't. Bowie wasn't stupid like Ira, or reckless like Johny. Now he'd have to pack his only sons off to Mexico and all because of Chance Cahill and his big nose.

He'd warned his sons to lay off the businesses until Chance blew out of town again. That boy never stayed anywhere long. Don had liked Chance when he was young, seeing more of Ruby's free spirit in him. The other two recalled Earl to his mind. Back then Chance had run with Ira and Johny for a time. But that hadn't lasted.

He wondered about the money. With Willem Van Slyck dead, he had no way to get to it. Damn, he hated bankers.

Don shaded his eyes with his hand against the setting sun.

"It's Doc Lewis," called Sydney from the gate. "Somebody's riding with him."

Who would be addled enough to ride out here? A hostage, he hoped. Give them some leverage.

"Who is it?"

"Ace Keating," called Sydney.

Damn, he liked Keating. He was a genius with a saddle, a regular artist. Bowie had chosen well.

"Send them up."

The eight armed cowboys beside him lowered their weapons. Ira came to the door.

"Can we come out?"

"No, damn it. Do you want them to say they seen you?"

Ira shut the door. A moment later Dr. Lewis pulled the buggy to a stop before him. Ace remained in the saddle as Lewis stepped down, sending the springs bouncing.

He held his arms stiffly at his sides. "I'm in possession of a letter from Marshal Cahill. He asked me to give it to you and wait for a reply."

Don nodded and the doctor reached inside his long black coat, retrieving an envelope. Then Lewis placed one boot on Don's step and leaned to deliver his message. He stood back as Don tore into the flap and opened the folded page.

He snorted as he read, then scowled as a finger of dread writhed in his belly. Bowie mentioned Muddy as a witness.

Don thought back to that day. Newt had been there, all right. His business was going to be affected by the decision since his ferry already had use of Cahill land and was near the site Earl proposed for the town. It was one of the reasons they had picked Earl's property. He had the ferry already, but only because he was a damned fool and let Muddy operate the thing on his land for free. But it turned out he was no fool, because the men from the committee had mentioned the advantage of having a ferry in the town. Muddy had left Wolf Grove that evening. Don had seen him go. But he'd been real drunk from celebrating. Had he passed out at Ghost Canyon, as Bowie stated? Don read on. Bowie mentioned details that only an eyewitness would know. Had that damned drunk seen it all? Why hadn't he come forward till now?

Bowie had him. Don was certain. And just like Earl, Bowie thought he'd outmaneuvered him. But he was just as wrong—dead wrong. He hated Earl and he hated Cahill Crossing. As of right now, he no longer wanted to own it. He wanted to wipe it off the face of the earth.

He wadded up the page and threw it in the dirt.

Lewis followed the balled paper with his gaze. "That your answer?"

"No. You tell him we'll be along. They can expect us."

Chance sat with his brothers at Leanna's table in the little house she shared with her husband and Melvin, the baby, Cabe, and her surly cook, Dorothy, who Chance did not like any better here than he had in Deadwood. The woman hated men, but seemed to tolerate Cleve, for reasons Chance did not understand.

The knock at the front door brought all the men to their feet, guns drawn.

Leanna rose belatedly and wiped her mouth on her napkin. "Do you really think Fitzgerald would knock?" She turned to Dorothy and nodded. "Go see, Dottie."

They remained standing, listening, until Chance recognized the voice of Ace Keating. He holstered his pistols. A moment later Keating and Dr. Lewis appeared with Dorothy, looking like she just sucked a lemon.

Bowie greeted them with a handshake and a few words.

"You think he's coming in?" Bowie asked Dr. Lewis.

"Oh, he's coming, all right. But not to turn himself in. I also saw Ira in the window of the house. So they haven't gone anywhere."

"You see Whitaker?" asked Bowie.

Lewis shook his head.

Bowie turned to Quin. "You think they'll come tonight?"

"Maybe. But they've got to prepare. We best do the same."

The men headed for the door, Cleve a step behind because he had to pass off the baby first.

At the jail, Bowie unlocked the rifle case and retrieved something from beside the ammunition boxes. He spread three badges on the desk.

"I want to deputize you."

Quin and Cleve stared at the silver stars. Chance scooped one up.

"Raise your right hands first," said Bowie.

Two minutes later they had all been duly sworn.

Bowie recruited a number of volunteers, but the total was less than he had hoped. It seemed most men who owned businesses were not willing to take up arms to defend them against a mob of killers.

Quin's men arrived from the 4C and he posted lookouts on every road but the night passed quietly. The signal shots sounded the following day at midmorning, announcing the Fitzgerald gang had chosen the most obvious of paths to town and were riding in in broad daylight.

All the Fitzgerald men, the turncoat deputy plus a dozen hands, all armed with rifles, charged straight past the general store, but they did not turn toward the bank, as expected.

Bowie, Chance and Quin had taken up positions across from the bank in the drugstore.

"What are they carrying?" asked Quin.

"Torches," said Bowie, leaving cover in favor of the door.

All three reached the street.

"He's headed for Leanna's Place," yelled Quin, running now.

Fitzgerald's men carried bottles, stuffed with rags. Chance watched in horror as they lit and threw the incendiary bombs. Kerosene exploded like liquid fire, sticking to the planking and igniting the porch of the general store. A second bottle shattered the front window. Screaming echoed from within.

The Cahills ran, trying to catch riders who now separated into two groups, Don and his boys leading one and Whitaker taking the other. Quin's men fired from the roof of Arthur Slocum's law office and two riders went down, but now the store was blazing and men scrambled from the interior, which had black smoke pouring out of it. Chance watched another grenade sail through the air, exploding into flame on the porch roof of Leanna's Place. Windows flew open and her girls, who had been hiding upstairs, beat the flames into submission with wet blankets.

The second group of riders charged past them.

"Ellie," Chance yelled. "The hotel."

He turned and ran after Whitaker's group, leaving Bowie and Quin firing at Ira and Johny, who now returned fire from horseback. Smoke burned Chance's nostrils and obscured his vision as he ran past the burning store. Burnett stood on the porch of his wife's boutique, taking slow aim at the riders as they passed. The former Texas Ranger did not miss and three more men fell from their horses. But there were so many.

It looked as if Don Fitzgerald was preparing to burn Cahill Crossing to the ground.

By the time Chance reached the hotel there were at least five fires burning. Screaming, smoke, flames, chaos.

Chance had to find Ellie.

The riders whirled in the street, charging back past the Château Royale. Smoke burned his eyes, but he saw what they held in their hands—dynamite, with the short fuse already burning.

"No!"

But no one could hear him as he shouted into the chaos. He lifted his rifle, taking aim at the rider lighting another stick even as the first turned the front of the hotel to splintered kindling.

The man lit the fuse with his cigar, drawing his last breath as Chance's bullet struck him in the chest. He tumbled backward, the dynamite rolled forward.

Chance dove away as the blast deafened him. Where were his brothers? Where was Ellie?

Johny and Ira charged past him as Chance staggered to his feet. He couldn't hear. The whole world was burning, screaming, and he couldn't hear a thing but a sound like a waterfall coursing over rocks. Someone emerged from the smoke.

Oscar Jenkins. He took Chance's shoulders and shook him. Chance could see his mouth moving, but there was no sound.

Then he heard him, his voice coming from far away. A tiny voice, like an echo thrown off a canyon wall.

"Are you all right?"

That snapped Chance back to his surroundings.

"Where's Ellie?"

"Safe. She led the guests down the back stairs. They're all holed up in the depot until this is over.

Leanna's with her and Cleve. They ran down the tracks with the girls."

The depot was directly behind the hotel, so new arrivals could walk from the depot to the hotel or restaurant along the new boardwalk.

"Is Annie safe?"

Oscar nodded. "They all got out."

"Her place?"

"Don't know." He looked back at his hotel, the lobby blazing. "Go after Don, Chance."

Oscar ran back toward the fire and Chance took off after the Fitzgeralds. Ellie was all right. Her father had said so.

Chance raced after Ira and Johny. He ran through the smoke, jumping over debris and past downed horses kicking and screaming from their wounds. The booming town had turned into a battleground. Men beat at flames with their coats and bucket brigades were already forming at the general store. The flames had leaped from the Royale to Steven's Restaurant. The bakery was next door and then Rosa's Boutique. He saw Rosa Burnett on the roof of her porch, throwing a wet bedsheet over the cedar shingles. Below her, Burnett pointed.

"Toward Town Square!"

They were going for the bank now. Why hadn't they thought this might happen when they had dared Don Fitzgerald to come to their town?

Because he just couldn't picture anyone killing innocents or burning down businesses. But neither could he picture a man so filled with rage and spite that he'd kill their mother and shoot Bowie's girl.

A man like that might do anything at all.

He found Quin first, or Quin found him, pulling him

to cover behind the brick base of the half-finished stone barricade that would someday be the fountain at the center of the square. Bowie was already there, loading cartridges into his rifle.

"What did you see?" asked Bowie.

"The Royale is burning. They're using dynamite."

"Heard it," said Bowie, his voice sounding tinny to Chance's ears.

"They cleared the hotel and are all holed up at the depot. Annie is there with her girls," yelled Chance.

"Good. Don and his boys are in the bank. They're on foot. We took out their horses," shouted Quin, his voice still sounding strange to Chance's ringing ears.

"We can pin them down in the bank."

A boom accompanied an explosion that took out all the bank windows, sending shards of glass showering into the street.

"They've blown the vault," said Bowie.

"But they can't get away," insisted Quin.

"Unless they also blow out the back of the building," countered Bowie.

All three scrambled to their feet, but Bowie and Quin halted. Chance glanced about but could see no threat. He looked to them for explanation.

Both his brothers turned their heads as if listening to something Chance could not hear. He didn't like the look they exchanged.

"The train," said Bowie. "They've been planning to take it out all along."

Panic flashed through Chance like a pistol flash.

"Ellie's at the depot!" And so was his sister and who knew how many others. Chance started to run again, back into the smoke that billowed from the general store, now consumed by fire. His heart crashed against the walls of his ribs like a mad horse throwing himself against the fences.

Ellie, he had to get to Ellie.

Chapter Twenty-Three

Chance had been prepared to die to avenge his parents' murders. But he hadn't thought anyone else would have to. And now all he wanted was to find Ellie. If he could only see her safe, he didn't care what happened to Don Fitzgerald. His world narrowed, obscured by smoke and death, to that which was most essential. All that mattered was protecting Ellie.

What if they hurt her? What if they threw a stick of dynamite into that depot and killed them all?

Bowie and Quin were fast, but Chance, bolstered by the rush of pure panic, outdistanced them both. He'd lost his rifle, but not the pistols strapped to his thighs. Six shots apiece and more rounds in his gun belt. He recognized that now he wasn't fighting for revenge; he was fighting for the woman he loved and he'd kill anyone who stood in his way.

They streaked between Rosa's Boutique and the bakery. Every window of the wooden house now hung with wet blankets and sheets against the blaze of Steven's two doors down. The restaurant already had flames lapping out of the windows and lines of men swung full buckets from one hand to the next, wetting the clapboard of the bakery.

Smoke burned his eyes. From down the tracks he heard the whistle shriek, announcing the train's on-time arrival at Cahill Crossing's depot. Only today the world had turned upside down and the newly emerging town blazed with the fires of hell. Chance cleared the alley and made it onto the boardwalk. Steam from the engine blasted across the platform, merging with the smoke.

And then he saw them. The walkway was crowded with people, herded like cattle by Fitzgerald's men, trapped between the fire and the train.

Where was Ellie?

"Leanna!" shouted Quin, now just behind him.

Ira had their sister, holding her about the waist, pressing her up against him as a human shield. Don had hold of Maria, the chambermaid from the Royale. She clawed at his face as he used her hair to bring her along. Whitaker came next, holding Cassie in the same fashion. The woman made no protest for he held a gun to her head, next came Johny dragging Ellie. Each man had a saddlebag slung over his shoulder. Chance knew it must be stuffed with cash and gold coins from the bank.

Their men pushed the crowd toward the locomotive.

Quin raised the rifle. "They are not taking them on that train."

Chance stared in horror at his brothers and then at the nightmare before him.

"Shoot, Chance. What are you waiting for?" It was Bowie's voice.

Chance had never hesitated before, never felt this

terror pooling in his belly at the prospect of drawing his pistol. What if he missed?

"Whitaker," said Bowie, choosing his target and the man who had betrayed him all in one breath.

"Ira," said Quin, picking the man who threatened his sister.

That left Johny and Don.

The Fitzgeralds had seen them now and they fired. The Cahills ducked back into the alley. They'd be gone in a minute, would have boarded the train and been safe behind the steel walls.

Chance drew his pistol, aiming at Johny.

"Now!" he shouted.

All three guns fired in unison.

Ira dropped to his knees, clutching his throat, blood pouring between his fingers. Whitaker stumbled, then fell backward, dragging Cassie along. Don continued to the steps of the train, turning to see Johny dropped like a stone, still looking up at the bullet hole Chance had planted between his raised eyebrows.

"Don," yelled Quin.

Chance turned his pistol on Don, but he had no shot, because Don now hunched behind Maria like the coward he was.

Don never got that second foot off the platform, but the shot did not come from Chance's gun. Don released Maria to grab his chest. Maria leaped free as Don stared out at his fallen sons strewn before him like butchered buffalo and pressed both hands to his chest, gasping. Blood welled between his fingers and soaked his vest. He turned to the shooter, staring, wide-eyed.

Leanna stood with her arm extended, the tiny pistol that Chance had told her to keep close now clutched in her hand. Don dropped to his seat on the bottom step of the train, hands over his heart. A moment later he slumped to the side, lilting like a drunk as he collapsed against the steel wall of the narrow stairwell.

Leanna stooped and retrieved Don's pistol.

Two more shots sounded. Two more of Fitzgerald's men, the ones herding the citizens from the depot, dropped.

"The roof!" yelled Quin.

Chance glanced in the direction he pointed. Oscar Jenkins and Cleve Holden were firing from the top of the Royale.

Bowie lifted his rifle as all three brothers advanced.

"Drop them!" he shouted at the remaining four men.

Don's men did as he ordered, throwing down their weapons and lifting their hands. Bowie moved forward, shouting directions.

Leanna ran to Chance, hugging him, and then turned to Quin to do the same. Chance found Ellie, reaching her a moment later.

"Are you hurt?" he asked.

She shook her head. He dragged her into his arms.

"I almost lost you," he whispered.

His ears must still be playing tricks on him because he thought she said, "Never."

He drew her away from the carnage, away from the citizens gawking or making their way to safety. Away from Bowie and Quin, checking the bodies of the Fitzgeralds. Away from the revenge he thought he'd wanted more than life itself.

But now he held what he wanted most. Ellie was everything to him and he'd almost lost her.

He didn't expect he'd make much of a husband and still believed she could do better, but he knew now what he wanted. Maybe she'd be foolish enough to say yes.

Trouble was, he had nothing to offer her. All he had
was the clothes on his back, his guns and his saddle.
It didn't sit well to have to work for her father and it
didn't sit well to ask Quin to take him back.

But he couldn't have his pride and Ellie.

"Ellie, I got something to ask you."

She stared at him, soot blackening her cheeks and
her gray-green eyes shining up at him.

"All men to the bucket brigade!"

Ellie turned away. "The hotel!"

Together they returned to the Royale where Ellie
was swept up by her mother, while Chance joined the
line, throwing water first on the hotel and then on the
charred remains of the restaurant. The bakery suffered damage to the roof; Rosa's had survived with
only a scorching, but the general store had burned to
the ground. The bank, made of brick, had a hole in the
back large enough to drive a wagon through and the
vault had been destroyed. The Château Royale suffered
structural damage from the dynamite, but the fire was
staunched quickly thanks to Oscar's natural ability to
rally, organize and lead men. By late afternoon the
remains of Fitzgerald's men were locked up, the fires
were out, the bank shorn up with wood and a guard
posted. And the noon train had departed late for the
first time since it had begun its daily stops in Cahill
Crossing.

That evening, sweating and stinking of smoke,
Chance stumbled over to Leanna's home and took
advantage of the bath and meal she offered. Afterward
he joined her downstairs to find that Cleve had taken
over the job of putting the boys to bed, leaving him
alone in the quiet parlor with his baby sister whose hair
was still wet from her bath.

"Everybody all right?" he asked her.

She nodded. "I couldn't let him take Maria on that train."

"You did right."

They stared at each other. Was she thinking what he was, that it was finally over? Their parents could rest and they could rebuild.

"What will you do now, Chance?" she asked.

He knew what he'd like to do, but he scarcely dared say it aloud.

"I'd like to stay."

Her smile lit up the room. "I'm so glad."

"I'd like to ask for Ellie's hand."

"Wonderful."

"It's not. I got nothing, Leanna. No money, no job except killing outlaws. What kind of life is that for her? If I stay I'll have to work for her father or ask Quin to take me back. I don't favor being a hired man, but I can't see any way out of it."

"If you had money, what would you do?"

"Buy land. That's what Ellie wants."

"What do you want?"

"Land. Land of my own."

"Chance, you remember all those bounties you gave me?"

He didn't like the way this was going. "I don't expect you to pay me back, if that's where you're headed. That money was meant for you, to keep you safe."

"And so it did. I just wanted to say that I couldn't have gotten on without your help. Especially at the beginning. If I didn't have you supporting me, I might have ended up like one of those girls in the red-light district. I owe you for that, Chance, and I'll never be able to pay you back. Because of you, I have a business and we're building a ranch. I have a husband and two beautiful boys." Leanna gave him one of her mysterious smiles. "Oh, and Chance? You're going to be an uncle again. Cleve and I are expecting a child."

His jaw dropped. Leanna patted his forearm. He recovered enough to kiss her cheek and clasp her hand.

"That's wonderful," he stammered, a little afraid for Leanna. But she glowed with a happiness that reassured him.

"Don't you see? None of this would have been possible without your help."

"You don't owe me. It wasn't a damned loan."

"I know that, but the thing is, I'm good at business. Very good. I only ever used the first two bounties you brought in."

Chance remembered the first. Two hundred and fifty dollars for the man who'd killed the driver on a Fargo stage. The second was for six.

"I put all the rest in the bank in an account under your name. There's over three thousand dollars in there, Chance."

"The same bank that got robbed?"

"Oh, we got all the money back. Bowie said so. Stop dodging, Chance. You have the money. So go ask Ellie to marry you."

He remained where he was. He had enough to buy land. So why was he more afraid now than before?

"Well?"

"What if she says no?"

Leanna gave him a gentle smile. "She won't."

He stood and took a step toward the door, then turned back. "This is harder than tracking outlaws."

Leanna gave him a push in the right direction as she had always done.

But what if she was wrong? What if Ellie didn't want him, after all?

Ellie directed the workers, deciding what to keep, repair or discard. The dynamite hadn't killed anyone, because of her father. He'd cleared the lobby and sent all the guests out the back entrance facing the depot as soon as the Fitzgeralds had started torching the general store four businesses down. But the explosive surely had played havoc on the interior. Debris was strewn all over the floor, splintered wood, charred upholstering, hunks of wall still hung with wallpaper and pieces of the crystal chandelier all lay scattered across what had been the lobby. She was filthy, reeked of smoke and her muscles ached from the cleanup. She'd never felt so utterly exhausted.

"Ellie?"

She looked toward the familiar voice and saw Chance heading straight for her. The purpose in his stride and the grim expression on his face set her on guard, for he looked like a man on business he wished dispensed with in haste.

Ellie felt her feet stick to the floorboards. She stood as immobile as the broom she held except for the bead of perspiration rolling between her breasts. Chance Cahill had done what he'd set out to do and now he had come to say goodbye.

Ellie set the broom against the wall and placed a hand over her pounding heart, surprised to feel it still beating. Would he stay if she fell to her knees and begged him?

She would, if she thought she had the least chance of

success. But this was a man who knew what he wanted and no one, not even her father, could dissuade Chance Cahill once he'd fixed his sights on something.

He drew up before her. "Hello, Ellie."

The awkwardness between them hung like a fog.

"Hello," she murmured.

Making love to Chance, being in love with Chance, had changed her forever. Ruined her, but not in the way her mother meant. This man had ruined her for any other because now she was not willing to settle for a decent man whom she did not love. She wanted Chance and, like him, she would have what she wanted or nothing at all. She swallowed, but the knot in her throat only seemed to grow.

"I came to say something."

She folded her hands before her and told herself not to cry. But her throat was already closing up and his image swam before her eyes. He was leaving.

"I wondered…" He stopped, glanced about and then rubbed his neck as if it pained him. Perhaps all that pained him was the task at hand. He was clean-shaven and his damp hair curled against his neck. She drank in the sight of him, trying to capture every detail, trying to seal his image in her mind, to save it for the endless nights without him.

How could she have been so stupid as to fall in love with the wildest of the Cahill men, the one they all warned her would ruin her reputation and break her heart?

He remembered belatedly to remove his hat and stood turning it nervously in his hands.

When he finally spoke, his words were a rush, as if he raced to get them out. "I came to ask you to marry me, Ellie."

Ellie's knit brow dropped low over her flashing eyes. "I'm not marrying you."

Chance wrinkled his brow, feeling the sting of her rejection.

"Why not?" he asked.

"Because I'll not marry a man who wants nothing more than to leave me behind, but who has too much honor to do so."

"Ellie, you got it all wrong."

"I don't. This is not your fault, Chance. It's mine. I tempted you—I knew what I was doing."

He dropped his hat to his side and stood still and silent, scowling at her now, his eyes stormy. "That's not why I'm asking."

She threw up her arms in frustration. "Well, why, then, Chance?" She hadn't meant for her voice to sound so sharp, but having a man propose out of guilt, especially the man she loved with all her bruised heart, was worse than watching him leave.

"I'm asking because I love you, Ellie, and I reckon I can't give you up even though I know it would be best for you if I did."

Suddenly she could scarcely draw breath. "You love me?"

He nodded once and then replaced his hat, pulling it low, so she could barely see his eyes. He fidgeted with a bullet in his gun belt as he waited for her to speak.

"You love me." This time it wasn't a question, but a statement of fact, as she grew accustomed to the idea, bringing the sentiment into her heart. A smile blossomed across her face, but she didn't say anything else.

Chance squirmed. "Ellie. You got to answer the question."

She stepped forward so that they almost touched

and then looped her arms about his neck. "Yes, Chance Cahill, I will marry you, because I love you, too!"

Chance gave a holler and threw his hat. It sailed across the room, but before it hit the ground, he was kissing her.

Epilogue

To Chance, Bowie looked about ready to faint. He swayed in his place beside the altar, waiting for his bride to make her appearance and Quin had had to right him once already.

"Still time to run for your life," said Chance, standing between Quin and Lucas Burnett, all dressed in black suits and white dress shirts with the scratchiest damn collars this side of the Red River.

Bowie shook his head. "I'm afraid she'll change her mind. Can't get that ring on her finger fast enough."

Chance knew how he felt, for it was the same with him and Ellie, not because he feared Ellie would get cold feet. He just wanted to be alone with her. Since announcing their intention to marry, Minnie had had Ellie occupied every spare second with invitations and guest lists and seating charts. It all made him long for her father and his shotgun.

"She won't change her mind," said Quin, staring from his place across the aisle to his wife, Adrianna, the matron of honor, who was just taking her place on the opposite side of the altar. She was dressed in a soft rose-petal-pink dress that dimmed next to the radiant smile she offered Quin. She had a row of small rosebuds threaded in her hair that made her look like some goddess of the spring. The woman obviously liked a challenge, for he could think of no other reason to wed someone as pigheaded as his eldest brother.

Next came Rosa Burnett, wife of their neighbor Lucas Burnett and cousin to Quin's wife. Rosa proceeded down the aisle and into her place. Her pretty blond hair was swept up in an elaborate hairstyle of braids and cascading curls and she also had pink roses in her hair. Quin had had them shipped by rail from Sacramento. Roses in October—what would that railroad bring them next? Leanna arrived three steps behind Rosa, in a dress the color of the inside of a lime, except for the wide pink ribbon about her waist that was a ringer for the roses in her hair. She glanced back at Cleve, sitting on the groom's side of the aisle, holding a baby against his shoulder, his arm wrapped around Melvin next to him. Her husband had more patience than any man Chance had ever met. He poked Melvin as the boy waved enthusiastically at Leanna. Directly across the aisle, sitting on the bride's side, was Lefty Gorman, one of Merritt's good friends, looking so happy his eyes were watering. It seemed Merritt had invited the entire town. Chance looked down the aisle at the sea of faces, searching for one in particular.

Chance found Ellie, scrubbed and dressed in forest-green that made her eyes look the same color as cedar boughs. She didn't need roses in her hair to outshine all the women before the altar, but Chance thought that a coronet of white roses would look lovely in her dark hair and determined to ask Minnie to add that to her wedding list.

Ellie sat between her mother and father. Minnie had taken wholeheartedly to the idea of Chance as her son-in-law only after she'd discovered that Quin, while keeping his promise to pour back the profits from the ranch into the 4C, had nonetheless seen that each of his brothers and his sister took all the revenue from the rents paid in Cahill Crossing, making them all wealthy in their own right. Quin had turned over the accounts to his siblings and that, combined with the money Leanna had put aside from his bounties, was more than he needed for land and livestock. He was glad they hadn't purchased land yet, because he still hadn't decided how far from Minnie they needed to be.

Oscar had wanted Chance all along, it seemed, seeing something Chance never saw in himself. He was grateful for the confidence but still had his doubts about whether he could be a proper husband. But he had no doubts about how much he loved Ellie.

The piano began to play something classical and the doors swept open. There stood Merritt in the door, a vision in a dress of soft moss-green satin that shone with flashes of silver as she moved, like fishes darting through the current. Chance smiled at the picture she made, carrying a bouquet of pink roses to match those threaded in her attendants' hair. Merritt's father, Thomas Jensen, also wore a pink rosebud in his lapel. The big man escorted his daughter slowly down the aisle, as if in no hurry to give her away again. Did she know how lucky she was to have both her parents here to see this day?

Chance felt his throat burn, realizing that his folks weren't here to see Bowie wed. It was a hard truth that finding the culprit had not brought them back. Quin placed a hand on Chance's shoulder and squeezed.

"I was thinking of Ma," Chance said.

"I know. We're all missing them today."

Jensen told Bowie to take good care of his daughter and then took his place beside his wife, Carolyn, who smiled as she dabbed her green eyes with a lace handkerchief.

Soon the service was underway. Chance listened to the vows, words he would soon speak to Ellie, if Minnie could ever decide on the color of the damn napkins. He'd never realized how much preparation went into weddings and he had been considering throwing a ladder up against Ellie's window and avoiding the entire thing.

Bowie finally got to slip that ring onto Merritt's finger; at that point Leanna was crying, of course. She always cried at weddings.

Bowie offered his arm to his bride and led Merritt Cahill out to sign the marriage license. Chance offered his arm to Leanna and walked her back down the aisle. She wiped her streaming eyes as she went. Cabe waved with Cleve's help and she paused to scoop the baby up. Chance continued along with her until they reached the street.

He figured he'd never know for sure whose baby that was or why Leanna chose not to tell any of them. And he realized it didn't matter much anymore. He was Leanna's. She'd claimed him and that was good enough.

"You're thinking about Boodle, aren't you?"

Leanna was like that. Always knowing what he was thinking. He nodded.

"Do you remember Arden Honeybee?"

That was one of Leanna's girls, but now that he thought of it, Arden had not come with her to Cahill Crossing.

"Yup."

"Her real name was Arden Holden. She gave Cabe to me. I promised to protect him from his father."

"Who's name is…?" She'd just said Arden *Holden,* which was Cleve's last name. He glanced back toward the church, more confused than before. "Is it Cleve?"

Leanna shook her head. "No. Cleve is Arden's brother and is Cabe's uncle." Her face grew deadly serious. "Preston Van Slyck was the father, Chance. He ruined Arden and he ruined others. It was some kind of a twisted game to him."

Chance set his jaw as he recalled Preston pursuing Leanna all the way to Deadwood. But it seemed, with Leanna, Preston had finally met his match.

"I couldn't tell you in Deadwood because I had given my word. Preston figured it out when he saw Boodle's eye color. They're very unusual—his grandfather had them, as well. After Preston died I was afraid that Willem Van Slyck might also notice and try to claim him." She kissed Cabe's little fist. Then she looked back at Chance.

"Is that why Preston took him?"

She nodded. "Yes. And he wanted us to stop poking around in his father's business and taking girls from across the tracks. I fear he thought that bringing Cabe to Willem would lift him in his father's eyes." Leanna grinned at Cabe, speaking in a tone meant for a little one, while her words were for Chance. "We love him like our own. Don't we?"

"He's a lucky boy. I appreciate you telling me. Will you tell Bowie and Quin?"

"Bowie knows and I'll tell Quin by and by. It's safe now."

Cleve appeared through the crowd and took charge of Leanna.

"We'll see you at the reception," she said, and off she went.

Both Quin and Leanna had offered their places for the reception and Merritt had chosen Leanna's Place, Chance thought, to add the weight of their confidence that Leanna's Place was most definitely on the correct side of the tracks. The new window had arrived, but Leanna wouldn't let anyone see it yet. It was installed, but still wrapped in brown paper. Having paid for it, Chance had been allowed a peek. Unlike the last one, this window did not depict the past. Instead, Leanna had chosen a rendering of a locomotive, rolling into a booming town set between the river and the cattle ranches beyond. Leanna's window now pointed toward the bright future of Cahill Crossing. And as for the shards from the old window, she had shipped them east where they had been transformed into stained-glass lamps that hung over the dining room tables.

Ellie appeared and Chance took her up in his arms and kissed her. She pulled back after a moment, flushed pink and smiling brightly, her ridiculous hat now askew. He grinned down at her, feeling happier than he could ever remember.

"Are you ready?" she asked.

He nodded, setting them in motion. He was ready— ready to begin living again, ready to rejoin his family and ready to marry the bravest, smartest woman in Cahill Crossing. She'd given him a reason to cast off his guilt and grasp what she offered with both hands. With her, he knew they would build a home and put down roots so deep they would nourish generations.

* * * * *

HISTORICAL

Where Love is Timeless™

HARLEQUIN® HISTORICAL

REQUEST YOUR FREE BOOKS!

 HARLEQUIN® HISTORICAL:
Where love is timeless

2 FREE NOVELS PLUS 2 FREE GIFTS!

YES! Please send me 2 FREE Harlequin® Historical novels and my 2 FREE gifts (gifts are worth about $10). After receiving them, if I don't wish to receive any more books, I can return the shipping statement marked "cancel." If I don't cancel, I will receive 6 brand-new novels every month and be billed just $5.19 per book in the U.S. or $5.74 per book in Canada. That's a savings of at least 17% off the cover price! It's quite a bargain! Shipping and handling is just 50¢ per book in the U.S. and 75¢ per book in Canada.* I understand that accepting the 2 free books and gifts places me under no obligation to buy anything. I can always return a shipment and cancel at any time. Even if I never buy another book, the two free books and gifts are mine to keep forever.

246/349 HDN FEQQ

Name	(PLEASE PRINT)

Address	Apt. #

City	State/Prov.	Zip/Postal Code

Signature (if under 18, a parent or guardian must sign)

Mail to the Reader Service:
IN U.S.A.: P.O. Box 1867, Buffalo, NY 14240-1867
IN CANADA: P.O. Box 609, Fort Erie, Ontario L2A 5X3

Not valid for current subscribers to Harlequin Historical books.

Want to try two free books from another line?
Call 1-800-873-8635 or visit www.ReaderService.com.

* Terms and prices subject to change without notice. Prices do not include applicable taxes. Sales tax applicable in N.Y. Canadian residents will be charged applicable taxes. Offer not valid in Quebec. This offer is limited to one order per household. All orders subject to credit approval. Credit or debit balances in a customer's account(s) may be offset by any other outstanding balance owed by or to the customer. Please allow 4 to 6 weeks for delivery. Offer available while quantities last.

Your Privacy—The Reader Service is committed to protecting your privacy. Our Privacy Policy is available online at www.ReaderService.com or upon request from the Reader Service.

We make a portion of our mailing list available to reputable third parties that offer products we believe may interest you. If you prefer that we not exchange your name with third parties, or if you wish to clarify or modify your communication preferences, please visit us at www.ReaderService.com/consumerchoice or write to us at Reader Service Preference Service, P.O. Box 9062, Buffalo, NY 14269. Include your complete name and address.

HH11B

New York Times *and* USA TODAY *bestselling author*
Maya Banks presents book three in her miniseries
PREGNANCY & PASSION.

TEMPTED BY HER INNOCENT KISS

Available March 2012 from Harlequin Desire!

There came a time in a man's life when he knew he was well and truly caught. Devon Carter stared down at the diamond ring nestled in velvet and acknowledged that this was one such time. He snapped the lid closed and shoved the box into the breast pocket of his suit.

He had two choices. He could marry Ashley Copeland and fulfill his goal of merging his company with Copeland Hotels, thus creating the largest, most exclusive line of resorts in the world, or he could refuse and lose it all.

Put in that light, there wasn't much he could do except pop the question.

The doorman to his Manhattan high-rise apartment hurried to open the door as Devon strode toward the street. He took a deep breath before ducking into his car, and the driver pulled into traffic.

Tonight was the night. All of his careful wooing, the countless dinners, kisses that started brief and casual and became more breathless—all a lead-up to tonight. Tonight his seduction of Ashley Copeland would be complete, and then he'd ask her to marry him.

He shook his head as the absurdity of the situation hit him for the hundredth time. Personally, he thought William Copeland was crazy for forcing his daughter down Devon's throat.

Ashley was a sweet enough girl, but Devon had no desire

to marry anyone.

William had other plans. He'd told Devon that Ashley had no head for the family business. She was too softhearted, too naive. So he'd made Ashley part of the deal. The catch? Ashley wasn't to know of it. Which meant Devon was stuck playing stupid games.

Ashley was supposed to think this was a grand love match. She was a starry-eyed woman who preferred her animal-rescue foundation over board meetings, charts and financials for Copeland Hotels.

If she ever found out the truth, she wouldn't take it well.

And hell, he couldn't blame her.

But no matter the reason for his proposal, before the night was over, she'd have no doubts that she belonged to him.

What will happen when Devon marries Ashley?
Find out in Maya Banks's passionate new novel
TEMPTED BY HER INNOCENT KISS
Available March 2012 from Harlequin Desire!